Shatterproof

by

K. K. Weil

Shatterproof

Cover Art by *Debbie Taylor*

The Wild Rose Press, Inc.
PO Box 708
Adams Basin, NY 14410-0708
Visit us at www.thewildrosepress.com

Publishing History
First Mainstream Women's Fiction Edition, 2015
Print ISBN 978-1-5092-0395-6
Digital ISBN 978-1-5092-0396-3

Published in the United States of America

Dedication

To all the boys strong enough to end the cycle

Acknowledgments

Many thanks to my editor, Cindy Davis, for believing in the potential of this book. Your wonderful suggestions, guidance, and creative editing have taught me so much and made *Shatterproof*'s message all the more powerful.

Thank you to the entire Wild Rose Press team, especially Rhonda Penders, RJ Morris, Roseann Armstrong, and Lisa Dawn for your warm welcome and continuous support. I'm so happy to be a Rose. Much gratitude goes to Debbie Taylor for the beautiful cover art and for imagery that enhances my words.

A thousand thank-yous to Kim and Jason for poring over my mess of a first draft and for taking the time to prod and probe all my plots.

Thanks, always, to my family, especially my grandmother, one of the really great storytellers.

And to Neil, for keeping me going, always brainstorming with me, and for letting my imaginary friends into our lives.

Finally, thank you to all the places like Holly's House. Your dedication to helping women in need knows no bounds.

Chapter One

Griffin

I've been down this road before. And I know where it ends.

Sneakers dangle from a street lamp. Garbage bags line the curb. A store owner smokes under the scaffolding. But none of that matters to me. Only one thing does.

The inconspicuous brownstone comes into view. I tuck my bag inside my jacket to protect it from the sheets of water falling around me. I pick up my speed, but not because I mind the rain. I don't. I love storms, the more ferocious the better. No, I walk faster because that's what I always do when I'm almost at Holly's House. It's one of the few places I feel at peace.

I bound up the steps two at a time and ring the bell. I know there are cameras on me, so I smooth the wet hair off my face.

A familiar voice comes through the intercom. "Yes?"

"Hey, Taylor. It's Griffin."

"Come on in," she sings and buzzes me in.

I stride through the entryway and graze my calloused fingertips over the plaque that reads, Holly's House, for Solace and Freedom. It's my ritual. Other guys rub a rabbit's foot. This plaque is my good luck charm.

"Hi, Griffin." Taylor greets me from her small desk in the corner. "Yikes, you're soaked! Do you need a towel or something?"

"Don't worry about it." I shake out my tousled hair with my palm.

"Who are you meeting with today?"

"I'm actually delivering. I've got this for April." I hold up the brown bag.

Taylor smiles and claps her hands. "You're about to make her day."

"I don't know about that."

"You are. I'll go find her. Make yourself comfortable in the sitting room."

I always consult with the women in this room first. It's a stark contrast to my warehouse, which, by comparison, is spare and cold. This room is warm and welcoming with soft couches, hoards of books, and a steady stream of music coming from some invisible speakers. Taylor keeps a candle burning, too, so it always smells like cinnamon. It's exactly what the guests here need.

Every time I'm in it, I'm grateful a place like this exists for them.

"Hi, Griffin. Thanks so much for coming." April approaches. She wears an easy smile that wasn't there the day I met her. I'm happy to see it.

"Hi, April." I stand up to say hello, but make no movement toward her. I'm always careful that way. "How are you?"

"I'm okay." She tilts her head to the side as we sit together. "I'm leaving at the end of the month, thanks to you."

"I'm glad." I run my hand through my beard in an attempt to dodge the compliment. "How is your arm?"

"Better. The cast should come off in two weeks."

When she lifts her bandaged arm, I chew my lip to suppress the surge of anger inside me. The environment at Holly's House may be soothing, but that doesn't mean the women's wounds don't affect me.

"Good." I swallow. "So, I've got your piece here."

Her face shines with anticipation. "Can I see it?"

"Of course. It's yours." I hand her the bag.

She removes the blue tissue paper, one layer at a time. When the paper has been discarded and all that remains is the sculpture, her smile is replaced by a pensive gaze. We sit in silence while she takes in every inch of it.

I think this is my favorite part. The initial silence as they inspect the sculptures. After the silence come the thanks. That part makes me uncomfortable.

April covers her mouth with her hand. Beads of water trickle down her cheeks in response to the sculpture of a smiling woman. Strong, proud. Swinging her daughter high over her head, with a silhouette of the moon in the background. With no broken arm. With no broken spirit.

"My God, Griffin. I don't know what to say. It's beautiful."

"*She's* beautiful," I correct. "She's you."

The tears come heavier now, and she scoots over to me on the couch. She wraps me in a hug that I gently, but reassuringly, return.

"I don't know how to thank you."

"Just be happy. And safe." And stay far away from the asshole that did this to you. I keep the last advice to myself, though I wish I could say it aloud.

She releases me and wipes her cheeks with the back of her hand. "Do you mind if I show it to Julia? She's napping, but I know she'll want to see it. She's been asking when the sculpture is going to be finished." She stands.

"Of course, go." I remain sitting.

"I'd invite you in to see her, but…"

I shake my head. I'm not allowed beyond the sitting room. "April," I say. "Go. Share the piece with her. And take care of both of you."

She nods and gives my shoulder a quick squeeze. "Thank you so much again, Griffin. You have no idea what this means to me." She leaves the room with more pep than before.

That is my thanks. And my reward.

I lean over to clean up the couch, which is littered with the bag and tissue paper.

"Can you leave that where it is?"

I'm caught off guard by the sharp voice and turn around, only to be hit with a startling piece of art. Alabaster skin that I'm sure is as smooth to the touch as satin. Flowing, almost uncontrollable, blonde hair. The kind my fingers would get lost in. Lips so full I couldn't perfect her pout with my own clay. And her eyes…they're a unique shade of green that reminds me of moss after a rainstorm, with bright clear droplets glistening in them.

I have a fascination with eyes. It's been my experience that people are inherently liars. They can't help it. They can lie through gleaming, perfectly constructed teeth and beautifully formed lips. The ones who are good at it can even lie through body language.

But not through their eyes. Eyes always tell the story. They tell us about love and hate; they tell us about embarrassment and desire. They tell us when a person is about to lose it and crack. I've been on the hunt for that one all my life, and I'm always right.

When I'm here at Holly's House, though, I try not to stare into people, or search their thoughts, which I do out of habit. These women have dealt with enough. They don't need some random guy intimidating them when he's supposed to be helping.

But it takes a few seconds to catch myself this time because I'm absorbed by the way she's focused on me. It's not only the hue. I'm also surprised by the expression in them. Ordinarily, the women here have been put through so much; it shows in every motion. Especially when they first arrive. But this woman is almost giving me an order with her tone and her glare.

"Sorry, what?" I ask, half of the paper in my hand, half still on the couch.

"The tissue paper. Can you leave it alone?"

Only then do I realize she's got a camera in her hands. I don't know anything about photography, but from all its gizmos, I'm guessing it's an expensive one.

"Uh, yeah, sure." I let it drop back onto the couch.

"Thanks." She practically shoves past me to adjust the tissue paper. "Here. This is how it was." She gets down on her knees in front of the couch and starts snapping off pictures, inches from the paper. I'm intrigued because to me this is just a crumpled mess, but she obviously sees something I don't.

"What's luring you to that paper?" I'm not supposed to be asking anything. Taylor's instructions have been crystal clear from day one. This is a safe haven for women. To be left alone. But the words escape from my mouth before I can stop them.

"The way the light was hitting it, with those raindrops...I had to capture it," she answers without lowering the camera. She inches over to get the paper from a different angle and the camera clicks a few more times before she rises

It's definitely time for me to go, but I keep standing here, stalling.

"The way it was hitting the paper?" I ask as she scrolls through the pictures on the screen.

"Yeah, here." She holds out the camera.

I step in closer to her so I can see and a few strands of her hair tickle the side of my face. At first, the camera screen is just filled with some blue tissue paper, but when she zooms in, I find bristled textures in it I've never noticed before. She's right; the light shining though the water marks does change its appearance.

"Once I play with the effects and come in a lot more, you won't even be able to tell what it's a picture of. It'll be really cool." She lowers the camera to her waist and smiles with her lips together. The right side of her smile is marginally wider than the left. It's a beautiful imperfection.

Without thinking, I look her up and down, which I'm embarrassed about in an instant. She'll definitely misinterpret what I was doing. In reality, I was scanning her for bruises, and I'm relieved when I don't find any. My relief fades as I realize the bruises might be where you can't see them.

Her smile transforms into a smirk, which means I was right. She thinks I was checking her out. But the fact is, no matter how gorgeous any of these women might be, I would never, ever check them out. That would be repugnant.

"Are you a friend of April's?" she asks, probably trying to figure out my connection with this place.

"Not a friend, no. Are you?"

"Met her this morning. I just got here last night," she volunteers.

"Are you okay?" The words spurt out. I'm ordinarily so careful here. I don't presume anyone wants to tell me anything, and I don't ask personal questions unless they start talking to me about their lives first. But something about those eyes makes me want to know the story behind them.

She blanches at the question, making me sorry I asked. She shakes her head. "No, I'm fine. Really."

"How's everything going?" Taylor's every-cheery voice croons. It's her way of telling me it's time for me to go. They trust me here and appreciate what I do, but this is a women's shelter, and they don't want men hanging around. If my work is done, I need to leave.

"I'm all set. Just collecting the garbage." I fix my attention back on the couch where it belongs. I gather up the tissue paper, before making my way toward the exit.

"Thanks so much, as always, Griffin," Taylor calls as I leave. "See you soon."

****

"Did you know there's an apartment for rent in this building?" I ask my friend Sarah as I throw myself on her couch and pull both of her legs over my lap. I toss away her shoes and massage her feet and calves.

"Mmm, so good." She slumps down and rests her tired head against the arm of the couch. "Yeah, I know," she answers. She sounds like she might fall asleep.

"Do you know which apartment it is?"

"Ground level studio, I overheard someone saying."

"Good to know."

"For someone at Holly's?" She scoots up.

"Just to keep in mind." I nod.

"Griffin," she says and I sense a speech coming. "I don't think this building is exactly…" She fades and doesn't need to finish.

"Just to keep in mind," I repeat. I know it's not a great placement.

Sarah's apartment building is, for lack of a better term, a complete shithole. Really, mine is a shithole too, but it's right above the warehouse where I do my sculpting, and I can afford to live there without a roommate. Sarah's apartment, though, is a tiny dump on a seedy block, which she has to share with two other girls. Even the *Apartment For Rent* sign taped inside a window downstairs is worn enough to be twenty years old, though it wasn't there when I was here last week.

But it's all she can afford. That's the price you pay to live in Manhattan.

As a result, she's at my place, a lot. She's quiet and unobtrusive, so I don't mind. Much. Sarah and I have known each other since high school. If there's anyone who can put up with my moody crap, it's her. She understands the darker side of me, and she loves me anyway. But then, I know her baggage, too, and since it makes her who she is, I embrace it.

"Well, the landlord's name is Benny," Sarah says. "I don't know if he'll care as much about helping those women as the other landlords you deal with. He's pretty uninvolved. But you can give it a shot. If you really think having one of them living here is a good idea."

Sarah's building isn't up to my usual standards for these women, but I'll keep it in the back of my mind in case something suddenly comes up.

"So, when is Kaitlyn getting here?" I fan through a tattoo magazine lying on the table and realize it might be time to get some new ink.

"Any time now." She yawns. Sarah and I have been friends with Kaitlyn since college. Though we're all busy and getting together with her has been challenging since we graduated a couple of years ago, we make sure to do it every so often.

Kaitlyn and I sort of dated in college, after we'd developed a friendship. I liked her and all, but I kept things casual. First off, the whole time we were together I suspected she had a thing for the guy she's with now. As soon as I was sure, I ended it, which was fine with me. We went back to being friends without skipping a beat. We worked better as friends, anyway.

More importantly, I always keep my dating relationships easy. Light and carefree goes against everything I am, but when things remain that way, there's no chance the red will come barreling through me. I know what happens when a man like me gets too comfortable in a relationship and starts thinking he can treat a woman any way he wants. It's better for everyone involved if I keep my distance.

"Is Jackson coming?" I ask.

As if on cue, there's a knock at the door and when it opens, Kaitlyn's alone.

****

"The play is going well," Kaitlyn tells us over Thai food. "Opened a few weeks ago, and it's sold out every night."

Kaitlyn's guy, Jackson, is a playwright. He does mostly small, underground work but has had larger success as well. Kaitlyn works on his sets sometimes.

"How about with you, Griffin? How are sales going?" she asks.

"Okay, I guess. Enough to pay the rent."

"Oh lord, here we go." Sarah sighs. "He's so annoying. Try to get him to ever accept a compliment without making some self-deprecating remark after it. If you can manage it, you're a better woman than me."

"Yeah, I know. He's ridiculous." Kaitlyn smiles.

"It would be nice if you two wouldn't talk about me as if I can't hear you," I say.

"Who cares if you can hear me? Are you going to deny it? You're shit at taking a compliment." Sarah flicks me in the shoulder with her finger. "Anyway, he's doing great. You should see the waiting list he's got."

I roll my eyes. She's right; I am backlogged with clients, but this conversation makes me want to leave the table. But when my cell rings and I see who it is, I realize how much I'd rather be at this dinner with my friends than anywhere else at all.

Chapter Two

Frankie

The pictures from the other day came out better than I hoped. I'm flipping through them on my laptop, admiring my editing skills.

Not bad for a complete amateur.

My goal wasn't to shoot close-ups of the tissue paper, even though that's what I ended up getting. What I wanted was a picture of those hands holding the tissue paper. If I'm honest, what I really wanted was the expression on that guy's face while he was holding the tissue paper, but I would have settled for the hands. I don't usually take pictures of people. I'm much more interested in macro-photography, using *things*. Finding beauty in objects that no one else sees. But his expression was so strange. It was like he was happy and sad and tortured all at the same time. He didn't even notice his hair was dripping all over him. I would have given anything to capture it. But I would have had to get up much too close to take my kind of picture. Soliciting a strange man in a women's safe house, to take a close up inches from his face, didn't seem like the best idea at the time.

Unfortunately, when I asked him to leave it alone, he dropped it, thinking that's what I meant. I could have asked him to freeze, instead, so he'd still have the paper in his hands, but that might have been a little too forward. Plus, he might have thought getting so close to him to take a picture was weird. But that's the only way I can catch all the lines and creases. I would have killed to get a shot of one of his tattoos.

I don't know why he was here. I didn't think men were allowed in places like this, but I could be wrong. At first I thought he was visiting someone, but in the end it didn't appear that way.

He seemed to be trying to figure out why I was here, too. Looking me over, but not in a sexual way. More like he was curious and thought I didn't belong. If that's what he thought, he was right. I don't belong here. I've been guilty about being here for the past four days.

It's not like I'm scamming or anything. Holly's House provides temporary refuge for women in abusive relationships. Even though that's not technically me, my stay here was approved.

I came down to the city from Buffalo two months ago, when my boyfriend, Randy, told me he was moving here to pursue his music career. We'd only been together a couple of months, but he was fun and I'm always up for an adventure. My photos weren't selling at home so I figured a change of scenery was a good idea, and what better place to try to make it than New York City? My parents thought it was a terrible idea, which I'll admit, made it that much more enticing. I packed my crap and left.

At first, everything was fine. I got a waitressing job at a bar in the Village, and Randy was scouring the city for gigs. I guess he got frustrated with his lack of immediate success, because after the first month or so, there was a change in him. He started picking fights with me, getting angry over nothing. It made me a bit uncomfortable, but I had no reason to be nervous.

Until I did.

One afternoon, he came home after an audition, which I assume he bombed. When I asked how it went, he snapped at me and told me to mind my own fucking business. I'm not used to being spoken to that way, and I never hold my opinions in, so I snapped back. I don't even remember what I said, but the next thing I knew, Randy was screaming about not wanting the added pressure of supporting some girl he just met and how New York was a scam of a town that doesn't give the little guy a chance. He started throwing things and breaking them, and I knew it was time to go.

There is one good thing about being impulsive. It makes it very easy to pick up and leave when things don't go your way. As soon as Randy calmed down and I could get a word in, I told him this wasn't what I signed on for. He wasn't any more invested in our relationship than I was and didn't give me a hard time about leaving.

I didn't have anywhere to go. I was embarrassed to return home after only a couple of months. I don't like proving my parents right. Going back to Buffalo, living the dull life they wanted me to live, was not an option that interested me.

I needed to get my head on straight. I stayed in a hotel for one night, which cost about two weeks of my salary. I found this shelter online and thought maybe I could stay here until I could figure out my next move. I didn't realize until I got here how limited the spots were and how much these women needed this place. The entire building had been converted to a safe haven, but even still, its maximum capacity is twenty-four women. I could be keeping someone out who needs refuge. I explained my situation to Taylor, the woman who runs Holly's, and asked if she wanted me to leave straight away. She thanked me for my honesty and we worked out a deal. If she needs the space, I'll leave. Otherwise, I am free to stay for up to the ninety days normally allowed, or until I could find somewhere decent to live.

For the past few days, I've been checking out rentals. It's become very clear I won't be able to afford an apartment on my own. Looks like I'll either be needing a roommate or a giant stroke of magic. A broke waitress/aspiring photographer in New York, living with complete strangers. The American Dream. But as I think about where I am, I count my blessings and say a silent prayer for those who weren't able to get out as quickly as I did.

There's a little bit of commotion in the front of the building. When I open the door of my shared bedroom, my first impulse is to slam it back shut. I'm sorry I looked. My second impulse is to run and help.

Taylor is holding up a woman who is so badly beaten, it's hard to make out her face. She's weak and needs support to stand.

"Frankie," Taylor calls to me. "Go outside and hail a cab. We have to get her to the hospital."

****

Taylor consoles the woman for the duration of the cab ride, assuring her she's safe now and everything is going to be okay. As soon as we arrive at the ER, they take her in, thank God. She's in very bad shape. Taylor leaves to make a couple of phone calls but asks me to let her know if I get any updates.

I find a seat in the waiting room, which is as crowded as I'd expect. I'm always curious about everything around me, so I try to be inconspicuous as I take in the patients with less urgent injuries. There's a kid with a broken finger, adeptly playing his video game with the other hand. To the far left is a young man with a nasty, deep gash on his head. I look away. I have no stomach for anything medical. On the other side of the room, a familiar figure sits in a chair. He's slouched over with his head in his hands, but I'm pretty sure from the brown hair, the broad shoulders and the disheveled clothes, it's the guy who was at Holly's the other day. The guy Taylor called Griffin. When he pushes his sleeves up to his elbows, exposing his tatted-up arms, I know it's him for sure.

Before I can question what I'm doing, I walk across the waiting area to say hello. As if he senses me approaching, he raises his head from his hands. He frowns a little before he catches himself.

"You." I smile as I approach him.

"You," he repeats to me. "What are you doing here? Are you okay?"

It's the second time he's asked me that.

"Yes, I'm fine. I'm here for another woman. How about you?"

"My mother..." He pauses as the exit door opens. When he doesn't recognize anyone, he continues. "Got hurt."

"Oh, sorry," I answer. "Is she okay?" I sit in the empty seat next to him.

He lets out a hollow laugh. "She could be if she wanted to." He says nothing else, and silence hangs between us.

I get very uncomfortable with awkward pauses so the absolute quiet is disarming.

"What were you doing at Holly's the other day?" I ask him, then snap my mouth shut. I always speak before I think. It's none of my business what this stranger was doing there.

A few seconds tick by and he says nothing, possibly deciding whether he wants to answer or not. I'm about to get up and walk away, because this is a little too weird. But right before I move, he speaks.

"Sometimes I do sculptures of the women who stay there." He plays with the tattoos that adorn his knuckles.

"What kind of sculptures?"

He frowns. I really am too nosy for my own good.

"It's involved." His clipped, evasive response should shut down my questions, but it doesn't.

"Why do you sculpt them? Do you know someone who stays there?"

"Why are *you* staying there?" His question comes at the tail end of mine, throwing me a little. I wasn't expecting him to deflect my question with his own.

Rather than explain that I'm taking up space at Holly's House when I shouldn't be, I play the evasive game, too. "I won't be there long. They're just letting me stay until I can find a place of my own, which is kind of hard, because I can't afford much rent."

The way his eyes dart back and forth between mine makes me a little uneasy. I force myself to maintain his glare, more out of defiance than anything. I mean, really, social convention says look away every now and then.

It's the first time I've had a chance to give him more than a quick glance. His dark hair has some auburn highlights you can only make out if you're inspecting him. It's kind of long, and he's got heavy facial hair. He wears earrings and rope bracelets and his clothes…God, I don't know. Maybe he picks them off his floor and throws on whatever random item he grabs. I guess he *looks* kind of like a hipster. These days, you see beards and tattoos on people more often than not. But I don't think he's hipster at all. His appearance is more "screw the world" when I think about it. But I've got a knack for seeing what others don't at first. Hidden underneath his sloppy exterior is a very handsome guy. Why does he hide it?

He says nothing in response, and I need to fill the air with something.

"Right now, I'm just a waitress."

"Just a waitress? What's wrong with that?"

"Well, nothing, except…" I shrug. "I don't know."

"What do you want to be?" I'm about to answer, but he speaks first, answering his own question. "A photographer." He nods once.

I'm flattered that he remembered, but I probably shouldn't read so much into it. I did order him to put the tissue paper back and all but crawled on the floor in front of him to get the shot. What a first impression.

I smile. "Yes."

He returns the smile. Even though it's small, it softens his harsh exterior and transforms him. He's even hotter than I thought.

"The picture you showed me was—"

"Hi, honey." A tall, attractive woman walks over to us. She's got a bandage across her nose and shades of blue and purple surround it.

Griffin's attention is redirected to the woman who is obviously his mother. "Is it broken?" His tone has a sting to it.

"No," she murmurs. "Just bruised."

"Wonderful." The word drips of sarcasm. "Let's get the hell out of here." He scoots forward on his seat to get up.

I'm tempted to stop him. My picture was what? But why do I care what he thinks?

"Take care of yourself," he says to me, all traces of his small smile gone.

I'm a little disappointed he's leaving so abruptly, which is stupid. Did I expect him to hang out in the emergency room all night?

Then he stops as if he forgot something. He leans back. I don't know if he realizes it, but he's kind of on top of me...so close his shaggy hair is practically in my face. The scent of his shampoo is overpowered by...what is that...paint? A strange combination.

"Thought-provoking," he says, and I realize he's finishing his sentence. "Where do you work?" His voice is low and gruff. He doesn't want his mother to hear him.

"Sam's Tavern, in the Village." I expect a follow-up question or something. But he rises, puts his large hand on his mother's lower back and leads her out the door.

I watch him walk away until the nurse comes over to give me an update about the poor woman we brought in, pulling me from my daze.

Chapter Three

Griffin

When that girl from Holly's sauntered toward me in the hospital, I nearly hissed through my teeth. She was the last person I needed to see right about then. I was angry enough about the entire situation. Being at the hospital with my mother, once again. Sitting in the ER waiting room, once again. Hearing her make excuses for him, once again. My blood was already almost at its boiling point, and then she appeared.

At Holly's, there was something jarring about her. I don't know if it was the way she ordered me to leave the paper alone or the fact that she reminded me so much of how my mother was, years ago. Bold, interesting, inquisitive. She seemed like exactly the type of woman who would challenge me to dig deeper into myself, forcing me to look at things in ways I never have before, which is why she's exactly the type of woman I've got to steer clear of. Besides, she's staying at Holly's. The last thing I need is to get involved with a woman who's in a position similar to my mother's. I already have enough on my plate with her.

And yet, I can't stop thinking of a reason to go to that bar where she works. I really shouldn't have asked.

"I'm craving a burger," I tell Sarah.

"A burger?" she asks, skeptical.

I concentrate on my sculpture rather than Sarah because, while I'm excellent at reading people, I'm terrible at deceiving them. I was better at it when I was younger. But as time went on, I developed such a disdain for liars that somewhere along the way I lost the ability to do it. She'll know I have an ulterior motive the second she gets a full view of me. She probably knows anyway because I keep my head and shoulders down. But I play it off as if I'm focusing on my work.

I usually don't let people hang out with me in the warehouse while I'm working. My mind goes somewhere else when I sculpt, and I don't want to be pulled from it with meaningless small talk. But Sarah's different. She understands my work because she's an artist herself. She doesn't babble. So I'm sure this random statement seems as out of place to her as it feels coming from my mouth.

"Yeah. I know a place with good ones."

"Good burgers," she repeats, her voice full of amused suspicion.

"Yes."

"You're going to leave here in the middle of working because you feel like eating a burger?"

It's not surprising that she's questioning me. I never stop to eat when I'm in a groove. I've missed more meals than I can count. But I'm not in a groove now because all I can think about is going to that fucking bar.

I'm impatient. "Will you come or not?"

"Well…" She sits up on the couch. "I guess it's either come with you or go back to my place, so let's go."

Sarah won't stop bitching the whole way to Sam's

Tavern. It's making me wish I hadn't asked her to come and had just taken care of whatever this is on my own.

"Tell me again why we're trekking all the way across town when there are a dozen restaurants within a two block radius of your apartment?"

I've been evasive about why we have to go to this particular place. Probably because I shouldn't be going there at all. But I keep reminding myself why I am. The girl told me she needs a place to live. There's a vacancy in Sarah's building. This is simple math. I'm going to help her out of a bad situation. I'm doing her a service. The same as always. It has nothing to do with me.

Right. If that's the case, why haven't I told Sarah? I'm not even good at lying to myself.

Sam's Tavern is pretty crowded when we arrive, and reeks of stale beer more than it should for this early in the evening. I scan the place and realize I have no idea when this girl works. I can't even ask for her, because I don't know her name. How did I not ask her name? I don't usually do stupid things, but this ranks up there among the more asinine.

She may not be here. A disturbing knot forms in my stomach.

"Can I help you?" the hostess asks. But we can't sit yet because I need to see if the girl is waiting tables or not.

"We're going to the bar," I answer.

Sarah huffs over my shoulder. I'm blowing my cover, which is already full of holes. I'm well aware that my behavior makes no sense. I pretend not to hear Sarah grumbling as a figure with wavy blonde hair emerges from the kitchen.

It's her. My pulse lurches, taking me by surprise.

She brings drinks and appetizers to a bunch of rowdy guys who appear to be flirting with her. She teases them back. I'm amused by the way she deals with them, until one of them tugs at her apron, pulling her close to him. My ears immediately burn and I take a step in her direction. Before I reach her, though, she pushes off him and says something that causes his friends to laugh. I laugh at the guy, too, before something occurs to me.

I'm just like one of these guys, showing up here unwanted, simply because I ran into her and she's in my head. I can't offer her anything real. I don't do real. It's too dangerous for whomever I'm dating. I have no business seeking her out. I'm as sure of that as my own name.

Then why am I here?

"Who is that?" Sarah whispers, as I'm watching the girl like a goddamn creeper. My mind searches for an answer.

"I don't know." That's not a lie. I don't know who she is.

"Is she why we're here?" Sarah asks. Before I have to say yes, there's a silky voice in my ear.

"You."

I turn around and am greeted with those same moss eyes that have invaded my thoughts for days.

"What are you doing here?" she asks.

"I'm hungry." I sound like a fool. I might as well have just said *me, caveman*. This is very unlike me. Sarah chuckles from behind. I ignore her again.

"Well, do you need a table?"

I take a second to assess the situation. If I sit at a table and she's not my waitress, I won't be able to talk to her about the apartment. Or anything else.

"We'll just sit at the bar," I say. That way at least we can have a quick exchange as she picks up drinks.

"We?" she asks.

I'm not sure if she doesn't see Sarah or if she's fishing to find out who she is to me.

"Yes, the two of us." I motion toward Sarah.

"Go help yourself to some stools if you can scrounge them."

Miraculously, we find a couple of open seats at the bar, which give me a clear view of the whole place. This girl's got the most interesting mannerisms. She's polite to the customers, but she's not interested in them. She's much more focused on the things around her. She runs her fingers over the smooth bar counter. She examines the chunky beaded necklace a customer is wearing. I even find her staring at the clock, not to check the time, but as if she's analyzing the design of the hands. I think back to the way she described those scraps of tissue paper, like they had artistic value. She's fascinating. She's not even doing anything, but my heart is thumping against my chest for no apparent reason.

This was a mistake. This is a girl I need to avoid.

She comes to the bar and asks the bartender for two beers and a Jack and Coke, before acknowledging me. "So, you. Need anything?"

"Griffin," I correct, even though there's something I like about her calling me "you." She nods as if it's not new information.

"Frankie." She smiles.

"Just an answer, Frankie." There's a flirtatious tone in my voice when I say her name, which I definitely did not intend.

"An answer? You've piqued my interest. What's the question, Griffin?" She's playing back, with the same tone.

"You mentioned needing an apartment. Do you still?"

Her brows shoot up and her lips crinkle, giving her chin a more pointed appearance than before.

"You know of one—cheap?" Before I can respond, she continues. "It's not with you, is it? Because no matter how much you beg, I'm not moving in with you, becoming your sex slave and having your love child babies."

I'm dumbfounded. My jaw hangs a tad. She's not what I expected at all, considering her circumstances. She notices my shock and chuckles.

"I'm kidding, Griffin. Tell me about the place."

Next to me, Sarah is suspicious, but keeps it mostly to herself. "The place is in my building," she interjects. "The building is kind of…what are the words…"

"A complete shithole," I volunteer.

"Thank you," she says. "Yes, but what I was going to say is it's kind of bare-bones, but the landlord's a decent guy and the location isn't great, so even though it's not cheap, it's cheaper than anything else you'll find."

"I'll take it," Frankie says.

"Don't you want to see it first?" I ask. "I don't know what the apartment looks like, or if it's even still available." I wasn't expecting her to jump at it like that. In truth, I don't know what I was expecting. Clearly, I had no plan here other than to find an excuse to run into her. I haven't contacted the landlord or checked out the place. I haven't done anything I normally do to prepare for a transition. And yet, something tells me it doesn't matter.

"Nope. You said the magic word. Cheaper. If the landlord throws out a number I can pay, I'll move in tomorrow."

"Do you want me to call for you?" I ask.

Frankie's face curls into a tiny, cute knot. "Why would I want you to do that?"

"I d-don't know," I stammer. It does seem like an odd question, in this context. "Sometimes I-I don't know. Here's the number." I dig a crumpled paper out of my pocket and slap it on the bar. "I copied it off the sign."

"Great. Be right back." She grabs her cell and walks outside.

Sarah jabs me in the ribs. "Doesn't Taylor usually handle the arrangements with the women after you deal with the landlord?"

"Usually, yeah." I play with a couple of straws on the bar, trying to shape them into something. But they don't bend well and they do little to occupy my idle hands.

"So then?" Sarah prods.

"Can you check in on her for me if she lives there? Make sure she's all right?"

"What—me? Griffin, what's going on?"

"Let it go for now, okay?" I answer, sharper than I intend.

Frankie reappears. "Next round is on me, for getting me a place to live. What'll it be?"

"The landlord said yes?" I ask with disbelief. Things don't happen that easily in the city.

"Well," she chuckles. "He said three people came and went today, not very impressed with the space, so if I want it, it's mine." She retreats behind the bar to get us drinks, and my palms get clammy when she throws her ponytail over her shoulder. I rub them on my jeans. I'm unable to pinpoint why I find her every move so enticing. It's just her, overall.

"Maybe they don't like it because it's disgusting," I say, trying to maintain my distance, even though I want to jump over the bar to erase the divider between us. I'm also a little nervous about what I just thrust her into. People don't usually turn down available space unless it's outrageously expensive, or fucking gross.

"I guess I'll find out tomorrow." She grins, with no hint of fear or hesitancy. "So, what do you want to drink?"

We ask for a couple of beers. Frankie hands me my bottle and as I go to reach for it, she takes hold of my wrist and examines my tattooed forearm.

"I like this one." She touches her pointer to the words forever embedded there, which are surrounded by other tattoos. I'm reminded of what caused me to get it and fire runs into my arm. I yank it from her.

"Thanks," I answer as I back away. I need to get to the warehouse. I need to sculpt. Right now. I start to exit the bar, leaving the full beer behind. Sarah wishes Frankie luck with her move, then follows me in silence. She knows me well enough not to ask what the hell that was all about.

By the time I've reached my warehouse, my breathing has slowed considerably. Simply knowing I'm about to get my hands on my clay calms me. Just like it has since the first time I touched it.

I pull out a new block and start working it. It doesn't matter what I'm making today. All that matters is purging the memory through my fingers. Erasing the day I yelled at my mother, questioning her for the thousandth time about how she could allow herself to be so mistreated.

"You don't understand," she'd told me. "It's complicated, Griffin."

I hated it when she said that. It was such a pathetic excuse.

"You're damn right I don't understand. You're such a strong woman. How can you just let him do this to you? For all this time. He's a fucking monster."

"Don't call him that. He's flawed, certainly. This is his flaw." She ran her hand over her swelling cheekbone.

"You think?" I snarled.

She shook her head. "Stop. I can't stand the way you feel about him because he's inside you. Don't you see that? Don't you understand where the intensity you carry around comes from? I love that about you, honey. And you get it from him."

"I am nothing like him!" I screamed. But even as I spoke the words, the familiar heat rose through me. It started at my fingertips and toes, coursed up my legs, through my torso, up to the top of my head. It was an energy I could barely control, and I had to take deep breaths to have any hope of containing it. My hands clenched. The need to do something with them was overwhelming.

I flew from the house as quickly as my legs would take me. She was wrong. She had to be wrong.

Your origin need not determine your destination.

I trace over the words Frankie pointed out on my arm. I got them the day after that argument with my mother, to remind myself I would not be like that man. I would avoid that destination at all costs.

But avoiding the destination means avoiding all roads leading to it as well. Somehow I know Frankie, with her moss eyes, wise-cracking mouth, and whatever-goes attitude is one of those roads.

Chapter Four

Frankie

Okay, maybe accepting an apartment sight unseen isn't the smartest move in the world. As I wait to be buzzed in, I'm pretty sure the building next door is either a crack den or a brothel. Or both.

Awesome.

The landlord is a middle-aged caricature of a typical building super, overalls and all. He brings me into the "garden apartment" on the ground floor. Describing it as tiny would be generous. I'm almost positive it was a storage closet at one point. A queen size mattress may not fit. Not that I even have a mattress. I'll have to order one. Almost everything in my old apartment was Randy's.

The bars on the apartment's single window do nothing to make it more appealing. Still, I try to imagine the place with lacy, patterned curtains, inspirational quotes on the walls and a coat of bright yellow paint to make the room pop. And I think about the rent, which is in the ballpark of my budget.

I can make this work.

I sign the lease, accept the keys, and say goodbye to the landlord. Then I stand in the empty room with my two bags at my feet. I don't really know what to do next.

"It's cute," a feminine voice says from the doorway. "But you might want to consider closing your door."

I spin around and am relieved to find Sarah, a familiar face. I laugh.

"I'd invite you in, but I guess you're already here." I gesture to the lack of space.

"Do you need help getting settled in? If you want, I can help you pick up the rest of your stuff from Holly's."

I'm surprised, and a little embarrassed, that she knows I'm staying there. "I don't have much more stuff," I answer. "Pretty much everything was my ex's."

Sarah nods. "Well, if you want, Griffin can probably hook you up with some things, like if you need a bed or a dresser or whatever. He's good like that."

I'm caught off guard by my stomach's flutter. I wouldn't be totally honest if I said I hadn't thought about the fact that living in Sarah's building would give me some access to Griffin. But I didn't know I'd react like that.

"Does he work in the furniture business?"

She crows like I said something hysterical. "No." She shakes her head. "It's just a thing he does."

I have no idea what that means, but getting hooked up with some cheap furniture would help me out a lot.

"Okay, sounds good. Thanks."

She checks the time on her phone. "He'll probably be in his warehouse. Why don't you stop over there and ask him?" She smiles again. I'm not sure if I'm being left out of a joke between Sarah and herself or if something else is at play here.

"Should you call him and let him know I'm coming?" Stopping by unannounced seems a little forward, even for me.

"He won't answer if he's working." She shakes her head. "Just go. I'm sure he'll be happy to see you."

****

Griffin's warehouse is a huge, empty space, sectioned off with metal accordion dividers. My heels echo on the concrete floor, so even though I can't see him, he must know someone's here. The only other sound is soft blues music playing in the background. Sarah told me his work area is the one on the right. I pop my head in.

"Hey, you," I say.

Griffin is behind a large table, molding something. He glances up from his work. "Hey. You. Come in."

This is definitely not a furniture warehouse. The space is impressive. This must be where he sculpts the women from Holly's. Supplies are set up on a cart next to him. There's a stool behind him, which is pushed back, because he's standing right now while he works. Then a few feet in front of the worktable, there's a simple couch and chair behind a small area rug.

Off to the side, next to a slop sink, there's a smaller table. This one has what I'm thinking is a finished piece of work on it. I move closer to get a better view. It's a sculpture of two adult figures and a child. Even though the adults aren't pulling at the child, their arms are wrapped around it like they're both struggling to possess it. There's definitely a story behind this, even though they're kind of abstract and you can't even tell if any of the people are men or women. I'm surprised to find it's causing a lump in my throat. It's beautiful and heartbreaking at the same time.

"This is incredible." I'm drawn to it and I go to touch it, then catch myself. I pull my hand back right before my fingers make contact. "What is it about?"

"It's a client's story." He stays behind his table as I inspect his work.

"What do you mean?"

He sits on his stool, with one sneaker hooked on its rung and the other on the ground. He crosses his arms in front of him "Well, my first love is creating sculptures for the women at Holly's. But I've got to pay the bills, ya know?" He pauses to wait for my answer.

I nod, but I don't really have any idea what he's talking about. Do they not pay him?

"So I started this sort of business on the side. People come and..." He pauses. "Do you want to hear about this? I know it's not why you're here. Sarah texted to tell me you need furniture."

Sarah texted? Then why did she say she wouldn't?

Right now, hearing the story behind his work is the only thing that interests me. This one sculpture alone is so powerful it makes me want to know more.

"No, tell me. I want to hear all about it." I walk over to the couch and sit.

"Basically, people come in and they sit where you are now and they talk to me about their lives. Sometimes they tell me stories they think they want the sculpture to be about. But as they speak, I can tell if there's something more important they're not sharing. I try to get it out of them. It doesn't make sense for me to do some simple sculpture of a Norman Rockwell family. They can go anywhere to get that. People come to me for what's raw, underneath the surface. They model for me while they're here. But I'm more getting a feeling for their kinetic energy than worrying about their physical position. It's what's behind their body language that I'm reading." He stops for a second. "Sound stupid to you?"

"Stupid? It sounds amazing. I never heard of anyone doing that before."

He gets up from the stool and comes to sit beside me on the couch. "But they agree ahead of time not to know what I'm going to create. It's part of the process. If I'm locked into something before I even start, it'll come out like shit."

"Your clients must be so moved when they see what you've done." I don't even know those people and that piece almost had me in tears.

Griffin shrugs. "As long as they don't complain, I guess I'm okay." He shifts around on the cushion, pulling at his jeans, obviously uncomfortable with the compliment.

"And you charge for the pieces? That's how you make a living?"

"Yeah," he nods.

"But not for the statues you do of the women at Holly's?"

He shakes his head. "That's different."

"How?"

He frowns. Maybe because he sees me as a woman from Holly's or maybe because he doesn't like talking about that part of his work.

Or maybe because I ask too many personal questions.

He doesn't answer right away. He just breathes deliberately for a bit, as if he's trying to figure out what to tell me. I fidget a little, too, hoping he'll answer soon before my discomfort forces me to say something stupid.

"Those sculptures…" he says, much to my relief. "They're the women who stay there…" Griffin looks away from me for the first time, and I notice a change in his eyes. They become darker, redder, much the way they did when his mother greeted him in the emergency room. "You've all been through so much. Trying to get your lives back on track. To get away from the bastards who've hurt you. The amount of courage and strength it takes…Holly's means everything to me. The fact that there are places where women like you can go to get a fresh, safe start…I don't even know how to say how grateful I am for it." He scoots a little closer to me and his expression becomes more solemn.

"I've always wanted to find some way to help women in these situations. But I didn't quite know how. Then I realized I could do this. It's small, but at least it's something. Basically, I talk to women there and they tell me whatever they're comfortable sharing. About their lives before abuse. Or about what they most want out of their new beginnings. I sculpt them to give them a concrete example of what their lives can be or to remind them how beautiful they are behind their scars, whether they're emotional or physical. I think a lot of them have forgotten. It's been stolen from them. If my sculptures can give even a fraction of hope, my existence is validated."

I pretend to cough because tears threaten to make an appearance and I'm responding like a typical, emotional girl. But what he's just said is amazing. "Griffin, that's really…"

He thinks I'm one of the women he's talking about. It's obvious because, all of a sudden he's rigid, trying to read my reaction. I need to clear this up, because I feel like a fraud. But for some reason, I think he's going to hate me. Hate me for staying at Holly's, for not telling him right away and letting him find me a place to live, for asking for a deal on furniture when I'm not really facing hardship. I'm just kind of broke.

But I need to tell him, anyway. And if he doesn't want anything else to do with me, I'll have to deal with it. Why does the thought of that bother me, even though I've only just met him? "Griffin, I..." I find myself inching forward as well.

"Oh God, were you two in the middle of something?"

I jump at Sarah's voice and the moment is over.

"I was just telling Frankie about my work." Griffin sounds defensive, like we were doing something we shouldn't have. Evidently, he's surprised by her appearance as well. He moves back toward the edge of the couch, and his body loses the tension it had a second ago.

Sarah smiles as if she's got some inside information. "His sculptures are breathtaking," she tells me. She sits in the chair, rests a foot on it, and wraps her arms around her bent knee. She's wearing sneakers. That's why we didn't hear her approaching. Then she turns to Griffin. "You should sculpt her."

Griffin shoots daggers at Sarah, but I have no idea why. This guy's face has too many complex expressions for me to even try to read them.

"No." He says it to Sarah, not to me, but his emphatic tone tells me she intentionally said something to provoke him. So does her smug expression. They're having some kind of standoff, and it's making me very uncomfortable. The longer it goes on, the more I want to run out of here, but in order to do so, I'd have to redirect their attention to me. With this silent war going on, that's not something I want to do.

So I wait.

"Why not, Griffin?" Sarah finally asks, grinning.

Griffin seethes through his nose and clamps his jaw. He's furious.

"Anyway," Sarah says to me, unaffected by his demeanor, "he's amazing. He only takes clients through word of mouth, and he can't keep up with the requests. He's got to turn people away."

"Believe me, I don't want to." Griffin's anger appears to melt away as he talks about his work again. "I need the money. But if I do too many at once, all the contours will be off, and they'll come out half-assed."

"I understand," I answer. And I really do. I'm certainly no artist. Right now I'm just fooling around with a hobby I'm hoping will turn into something. Even still, I want my pictures to be as good as they can be. I can't imagine how it would be for someone like Griffin to do a rushed job. I'm sure he'd rather starve than create something that didn't make him proud.

"People are lining up to have him sculpt them." Sarah beams like a proud sister.

"I don't think that's the case. I'm probably just so slow it seems like there's always a wait."

Sarah sighs at his comment. "Ugh. Anyway, did you tell her about the stuff you can get her?" she asks him and he shakes his head. Then, to me, she says, "Let's see if he can find you a bed."

Chapter Five

Griffin

"Why the hell did you do that yesterday?" I sneer at Sarah.

Yesterday I managed to scrounge a brand new, still-wrapped mattress and box spring set for Frankie. Kaitlyn's guy, Jackson, always has extra stage props. We've worked out a situation through Holly's where he donates them and he can write it off as a charitable contribution. I arrange for the furniture to be delivered, so there's no cost to the women who need it. You'd be surprised how often you use a bed as a prop for a play. It's also possible Jackson includes them because he knows they're going to a good cause. He's good that way.

In any event, I couldn't get a dresser for her clothes, but she was happy to not have to buy the bed. I doubt a dresser could even squeeze into her crappy studio apartment anyway. I'm a little guilty for suggesting she live there. I'm still convincing myself I had no ulterior motive.

After I arranged the delivery of the bed without letting Frankie know I was picking up the cost, Sarah insisted the three of us grab dinner. I know what she was trying to do, but it was one of the more awkward meals of my life. I don't divulge my innermost feelings to people. I don't discuss my work at Holly's with anyone outside of Sarah and Mr. Rothman, the man who showed me how to channel my anger productively, rather than fighting with every poor bastard who got in my way after a bad day at home.

Yet, in that moment with Frankie at the warehouse, I had to make her understand that I must have this purpose in my life. But I regretted the words as soon as they left my lips. I was shocked and paralyzed by my own candor. I sensed Frankie was about to divulge something important too, but Sarah interrupted before it was possible.

I was glad she did. The warehouse was getting a little too cramped, we were getting too close, and I didn't know what was about to come next.

Frankie was quiet at dinner, too. It felt like she was concealing something. Embarrassment or shame, probably. It wouldn't be surprising. Many of these women feel that way, even though they have nothing to be ashamed of. Quite the opposite.

"Do what?" Sarah asks. But she knows exactly what she did.

"Why did you put me on the spot like that? Saying I should sculpt her? You know I can't sculpt her."

"No, I don't know that, Griffin, because you're not telling me what's going on. First, for no apparent reason, you drag me to the place where she works. When we get there you offer her an apartment you know nothing about and ask me to keep tabs on her. Then when she touches you, you run out like her fingers are on fire. There's clearly something happening here. But you're acting all weird about it. So would you like to tell me whatever it is you're not telling me?"

"There's nothing to tell." I walk behind my sculpting table. I pick up the clay and mash it back into a ball. I wasn't far along with whatever it was going to be, anyway.

Sarah comes over to me. "Don't hide behind the clay." She stops my moving hands with hers. "Are you interested in her? She seems like exactly the kind of girl you'd want."

"I can't."

Sarah, of all people, should understand.

"Why?"

"She makes me...unsettled...and frayed...and..."

"Griffin." She pulls the clay out from under my palms. "You are not him."

"You don't know that."

"Of course I do. I've spent practically every day with you for how many years. You pulled me from that. Do you think I'd stick around again if I thought you were anything like that?"

"It simmers in me when I'm around her, Sarah."

"What you feel isn't the red stirring, Griffin. It's..." She laughs. "Well, you know what it is. I don't have to spell it out for you."

My face gets hot and I want to change the subject. "Speaking of which, I have to go see my mother."

She sighs. "Now why do you have to ruin my day by saying that? You were with her at the hospital a few days ago. Why are you visiting again? You know what she does to you."

"I have to. I need to check in on her."

"One of these days, Griffin, you're going to have to accept that this is the way things are."

Her words make me incensed. I'll never accept it.

39

"And what if I'd accepted the ways things were with you and ignored what I knew? Maybe you'd be dead in a dumpster right now." My voice booms and Sarah shudders. "I'm sorry." I pull her in to hug her. "I didn't mean that. I shouldn't have said it."

"No, you had every right. You're right. I know you have to go."

"She's my mother, Sarah. I'll never be able to walk away from this. No matter how much I want to."

"Can I come with you?" she asks.

"Nah. It'll be a quick visit. Hopefully he won't even be home."

****

My asshole father's BMW parked in the driveway proves that hopes rarely come true. I wanted to get in and out without having to deal with him, but as usual, life has other plans. When I walk through the front door, he's sitting on the couch, feet on the coffee table, computer on his lap. The slamming door grabs his attention.

My father is stunning. At least that's one of the words my mother uses to describe him. By the way women gawk at him, I know it's accurate. It's one of the things that lured my mother to him in the first place. And her attraction to him is one of the things that keeps her coming back for more abuse.

That, and the fact that he's just about the most disgustingly charming, wickedly persuasive man I've ever known.

Unfortunately, I was cursed with his face. His intense, unforgiving eyes. His defined cheekbones. Even his dimples. Our resemblance sickens me. I do whatever I can to distinguish myself from him. He hates that I keep myself this way, that I can take the beauty he has and destroy it. It gives me pleasure to know I can irritate him.

Because after all, he destroys the thing that should be most beautiful to me.

"Griffin." He smiles at me. "I didn't know you were coming by today."

"I didn't tell Mom I was coming. I just stopped in to check on her. See how her nose was healing." My words never hide my anger toward this man.

"Right. Two left feet, that one." Ever since I moved out, he plays this game with me. Pretends I don't remember how many times I witnessed him hitting her and begged him to stop. Like I'm supposed to act as blind as everyone else.

"Funny. Sure looks to me like some asshole punched her in the face." He can pretend, but I won't. I tramp past him through the kitchen to the back porch where my mother is drinking coffee.

"Hi, Mom." I kiss her on the forehead and sit next to her.

"Hi, honey. Why didn't you tell me you were coming? I would have put up more dinner."

"I'm not staying. Definitely not now." I tilt my head in my father's direction.

"Griffin, stop. I'm sure he'd love for you to stay. You two haven't spoken in a while. He probably wants to catch up."

"As if I give a fuck what he wants. Let me see your nose." I take her chin in my hand and examine the bruises. The swelling has gone down and some of the colors marking her skin are turning an ugly yellow.

She's healing.

"I'm fine, Griffin." She pulls her face from my hand. "You have to stop worrying about me."

"Then stop giving me a reason to worry."

She sighs and gives me the disappointed expression I've become accustomed to. "You're here. Stay. Let me throw something else on the stove and we'll all have a nice meal together."

"Do you remember the last time that happened?" I ask.

She thinks for a moment before answering. "Actually, no. See, we're overdue."

"Nope. Not gonna happen. But I would come more often for dinner with you if you'd leave his ass already."

Before the sentence is out of my mouth, my mother is shushing me to cover up the words she knew were coming. This is the way it always goes. She tries to quiet me. She tells me she accepts my father. She talks about all the wonderful things he does for her, the romantic poetry he writes her, the exotic places he takes her. No matter what I say, she counters my statements with her own distorted version of that man. She's been doing it all my life. It aggravates me beyond words.

She whispers. "You need to stop this. I'm not going anywhere. I've told you a thousand times. Now you can either stay, have dinner with us, and put on a happy face…well, at least take off the scowl. Or give me a kiss goodbye, and tell me you'll see me soon."

I stand and kiss the top of her head. "Goodbye, Mom. I'll see you soon."

When she acts defeated, it always makes me feel guilty. "Goodbye, Griffin. I love you."

"Yeah. Love you, too." I storm back through the

house, not acknowledging my father when he asks why I'm already leaving.

Chapter Six

Frankie

It's wonderful to have a day off. They've been giving me lots of hours at the tavern, which is great, even though it's exhausting, because I need the money. Plus, Sarah and Griffin have been stopping by on a pretty regular basis, which always makes me happy for reasons I'm not fully willing to admit to myself yet. I can't completely deny them either, though, because every time Griffin wanders in, I hope he's alone for a split second, until Sarah strolls in next to him. I'm pretty sure they're just friends, but they seem so close it makes me wonder.

When Griffin told me what he does for those women, I swear my heart cracked in half. I'm not sure if he realizes how beautiful it is. If he does, he certainly doesn't acknowledge it. He's been showing up unannounced a lot. Sometimes at the tavern, and other times he stops by my place to say hi, after visiting Sarah. He'll come in, talk and have a drink. But he always acts like he's not sure if he should be there, or like he can't wait to leave. Yet he doesn't leave. He sits, as if something is preventing him from going, or he's waiting for something else to happen. I ask him random questions to prolong his visits, and I always get the same ruminating pause before he decides if he wants to answer. Eventually, he does, and his answers are consistently complex. Everything he says affects me, making me like him a little more every day. And every so often, when I'm lucky enough to say something that tickles him, his mouth breaks into this amazing smile, brightening his whole face.

As attractive as I've tried not to notice he is, the clincher was last week. He came over after a meeting with a client. He was dressed up, with his hair pushed back. His full beard was trimmed to a thin scruff. And he's got these long, gorgeous dimples that I didn't know about. They start just under his cheekbones and extend down his face. When he walked in the door, I did a double take. I knew he was handsome. I could see it under his mess. But gosh, when the guy cleans up, he's breathtaking. I couldn't take my eyes off him. I was tempted to ask him why he conceals this version of himself. But for once, I had the decency to hold in my verbal diarrhea.

Historically, I haven't had the best judgment when it comes to guys. I mean, that thing with Randy was the only time I was in a situation that had the potential to turn ugly, but in general, I don't pick winners. I tend to jump into relationships, and I've been cheated on more than once. Since graduating college last year, I've found many guys who ended up wanting a one- or two-night stand. So even though I'm attracted to Griffin and would love a shot at something with him, I'm trying to hold back. Because as much as I'm sure he and Sarah are just friends, I'm not *really* sure. Sarah keeps insinuating that Griffin's been finding excuses to come over lately, but I have no idea how often he visited before I moved in. And every time I think Griffin and I might be about to cross some invisible line, he pulls back, holding himself at a casual arm's length. It's pretty confusing.

And then there's the fact that I still haven't explained why I was staying at Holly's. It may not even matter at this point, but now that I know how much Holly's means to him, it feels like a big deception.

I haven't intentionally withheld it from him. But either Sarah's around or we're in the middle of a great conversation and I don't want to ruin it. The longer I go without telling him, the harder it's becoming to bring it up. I just need to find the right moment.

Today, though, I'm taking advantage of my day off. I must have shot a thousand pictures this morning. The spring weather is gorgeous in Washington Square Park, where there is no shortage of interesting subjects. Everyone in the city is out and about today and the streets are saturated with color. I got a good shot of water spurting from a fountain. A close up of a rusty, broken spoke on someone's chained-up bicycle should come out nice. And some girl let me get about two inches away from her so I could take a shot of one of her striped knee-high socks. I'm excited to see what I can do with that one.

Most people don't get my pictures. I know that. Sometimes, I don't get them myself. But most of the time, when I study one after I've zoomed all the way in and distorted the light, it speaks to me. My pictures prove to me that all around us, things aren't what we think they are at first glance. The deeper we look, the more we find.

Maybe that's why I'm so quick to jump into things all the time. I don't just see a situation as it presents itself, with all its negatives. I see it for what it might become, if I explore some more. And if it doesn't work out, there's always something else behind it, waiting for me. One day my thinking might come back to bite me in the ass, but so far in my twenty-three years, it hasn't.

The sun beams and something shiny reflects off the ground. A tarnished silver hoop earring stuck in a crack in the sidewalk, calls me. I kneel to take the shot, but I can't get it the way I want from this angle. I'm too far above it. I need it head-on. I lie flat on my stomach, which allows me to catch the sun through the hoop.

"That's a fantastic way to catch impetigo." His low voice would have caused me to drop my camera if it wasn't already on the ground.

"What, are you following me?" I joke as I find Griffin through the lens. I snap a quick picture before he can process what I'm doing.

"Nah, I was on my way to deliver a sculpture to a client outside the square, and as I was walking through, I saw this crazy person splattered on the ground in the middle of Washington Square Park. I almost walked right on by because crazy isn't out of the ordinary here. But imagine my surprise when I realized I knew this particular nutcase."

I laugh as I stand and dust myself off. "Yeah, well. Had to get the shot."

He searches the ground but is blind to my treasure. "What were you taking?"

"Here. Look." I call up the picture and zoom it in. You can hardly tell it's an earring. A huge silver spiral and a blinding light shooting though it fill the screen. I can't wait to play with it when I get home. I hold out the camera for Griffin but not quite far enough. He's got to lean in close to see it. A strategic move on my part, I'll admit.

He breathes in and out a few times as he squints into the viewfinder. I'm not sure if our proximity is affecting him the way it is me, but when he rubs the back of his neck, I think it might be. I smile to myself. So much for holding back.

"That's that?" He points to the old earring stuck in the ground. I nod. "Wow." He smiles at me. "You have an incredible eye."

"Thanks." No one really compliments my pictures. They're often curious about them, and maybe give me a "huh" but that's it.

"Do you have more?"

"Are you kidding? How much time have you got?"

He smiles. Score!

We find a bench with some open space and sit close to each other, so we don't crowd the people already sitting. The lack of space is fine with me. I flip through the pictures taken today and try to find one he'll like. I stop when I come to a shot of a crack in a brick. The way I took it, it appears to be a deep canyon. Or a cut on a person's skin. I show it to him and wait with a tight stomach for a reaction.

He frowns at it for much longer than I expected. "What is this?" he finally asks.

"A cracked brick."

"Oh, I thought it was…" When he raises his head, our faces are closer than either of us expected, with me leaning over his shoulder to see what he's seeing. "How did you start taking pictures like this?" His voice is lower than before.

I shrug. "I don't know. I just like finding things

other people can't—you know? I don't think anything is either all beautiful or all ugly. When you get closer, there's a lot more to discover."

He doesn't respond. He just stares at me for so long it gives me chills. At first, I think he's going to kiss me, but when he doesn't it feels more like he's searching inside me, able to read every thought and see straight through to my organs. The idea makes me cringe and finally, I cast my eyes down.

"Don't do that," he says. "Don't deny me, Frankie."

I'm taken aback by his strange, forward comment.

"Deny you what?" I ask.

"You. Access to you." His words are tight and so is his expression. He definitely did not plan on saying that, because he tries to draw away from me as soon as the last word leaves his lips, but the arm of the bench doesn't let him. He stands.

"I've got to go. I'll see you." He stumbles on the bench as he bustles away.

Deny him access to me? I was right. He was trying to read my thoughts. I don't realize what his words did to me until my heart beats in my ears. I lift my hair off my neck for a second. All at once, it's gotten pretty hot out here.

When I lower my hand, it hits a brown bag sitting next to me. In his attempt to make a quick getaway, Griffin left his sculpture. He's nowhere to be found in the crowd of people. How fast did he book out of here?

There's no answer on his cell. Since I have no idea where he was meeting his client, I leave a message telling him I'll drop it off at his warehouse. Too bad he's too freaked to answer his phone. Now he'll have to make two trips.

****

The area behind the divider in his warehouse is empty, which disappoints me. Another sculpture sits on the table and I place the closed brown bag next to it. This statue is a woman. Tall, voluptuous, beautiful. She's wearing a sleek gown with a slit up the front, exposing a very long, slim leg. She's elegant and pristine, except one strap of her gown has fallen from her shoulder, forming an out of place contrast between the strap and the rest of her perfect posture. And though her body exudes confidence, her head is dipped down. She wears the most morose expression I've ever seen.

It is exquisite. Before I think about what I'm doing, I reach out for it. I can't help it. I caress the chiffon dress, and fallen strap. Then I touch her hair. The textures in it are wavy and unruly, almost to a sinful degree. An invisible breeze fans it around her. I breathe in through my nose to experience the breeze. She smells like Griffin. That scent on him the day I ran into him at the hospital wasn't paint, after all.

It was clay.

The woman's arm is raised and her fingers are running through her hair, moving it away from her face. I think I'm being gentle when I trace my hand over her arm, but my touch is obviously not as soft as I think.

"No!" I wail when the statue's hand separates from her wrist and her arm is limp in my hand. I panic. I can't even run away, because I know if I let go of this arm, the entire thing will fall off and I'll ruin it worse than I already did. Holy crap. Why would I touch his work? What is wrong with me? Beads of sweat form on my forehead and my chest. I'm stuck. I can't move a muscle for fear of destroying this beautiful piece even more. What the hell am I going to do?

Maybe if it let it go and run out of here, Griffin will think it fell off by itself. He never has to know I touched it.

"That wouldn't be very nice." Griffin's grumbly voice startles me from behind and I jerk, inadvertently removing the arm a little from the shoulder.

"Dammit!" The arm sags in my hand but I don't lower it. "I'm sorry. I'm so sorry. I shouldn't have touched it. I don't know why I did."

Griffin chuckles from somewhere deep in his stomach. My own stomach clenches with nerves.

"It's okay." He steps closer.

"Wait," I say. "What wouldn't be nice?"

"Making me think it fell off by itself. That I did shitty, unstable work."

I gulp. I'm glad my back is still to him, so he can't see my heart pounding through my shirt. "I said that out loud?" I do have a tendency to talk to myself. I scrunch my face in embarrassment.

"Yep." He's amused. I am not.

"I'm really sorry," I repeat. Who touches someone else's art? I'm such an idiot.

"I told you, it's okay." He moves within an inch of my back and reaches his arms around me. Before I realize what he's doing, his hand is over mine, guiding it. Together, we methodically rebuild the arm. First at the shoulder where it was still somewhat attached, then at the wrist.

Griffin's chest is on my back and every slow breath he takes accelerates my own. He's quite a bit taller and his chin is by my temple as he leans over my shoulder

51

to fix what I broke. Can he feel the moisture on my forehead through his stubble? I can barely focus.

"It wasn't set yet," he breathes into my ear. "Otherwise it wouldn't have fallen apart in your hands that way."

He's quiet as we finish smoothing the clay, blending it seamlessly. You can't even tell where it came apart. We're just about done, and I know when we are, he's going to back away again. I really, really don't want that. Before he can, I speak.

"Who is she?" My voice comes out hushed, which I didn't intend, but seeing how close he is, it makes sense.

"Just a client." His answer is low and dismissive.

"She's beautiful."

"Yes."

The word vibrates in my ear.

There's an inexplicable pang in my gut at the thought of him intimately sculpting this gorgeous woman, alone in this private yet open workspace. Especially since he said he wouldn't sculpt me. I have no right to that reaction. I'm nothing to him. Still, I stiffen at the thought. He must feel it because he releases my hand.

I turn around, but he doesn't back away, and now he's right in my face.

Ordinarily, if I'm attracted to a guy who's hovering in my space, I'd make a move without even hesitating. Just go for it. But Griffin makes me tongue-tied, which throws me. He shaved again, probably because he was on his way to meet a client. God, he's gorgeous. This close, every one of his defined features is clear. His bottom lip has a small indentation, like he bites it out of habit. What a picture his lips would make. I'd love to run my hand along them and feel him. But this time, I refrain from touching.

"Thanks for bringing back my statue." His soft breath tickles my nose.

"Sure. I knew you needed it."

At first, he says his usual nothing. I'm beginning to be irritated with this guy's complete comfort with silence and how long it takes him to say anything.

Then his lips part.

"I get so lost in you, Frankie. You make it too easy to slip away from reality." Even though the warehouse is completely open, it echoes like a cave and his gravelly voice surrounds me.

Okay, maybe some conversation is worth waiting for. I try to lean in a little closer but the camera around my neck jabs into both our chests. I pull it up over my head and wait for his next move. But his next move is to retreat.

"I guess I should go deliver this," he says, his voice assuming its normal tone. What? Are you kidding me right now?

Nope. That's enough. I have to speak up and confront him as he starts to walk away again. "I don't like this."

"What?"

"This. I think you're playing games with me, and I don't like it. You say these things and then you bail. There's no way you don't know you're doing it."

He's surprised by my directness. "I'm not."

I take step closer to him. "You are."

"I don't mean to play with you, Frankie. I swear." He sounds torn and genuine.

K. K. Weil

"Then why do you do that?"

"I'm trying...I don't want to do it." He dips his head down toward mine. "I just...I need to stay away from you."

These aren't the words I was expecting. "Why?" I lean into him. I have no idea why he thinks he has to keep away from me, but his body language says that's not what he wants.

His jaw clenches and his brown eyes become darker. I think he might back away and even though I'm acting poised and confident on the outside, all my organs feel like they're playing rugby inside me.

"I need to stay away from you. For *you*."

For me? That makes no sense.

"So stay away from me." I tilt my head up, daring him to kiss me.

He inhales a few times, thinking, with his frown growing deeper by the second. "I will...tomorrow." He pulls my head in, and both of his hands tangle into my hair. He kisses me with such force that at first our teeth crash together, before morphing into a kiss filled with starvation. It's a kiss that shoots straight to my toes and my fingertips, and I feel like a girl who's never been kissed before. And truly I haven't. Not like this.

It's exactly the kind of kiss I'd expect from Griffin Stone.

He pushes himself against me, and I boost myself onto his table, careful not to knock over the gorgeous woman this time. I pull him into me, between my legs. When our shirts both come off at lightning speed and his hands search my body, I have a sinking thought I might be throwing myself into one of those stupid situations again, with a guy who just wants a quick fix.

I have a feeling Griffin's not the kind of guy you sleep with, give a peck on the cheek, and are fine when he goes off on his merry way. He's the kind of guy you sleep with, he ravages your soul, and leaves you a puddle to clean up after he's gone. But while he's kissing me like his existence depends on it, I just don't care.

With a mind of their own, my fingers find his zipper. He pries one of his hands off my skin, pats the back of his jeans and groans. "Shit, my wallet's upstairs."

Luckily, I'm impulsive enough to know I need to always be prepared. I reach into my purse and dig out the little square he was searching for. I try not to imagine what he's thinking of me for having it on hand. "Here." I press it into his palm.

He contemplates the contents of his hand for a second. I assume he's going to rip open the wrapper and put on the condom. Instead, he crushes it in his fist and drops it on the floor. He pulls my mouth to his again and kisses me, almost desperately. Then with the same ferocity, he breaks our kiss, backing up only enough to allow us to catch our breath. He holds my face, unmoving for an eternity, inhaling and exhaling. I can't tell whether he's going to tell me to leave, because he said he needs to stay away from me, or tear off the rest of my clothes.

He does neither.

Instead, he lowers his hands from my face, pulls my shirt back on and scoops my hair out of it so it falls down my back. He coils his hand through its length for a minute before forcing himself to break free. Then he slips his own shirt over his head and takes my hand.

"Come with me."

He leads me down to the train. We sit side by side in complete silence for the entire ride. He doesn't so much as turn in my direction. In the reflection of the window, he's sitting straight as an arrow, oblivious of the people opposite us, with his thoughts somewhere in the blackness of the tunnel.

When we arrive at our stop, he takes my hand again, leading me onto the platform. We're in Brooklyn now, and I have no idea why. Asking would be pointless. Griffin will only tell me when he's ready.

We approach a modest two-story house similar to the ones on either side of it. It's made of brick, which is one of my favorite surfaces to shoot. So many unique crevices in a single brick. But Griffin's gait is purposeful, and I doubt he wants to be sidetracked so I can take a picture.

He pulls out a key and walks us in through a living room. "Mom?" he calls.

"Griffin?" a voice yells from upstairs. "Is everything okay? Why are you here?"

Quick footsteps tap the steps. Griffin's mother looks the same as the other day in the ER, except her bandage is gone and her bruises are almost no longer visible.

"Oh, hello," she says, startled to see me. Almost as startled as I am to be here.

Griffin walks us over to her and reaches out with his free hand. "Show her," he commands.

"What?" To say his mother appears shocked would be a gross understatement.

"Show her your side," he says, more forcefully.

"Griffin, I don't know what you're doing. What's

wrong with you?" She takes a step away from her son.

He raises his voice. "Lift your shirt." When she starts to protest again, he follows it with, "I need to show her what I'm capable of doing."

A flash of understanding crosses her face. After a momentary pause, Griffin's mother raises her shirt on her left side to expose her rib cage. The colors of the bruises are similar to the ones around her nose that day, but some spots are more discolored than others and I think I can make out the marks of knuckles.

My head snaps to Griffin. "You did that?" No way. No way in hell.

"No," he says, irises almost scalding me with their heat. "But I could." Without another word to his mother, he leads me out of the house.

"I don't understand," I say to him as we barrel down the block. What does that even mean?

Griffin finds a bench. I sit beside him in silence until he's ready to explain. Buses and people fly past and it's loud, but he doesn't care.

"My first distinct memory of my father hitting my mother is when I was seven. I remember some yelling before that, but details are fuzzy. This time, though, I was sitting at the dinner table. My mother made me grilled cheese and was leaning over the table, cutting off the crust when my father came in. She smiled and said hi, but he was scowling at her. He asked if that was what she wore outside that day. She said it was. He made a comment about her falling out of her shirt, and asked if she was trying to pick up some guys. Instead of taking him seriously, she laughed him off, made some sarcastic joke about him being paranoid.

"He started yelling that she was mocking him.

When she realized he was really mad, not kidding, she cowered. It was the first time it ever registered to me that she did that. Anyway, he stormed over, screaming, asking why she wore things that triggered him. He punched her right in the stomach. She keeled over, hitting her head on the table and knocking my grilled cheese to the floor. He yelled about that too, saying she ruined my dinner. I grabbed the food off the floor and ate every bit of it, cut-off crust and all, to show him she didn't do anything wrong."

Griffin pauses, deep in his memory, before continuing.

I wait.

"I don't know when it started but it's never ended, Frankie. She's stayed with him all these years. He hits her, then begs for forgiveness. And she loves him." He gives a brittle laugh. "The man punches her whenever the urge strikes him, and she loves him. She'll never leave him."

What he's telling me is horrible and my heart hurts for him. His pained expression makes him look as if he's going to break into a thousand pieces.

"Did he do it to you, too?" My voice is delicate, like a child's, but I'm afraid of the answer.

"No." He's hunched over with his head held low. "He reserved it for her. I would have gladly taken it, instead. But that's not his way."

I reach for his hand without thinking about it.

"But what did you mean when you said 'you could'? You haven't done anything, have you?"

He shifts in my direction. "Frankie, do you have any idea the likelihood that I'll be like him? Do you? Because I do. I've read every bit of research out there.

And it's likely. Too likely. It's in me. I would kill myself if I ever did that to a woman."

"So you're just going to stay away from women because you're afraid of hurting them?" I understand his point and respect him for it, but that's a little extreme.

He sighs and supports his head in his free hand. "Not all women." He stops talking for a second, thinking about what to tell me. "Frankie, you remind me so much of her. Of the way she used to be. I remember her being so lustrous and free-spirited, always jabbing at my father, seeing things around her the way no one else did. But he got worse as the years went on. He killed that sassy part of her. I don't think she even recognizes the change in herself. Or if she does, she's never mentioned it.

"That's why I have to stay away from you. From the second you ordered me to leave that tissue paper alone, I knew you'd be someone who could challenge me. You bring out my intense side, the side that wants something more, just like my mother did for my father."

"Is there another side to you?" I joke.

He gives me a mirthless smile. "I'm serious. You trigger things in me I'm dying to feel, but at the same time, with that comes a lack of control over myself and my actions. What just happened in the warehouse? So fast like that? I never... It's dangerous."

"Griffin, first of all, I'm sure he doesn't hit her because she's got a smart mouth. Men who hit, hit. Saying her personality provokes him is an excuse."

"That's not what I meant. I just meant they're more explosive together."

I interrupt before he can finish. "And second, you are not your father."

"I'm *like* him. And growing up in that house in itself, witnessing the abuse for all those years, puts me on a path to become an abuser. It's a fact."

"You're a good person, Griffin. You wouldn't hurt anyone like that."

His laugh is cynical this time. "You don't know, Frankie. The rage I feel sometimes when I think about him. The darkness takes over, and I have to fight to bring myself back."

"Everyone gets heated, Griffin. It doesn't mean you're going to hit me." I hate that he thinks this of himself.

"How could you even take that risk? How could you put yourself in that position again?"

"Griffin, I was never in a relationship like that." I don't even pause before it's out. There is no question that this is the time to confess. Still, I almost want to pull the words back before they can reach his ears.

"You don't need to lie to me. Please don't be ashamed. It's not your fault."

"I'm not. I mean, I'm not lying. I was in a situation that made me uncomfortable, so I left. I explained the whole thing to Taylor and she said I could stay at Holly's until I found somewhere else. But I've never been hit." I wish I could add, "Please don't hate me," but that's a little too needy.

He processes what I said for a couple of heartbeats, but there is no sign that he's angry. "Then you don't have any idea what you'd be getting into."

"But Griffin, you're not like that at all."

"Neither was he in the beginning. That much I

know. It started after they were in love, after he got comfortable. When he knew she was his. Then his true self came out."

"Just because that's what happened with your parents doesn't mean that's what will happen with you and me."

He shakes his head. "It's not a chance I'm willing to take."

Chapter Seven

Griffin

Another second with Frankie and I would have taken her right on that fucking table. I've never been with a woman in the warehouse. All the women who've been in there, except for Sarah, were clients, and I'd never sleep with a client.

But I'd be lying if I said I hadn't fantasized about it. From the first time I saw Frankie with her eye to that camera, her untamed blonde hair falling around it, I've thought about it a little too much. Something tells me being with Frankie would be even better than I've imagined. If I thought that's all it would be, I would have done it. And it would have probably been the hottest experience of my damn life. It took every ounce of restraint I had not to do it. Especially when she pressed that condom into my palm.

But I couldn't. She needed to know what I am. I've been a little on edge since bringing Frankie to see my mother last week. Well, on edge is putting it mildly. I've been a moody bastard. Storming around like some asshole who's got a beef with everyone and everything on the planet. Snapping at Sarah for nothing. I was even short with a client the other day, which is bad news if I'd like to keep eating.

Sarah's on her way over because she thinks

watching a comedy will be a good way to relax me, though I think it will take more than a few corny jokes and some bad acting to ease what's brewing inside me.

She knocks and peeks her head through the doorway. "Hey there."

"Hi, come on in. Everything is just about set."

"Griff?" She's tentative and it takes a mere second to figure out why. Mr. Rothman lags a step behind her.

Sarah really does get me. She knew damn well a movie wouldn't help. That wasn't even her plan. This was.

Just the sight of Mr. Rothman has a settling effect on me.

"Hi, Griffin," he says.

"Hi Roth. What are you doing here?" But I already know. He's here to be my mentor, my voice of reason, my sounding board, as he has been since the day he opened up to me about his shitty past.

He motions to Sarah as his answer.

"You tattled on me?" I ask her. But I'm not pissed, I'm grateful and she knows it.

"Come on, Griffin." She rubs my arm as a peace offering. "You know you've been in the bad place, lately. Maybe Roth can help. I'm going downstairs for a bit to check out what you're working on. We can watch the movie when you guys are done." She leaves without waiting for me to respond.

"Don't be mad at her." Mr. Rothman makes himself comfortable on my couch.

"For what, ratting me out to my high school teacher?" I joke.

"For calling me. You know she only wants to help."

"I'm fine," I say, but there's no point trying to conceal anything from him. All Mr. Rothman has to do is look at me to break my already-fracturing façade. "Okay, maybe a little less than fine."

"So what's been going on?"

I tell him about Frankie, how I'm frustrated because I found someone I think I'd be the real me with. How her words about there being beauty and ugliness in everything at the same time connected with me more deeply than it would ever be safe to tell her. I also share how my last couple of visits to my mother have been harder for me than usual. The older I get, the less I understand why she stays with him. And every time there's another incident, it chips away at me a little more.

I've been removed from the situation for almost six years, since I left for college. In some ways it's a lot better because I'm not living with it. But in other ways it's worse, because every time my mother's number pops up on the screen of my cell, my immediate reaction is to wonder if she's in the hospital.

My head's been all over the place for the past week. I keep replaying what almost happened in the warehouse. How powerful my craving for Frankie suddenly became. I went from zero to sixty in a split second. From restrained to losing control. I'll have it completely together, and then she says something, or looks at me a certain way, and I do something I wasn't planning on. The unpredictability of my responses to her scares the hell out of me.

It's much too familiar.

I haven't contacted her since that day, and she hasn't stopped by unannounced. I won't go to Sarah's apartment, because I'm afraid of running into Frankie. Every time footsteps smack on the ground, I stop working for a second, hoping it will be her, but so far it's only been the other guy who rents space in the warehouse. I don't want to hope it's her. I want to forget I ever met her at Holly's that day, and all our interactions since. It's better for her that way, safer. Pursuing her when I know that would be incredibly selfish of me.

Mr. Rothman is attentive as I ramble on. My thoughts don't follow any cohesive pattern. They just come out garbled, as they have been in my mind for the last seven days. Finally, I shut up and wait for his advice.

"You've come so far, Griffin. When we met, you were an angry kid, headed for nowhere fast. You got your life on track."

"*You* got my life on track," I say.

"No, son, I showed you an alternative road. You're the one who decided to follow it. But you're at a new crossroads, now. I know you're afraid if you let yourself out you won't be able to control it. But holding everything in and denying yourself will only eat at you."

"I do let myself out, through my work. You taught me that."

"Yes, and that's very important. And what you do for those women is invaluable. Except now you're hiding behind it as an excuse not to engage in relationships that might challenge you.

"My mother challenged my father for years," I say.

He shakes his head in pity. "Just because their situation is what it is, doesn't mean yours would be.

Griffin, you were smart to read up on domestic violence. You are aware of the facts, the statistics. If you weren't I'd be a lot more frightened of what you might become, honestly. Because let's face it, a lot of witnesses of violence go on to become perpetrators later. I don't have to tell you that, you know it better than anyone.

"But you *are* aware of it. I have every confidence you will not fall into that role of history repeating itself. You've got to have some faith in yourself. And you've got to stop running from anyone who can bring you real pleasure. Otherwise, your whole existence is going to be as bland and lifeless as those hunks of clay before you use your talent to mold them into something beautiful."

I put my head in my hands. "I don't know."

"I do. Now, I don't mean I know if this woman is the one for you. I haven't met her, and I've heard very little about her. What I mean is, I know you're afraid to be with her because she brings part of you to life. To me, that alone is a reason to try."

"I pushed her away. She hasn't contacted me since then. She's probably already moved on. She's not the type of girl who waits around for a guy."

"That's your fear talking. You won't know unless you try."

"I wouldn't even know where to begin." I sigh.

"How about with flowers? Women are suckers for flowers. I bring them to my wife whenever I'm in the doghouse." He laughs.

Flowers. I groan. Normal people aren't bothered by flowers. Normal people don't associate flowers with bribery and repentance. But then, normal people weren't raised by my father.

I can't even smell a rose without thinking of the day I came home to petals scattered throughout my home. The harsh floral scent permeated my nose before I even opened the door. There was a trail of red, yellow, and pink petals leading from the living room up the stairs. My hack father couldn't even think of a more original flower to bait my mother with.

God only knows what was waiting for her in the bedroom.

She was so happy. This was his latest extravagance for what my mother thought, or pretended to think, was no reason. But when she flinched as he kissed her split lip, there's no way she wasn't reminded of his handiwork from three days before.

I wanted to scream, "See, that's why he does all the things he does. To keep you distracted." But there was no point. My words would have fallen on deaf, stubborn ears, one more time.

They were playful, showering each other with petal after petal and each time the petals shifted, their fragrance scorched deeper into my psyche.

The only smell that makes me sicker is the sterile scent of hospital.

"You have a petal stuck to you," my father whispered, pulling a yellow one from the collar of her blouse. "Here, make a wish." He held it to her mouth.

She blew it and smiled. "I already got my wish."

I was sick at the way she adored him. He bent and scooped two handfuls from the floor, sprinkling them over her head. They got caught all over her.

"You're such a mess," he teased, nibbling on her neck. "What are we going to do with you?"

She giggled like a fucking middle school student. Man, did I hate that sound. I heard her whisper that she had a few ideas. I thundered out of the room, kicking any petals in my wake.

I will never use flowers to get what I want.

"No flowers." I'm adamant. "No bribes."

Mr. Rothman laughs. "Flowers aren't really a bribe, Griffin."

A Roth lecture is imminent, but I won't give in on this. "No flowers."

"Okay, well then you could just go talk to her."

"And say what?" I sneer. "That last week I was trying to protect her, but today I'm thinking about how hot she is, so the hell with her safety?"

He frowns at my sarcasm. "I think we both know it's not about whether or not she's attractive. Otherwise you wouldn't be so afraid of getting close to her. You'd have a quick fling and move on. Your past wouldn't be an issue."

He's wrong when he refers to it as my past. As long as my mother stays with my father, it's my past, present, and future.

But his point is spot on.

Chapter Eight

Frankie

My head is pounding. It came on while I was working the lunch shift. Even though I should have taken some pain reliever, it was busy and I kept forgetting. Now I'm lying in bed in the dark with a full-blown migraine. I've taken Motrin, but it hasn't kicked in yet. I'm afraid I might vomit. The cold compress across my forehead is doing little to help, and when my cell clicks indicating a text, there's no way I'm checking who it's from.

It clicks again. And again. When it clicks a fourth time, I ease my head up to reach for the phone so I can turn it off. Even that small motion makes my head throb and my stomach churn. I search for the button, but it rings in my hand. Whoever is texting me must really want to talk.

"Hello?" I murmur.

"Where have you been? Are you avoiding me?"

Uy. It's my sister, Gabby. And yes, I have been avoiding her.

I love my sister. Truly, I do. But talking to her is exhausting. Gabby is two years younger, which technically makes me the big sister, but it's never quite gone that way. Gabby has always been the driven daughter. The type-A girl who has it all together, who's

69

known since she was five what she wanted to be when she grew up and has never strayed from it. She gets great grades, she's been dating the same great guy since high school, and she even has great, weather-resistant hair. She's a pre-med major and will no doubt be accepted to the medical school of her choice when she graduates next year.

And then there's me. My parents see me as the flaky one, whose unpredictable life choices will lead nowhere fast and will, one day, bring me down a road of sadness and poverty. Of course they don't say it quite like that, but their passive aggressive comments about Gabby's success, followed by questions like, *So what is it you're focusing on these days, Frankie?* do little to hide who their favorite is. I couldn't even settle on a major until the last possible minute. Then I chose communications with a minor in ancient studies—yikes—not because I found them compelling, but because I'd already accumulated credits in those subjects. As a result, I spent an extra semester finishing school.

On paper, it doesn't sound good. I realize that. But I don't regret a single decision. I may not be the most focused person, but I enjoy my life. Some might think that makes me a quitter, but I think it makes me open-minded and interesting. I would never have even discovered photography if I felt bound to a certain path.

Less than a year ago, I was on my way to deliver coffee to an office full of people at my crappy, entry-level job. The coolest, most disgusting feather was stuck in a pile of dirt and something about it made me take pause. Bits of the dirt clung to the individual strands like they were holding on for dear life. I pulled out my cell and snapped a picture of it. When I got home later, I kept inspecting it, zooming in and cropping. For the next two weeks, I searched for weird things to capture on my phone. I asked my parents to buy me a fancy camera for my birthday. I doubt they would have agreed if they knew my next move would be to quit my crummy job and try to become a photographer. I know very well I'm a complete newbie, have tons of work ahead of me and might completely fail. But I enjoy taking pictures much more than anything else I've ever done. If I can waitress while I learn how to do this, then that's a pretty neat way to spend my time.

But when my sister's texts started last week, checking in, I didn't have it in me to list all my recent less-than-successful ventures. I like myself, and I'm not ashamed of who I am, but I don't always feel like harping on it. Gabby would never judge me, which is another one of her annoyingly perfect qualities, but she does report everything to my parents, and right now, I'm telling them things on a need-to-know basis. And they definitely don't need to know my short relationship failed, I haven't come close to selling a photo, and the guy I'm interested in thinks I'd bring out the worst in him.

It threw me last week when Griffin pushed me away. I'm not used to being turned down like that. But then when he brought me to meet...well, you can't call it meet...his mother and show me what his father does to her, I didn't even know how to respond. It's just awful.

I thought it was a good sign that he was sharing that with me. After all, I'd bet he doesn't go around exposing family secrets to just anyone. But then he maintained that he needs to keep his distance. I disagree. I mean, I get what he's saying: sons of abusers become abusers. But he's not saying he wants to be alone for the rest of his life. He just doesn't want to be with someone like me.

He said I'm not a risk he's willing to take. So I haven't contacted him since, and I'm not going to. I don't chase after guys. I move on.

But this time, for some reason, I'm dying to engage in the chase.

I did allow myself to fool around with that picture I stole of him in Washington Square. I zoomed in until the shot was nothing but his lips. I studied every groove until I made up my mind to delete it. No point driving myself crazy.

"Are you there, Frankie?"

"Yeah, I'm here." I speak low, to cause myself as little pain as possible.

"Why are you whispering?"

"Headache."

"Oh," she says and I think she might let me off the hook and hang up. No such luck. "Where are you? I called your apartment but Randy said you don't live there any more."

"Nope, that didn't work out. I got another place."

Gabby asks a bunch of probing questions, and I'm as evasive as possible, not telling her why I left Randy or about Griffin at all. I mention a couple of the shots I've taken and make up some places I tried to sell them. I feel a little bad about lying, but I want my parents to think I'm being proactive about my career. I'm about to cut her off and hang up because I don't think my head can take another second of conversation, when she interrupts.

"I'm thinking of coming down to the city to visit you soon, when I have a couple of days off. Would that be okay?"

So she can see my shoebox apartment next to a crack den? Sure, can't wait.

"Of course."

"Okay, Frankie. I'll talk to you soon." The phone clicks on her end, and I'm happy the conversation is over. I reapply the compress, close my eyes and try to will away the pain.

A soft tap at my door lulls me back to consciousness. I must have fallen asleep. I have no idea if it's still late afternoon or the middle of the night. I'm completely disoriented.

"It's open," I call. At least I don't think I locked it. I should get better at doing that.

The door opens a crack and a gale of light rushes into the room. I don't even have to pick up my head to know it's Griffin. Somehow, I sense him standing there. Maybe it's because he's so quiet at first. No one else would stand in a shadowy doorway for this long and not speak a word.

Or my spiked pulse rate might be the clue instead.

I don't look up.

"Frankie," he says. "Are you okay? Why are you lying here in the dark?"

I guess it's not the middle of the night yet, or darkness would be appropriate. "I had a headache. But it seems a little better now." I raise my head an inch or so. The wet cloth has fallen off my head and lies on a soaked pillow.

"No, don't…" He stops me from sitting up. "Rest your head. Do you want me to go?"

"It's fine." I try to sound casual, even though I'm dying that he's here.

"Can I sit?"

I nod and rest my head back down. I'm flat on my stomach with my arms nuzzled underneath my pillow. The mattress dips as he sits beside me.

"I tried to text you but when you didn't answer, I figured you might be mad, so I thought I'd come over in person."

Not all of those texts were from Gabby after all. Oops.

"I was sleeping. I didn't see it. I'm not mad at you." Disappointed, yes. A little insulted maybe. But not mad. I don't get mad that easily.

"I wanted to talk to you. I wanted to explain…" He pauses, and if I wasn't so used to his silence, I'd probably be concerned. But I already have a picture of him in my head. His slight frown filled with rumination, his dented lip.

Griffin sighs right before the mattress shifts again. In a soft, fluid movement, he throws his leg over me so he's straddling me. He's holding his weight up on his legs, and I don't move even a fraction of an inch. I'm very curious to see where this is going.

His open hand cradles the side of my head and his thumb draws circles on my exposed temple, with the perfect amount of pressure.

"Is it bad?" he asks.

"Better now." I let out a small hum because his touch feels that good on my tender pressure point. I savor every rotation of his thumb.

When he removes his hand from my face, I frown into the dark. But just as I'm about to turn to him, it's on me again. This time, he collects the hair at the base of my neck in one hand and slides his other hand down its length, until he reaches its tip. He twists it up and lays it on the pillow beside my head. Placing both hands on my shoulder blades, he presses first his palms, then his fingertips into me. My heart pounds through my chest into the mattress, which is resistant and shoves my heart right back.

Griffin's breathing is the only sound in the room. His palms glide over my arms, following them under the pillow, until they reach my hands. He has to lean forward to reach them, causing his chest to press into my back and my lungs to fail.

His cheek is flush against the side of my head. "I'm sorry, Frankie," he whispers in my ear.

I swallow before I speak because I want my voice to be steady. "You were just being honest. You didn't do anything to be sorry about."

"Maybe not," he breathes out, tickling me. "But I think I hurt you, nonetheless. I've been so worried I'd hurt you physically that I may have been careless about hurting you emotionally, instead." He draws his hands back up my arms and over my shoulders. He's sitting up on his legs again and then the most delicious pressure flows down my spine.

He's not just massaging me. He's kneading me, the way he does his clay. His fingers press into the sides of my ribcage and down to my waist. I'm very ticklish right there, but there's so much heaviness in every inch of his muscled hands that the last thing I'd ever do right now is laugh.

He finds his way under the bottom of my shirt and pushes into the small of my back with his palms and fingertips at the same time. They move a little higher and his steady breathing tells me he's in the zone, somewhere far away. He continues molding me for a few more minutes before he speaks again. Then his deep voice cuts through the thick darkness.

"I carry a lot of shit with me, Frankie. I've figured out how to filter my anger for the most part, but it's still always there, beneath the surface. Festering like a boil my father planted in my soul. I'm terrified of becoming him. It's the absolute worst thing I can imagine. Because of this fear, I've lived my whole life avoiding people I think could bring out certain qualities in me. If you're like my mother, and I'm like him, our combination could be lethal. That's why I said I need to stay away from you. I'm angry all the time. At him. At her for staying with him, for subjecting me to seeing that my whole life. The only thing that has ever brought me any relief from it is sculpting.

"There's no better feeling to me than when my hands are on a piece of clay, with unlimited potential. Molding it, forming it into anything I want it to be. I become so connected with it that I can feel its pulse in my fingertips. When I do a sculpture from a model, the life I feel in the clay isn't even from the model herself. It's from what I imagine I'm molding her into. It's the pulse in the clay that makes my heart beat, not the pulse of the other person in the room. Because, like I said, it's the best feeling in the world to me." He pauses. "Except for this."

I draw in a breath at his words. He feels it. His hands stop for a split second before they continue molding me into anything they want, because right now, underneath him, I'm the most malleable clay there is.

"When I first saw you at Holly's, taking those pictures, I had to know you. This interesting woman who finds beauty in something plain and isn't afraid to bark orders at a stranger to get her picture. Normally, I'm methodical. I've worked hard to keep my impulses in check. But I started doing things that were out of the ordinary for me. Like finding excuses to go to your job. Or grabbing you in the warehouse.

"When I touched you the other day, when I kissed you, I felt a rush I've only ever had when I sculpt, except it was magnified by a hundred. I want to run my hands over every part of you. I want to feel that pulse in every inch of you. And it's not because I want to mold you into something I imagine you to be. It's because of what I've already seen you are."

It takes me a second to adjust to the lack of light in the room. I turn my head a little so I can look at him, because what he's saying to me is too beautiful to be said into the air.

"But feeling like this toward you...toward anyone, terrifies me. It's exactly what I've tried to avoid. Not because I'm afraid of what I'll do today, but because of what I'm afraid will happen in the future, once you're invested in me and don't want to leave. Once I'm comfortable with you. The problem is, unlike when I've avoided other people, I can't stop wanting to know you more, to get closer to you and take that risk. I know it's selfish to ask you this, knowing what might lie ahead. I'm all sorts of screwed up because of him. But I want to try. For the first time, I want to try. Because the way

I feel when I'm around you, or even thinking about you, Frankie, gets harder to contain every day. Not having any contact with you this past week has felt like someone bound my hands and told me I could no longer sculpt. Something I need in my life has been missing and I have to get it back."

I had no idea I'd affected him this way, but it shouldn't be a surprise. Griffin is more profound than most people. I feel exposed by his words, like I'm about to jump into something again, except this time, I might care too much. I might become too vulnerable and not escape without a broken heart because I know right now that if Griffin takes these words and leaves with them when he gets freaked out, I'll be crushed. But I know myself. There's no way I'll allow fear to make me say no to this, whatever it might become. I'm already too into him and shying away from a challenge is not in my wheelhouse.

"What do you think?" he asks. "Would you want to take a chance on a guy who knows he shouldn't ask you to but is asking, anyway?"

I smile up at him and he scoots up a little higher on his knees so I can turn onto my back underneath him. "Taking chances is my thing."

"I thought photography was your thing."

"I've got a lot of things. You'll have to put in the time to find them all out."

He smiles for the first time since he came here. Then he leans forward so his face is inches from mine. He pushes a few of my stray hairs out of the way with one hand while he uses the other hand to brace himself next to my head. He frowns at his hand as he pulls it off the pillow. It's wet.

"Were you crying?"

"No," I chuckle. "I was using a cool compress for my headache."

"Good. I don't want you crying. Especially over me."

I prepare for the kiss I know is coming, but he's not ready yet. He's got something else to say, first.

"Promise me something."

Promise him? It's a little early for promising each other things, isn't it?

"Promise if I ever hurt you...even if you think I'm going to...you'll leave and never look back."

Oh, that kind of promise. That's not a fun one. I shake my head. "You never would."

He takes my face in both hands so I know he's serious about this. "Promise me, Frankie. You'll leave and never look back."

"Ok, I promise," I say because he is tortured, and reassuring him is the only thing that will relieve the internal pain he causes himself. Plus, I know he's not going to kiss me until I promise. And I really want him to kiss me. But I have a feeling that with this guy, leaving is easier said than done.

At my words, his face brightens, and he leans all the way into me, allowing our lips to connect. This kiss is different from the last one. It's still passionate, but not frenzied. It feels like the first kiss of many, rather than a kiss that's rushing to get somewhere. It feels like a promise, but a much better one than the one I just made.

A promise of the future.

Chapter Nine

Griffin

A persistent knock this morning separates us from each other after what was possibly the best night of my life. When Frankie opens her door, Sarah stands there with a brown bag in her hand and a shit-eating grin on her face.

"I picked up some bagels. Thought you might like one." She lifts the bag for Frankie to see.

Frankie squirms a little. "I, uh, we…"

Sarah pretends to notice me for the first time, lying in Frankie's bed. As if she didn't know I was here. As if I didn't go storming into her apartment first last night, on a mission, questioning her for twenty minutes about whether she thought I should go see Frankie or not.

"Oh hey," she calls over Frankie's shoulder. "Want a bagel?"

I was here for dinner and through the night, and I don't know if breakfast is overstaying my welcome. But I would like to stay.

Frankie and I did nothing more than share lingering kisses and talk throughout the night. If I'm going to do this with her, I'm going to do it right, even though the idea of it makes me uncomfortable enough to tear my skin off. I need to keep replaying Mr. Rothman's words in my head. In addition to the rest of his honest advice, he said something intended to manipulate me. He said as long as my actions are dictated by making sure I'm not like my father, rather than by doing things that will make me happy, the bastard wins again. Mr. Rothman is painfully aware of how many of my decisions are based on spiting my father.

Well played, Roth.

Even so, it took me a full day to decide what to say to Frankie. When she told me, shrouded in guilt, the reason she was staying at Holly's, I was saturated with relief that she'd never been hurt. But I was also split between being petrified because that meant I could actually pursue her and being cautiously optimistic because there was one less thing keeping us apart. I still believe the fair thing to do is stay away from her altogether, but since neither of us seems to want that, I'm going for it. I desperately hope I don't give her a reason to regret giving me this chance.

"Have a bagel if you want. They smell like they were just made," Frankie says. "I'm just going to jump in the shower real quick. You guys start without me." She disappears into the bathroom.

Sarah makes herself comfortable on the small couch Frankie got since I was last here. She opens the bag and passes me a sesame bagel with sundried tomato cream cheese. My favorite. She didn't know I was here, my ass.

"This is, without a doubt, the longest you've ever voluntarily been in my building, Griffin." She ruffles my hair.

I chew wondering if I should make my exit after breakfast.

"That's because your building is a dump," I gibe,

but grin.

"Maybe, but obviously it's a dump with a new attraction." Sarah leans over and wraps her arms around my neck. She kisses the top of my head. "I'm proud of you."

"Whatever."

"Don't *whatever* me. I know this isn't easy for you and you're scared out of your mind right now, even if you won't admit it. But you deserve this, Griffin. You deserve to have some of the happiness you bring to everyone else. Maybe Frankie can get you to realize that, once and for all."

"Easy there. It's only been a couple of hours."

"Yeah." She releases me. "But we both know you're planning on being different with this one. Maybe even letting her in. Otherwise you wouldn't have come here last night, all *I need to speak to Frankie.* You would have just casually hung out with her the way you always do with girls you're hooking up with. Which is nothing like the real you, and we both know it."

Sometimes it irks me that Sarah knows me so well, especially when she throws it in my face. But I've needed her through the years. Not having a friend I could discuss the black times with would have been unbearable. Each and every time I've come back from an incident with my mother, Sarah's been there, to listen, to sit with me in the warehouse while I pour my rage into my clay, to commiserate about how much we hate my father. I hope she knows how much I value her, even when I tell her she's being a pain in the ass.

The shower turns off. I figure I've got about five minutes before Frankie comes out, dressed and waiting to see what I'm going to do. I'm wrong, though, because about thirty seconds later the bathroom door opens and she saunters out, wrapped in one towel, shaking out her long, wet hair with another. She reaches into her closet for some clothes. She has to lean over to grab something, and I whirl away, blushing as I imagine the view I'm missing. She walks back to the bathroom and grins over her shoulder before almost but not quite closing the door behind her.

I gulp down a chunk of bagel and Sarah laughs. I swat her gently with my hand.

"I think that was an invitation," she taunts.

Man, do I want to follow her in there right now. My pulse quickens. Just thinking of twisting my hands into her wild, wet hair is enough to send me over the edge. Her hair distracts me. I even accidentally gave one of my statues hair that was more feral than it should have been, because while I was working, I imagined how Frankie's would feel wound around my fists. It was the piece Frankie damaged. When I walked in and saw it in her hand that day, I was afraid she'd discover the resemblance, but she was too caught up in wrecking the statue to notice.

I shift on the couch, uncomfortable. I'm not going in there. It's much too soon. And presumptuous. And I'm definitely not ready to let her get that close to me. Sex means too much when there are feelings involved. I need to test myself and see if I can stay under control with her before letting us get that close to each other. I have to be careful.

I take another large bite while I try to reestablish a normal breathing pattern.

"Chickenshit." Sarah tosses a throw pillow at my lap. "Here. Better cover up," she blathers, amused with herself.

I'm humiliated.

My cell vibrates on the table, and I'm thankful for the distraction of a text. It's Jackson. *Do NOT come to the theater today. Call me.*

I'd completely forgotten I was supposed to go see if Jackson had any furniture I could take. April, one of the women I'd sculpted at Holly's, is moving out this week and Jackson said I could check what he's got. I told him I'd come by today, but with everything going on, it slipped my mind.

I dial Jackson.

He answers with, "Griffin, do not step foot in the theater."

"Why, what's up?"

"Bedbugs. The place is infested. It's being fumigated, or whatever the hell it is they do to get rid of them. It's a total fucking nightmare. Everything in there is off limits. Sorry man, but I won't be able to give you anything this time." He pauses to listen to something. "Oh, right, Kaitlyn is asking if you want to have lunch."

I laugh. "Lunch? Tell her thanks but I'll have to catch up with you guys another time. Looks like I'm going to be furniture shopping today."

"What kind of furniture shopping?" Frankie's voice catches me off-guard as I hang up.

I turn to see her fully dressed, hair up in a wet ponytail. Thank God. I'm strong but I'm not a saint. I explain what happened with the furniture and realize this is my exit strategy, if I want one.

The opposite flies out instead. "Interested in coming with me?" My mouth is acting on what I want before my mind has a chance to forbid it.

"Sure." Frankie shrugs. "I don't have to be at work until late this afternoon."

We head to the nearest mattress store and spring up and down on all their samples like children in a bouncy house.

"I like this one." Frankie lies on one mattress that, to me, is identical to all the others in the store. "Come, feel it."

I flop next to her, flat on my back. The paneled ceiling above us has water stains that resemble huddles of bodies. How appropriate for a store full of beds.

"Comfy, right?" she asks.

"They all feel the same to me. I guess I'm not a mattress connoisseur."

"Me neither. But I know what I like." She smiles and somehow that alone makes me feel lighter.

I give a small smile back and roll on my side, unsure of what to do next. I've seen people start kissing in situations like this in cheesy movies, but that is, without question, not my style. I wonder if it's hers.

"Can I help you?" The salesperson offers me more relief than she will ever know.

"I need a queen and a twin, good quality. Something that will last."

"You need a twin, too?" Frankie asks.

"She's got a daughter," I explain.

The saleswoman buzzes on and on about the pros and cons of each mattress. I'm bored out of my mind. If I were doing this for myself, not April, I'd point at the nearest bed and order it. Since it's for April, I suffer through the sales pitch and settle on whichever one the woman suggests. I ask her about some children's furniture to go with it. I choose a girl's headboard, nightstand, and dresser that Frankie says are cute. When the saleswoman rings up the total for the furniture, plus delivery, Frankie chokes.

"Griffin, who's paying for this?"

"It's fine." That's enough of an answer.

"You can write this off, right? That's what you said Jackson does."

"Yeah, I'm sure I can," I say, but I won't bother looking into it. It's not the first time I've done this and it won't be the last. It's the least I can do for these women. A little credit card debt won't kill me.

Frankie understands. I feel her gaping at me, but for once I don't meet her eyes. I know what I'll see in them if I do. Instead of saying anything, she runs the knuckle of her pointer over the back of my hand once, twice. Then she drops it.

As we're waiting for my credit card to go through, Frankie steps away. "Oh, man." She strokes one of the nearby mattresses. "I wish I had my camera. This piping would make an awesome shot."

I watch her studying the bed and find myself breaking into a small grin. There's absolutely nothing interesting or unique about that bed but to her, there's something worth capturing.

I'm coming to understand that Frankie sees in things what I see in people. Things that are masked, that you have to dig a little deeper to find. I fleetingly hope she'll stick around long enough to apply that vision to me.

Or that I will.

When we leave the store, Frankie stops dead in her tracks. I should have known I couldn't get away from this without a conversation.

"I can tell you don't want to hear it, so I'm just going to say one thing," she says. I don't respond. She'll say whatever it is anyway. "Those women are lucky Taylor found you."

They're lucky? No, they're not lucky our paths crossed. I am.

I was having a red day. The night before was bad, and my mother woke favoring one side, setting me off. Even though I was supposed to go to Spanish class, my feet led me to the one place I could relax.

When I got to Mr. Rothman's room, I froze. He had a class that period, of course. Someone called his name, and he noticed me in the doorway. I must have looked like hell, because he frowned.

"Come in, Griffin." He guided me to a table in the back and placed a sculpture I'd been working on in front of me. I shook my head. If I touched it, I would have put my fist right through it. He exchanged the sculpture with a brand new hard block of clay.

I kneaded it as if my very sanity depended on it. In a lot of ways, it did. With every ounce of pressure I put into this block of clay, rage seeped out, little by little. Mr. Rothman wrote a note to get me out of my next two periods and by that time I had a very angry abstract of a man in front of me. I was calm enough to make it through the rest of the day, but Mr. Rothman wasn't satisfied.

"I'd like to take you somewhere tonight, Griffin."

I didn't know that was allowed. "Where?"

"I'd rather not say because I'm afraid you'll refuse. I would just ask that you trust my judgment."

I did trust him, so I agreed to meet him outside school at 7:15 sharp.

Mr. Rothman drove us to a run-down church and my immediate thought was to escape. I didn't do church. I didn't pray. And no matter how much Mr. Rothman had helped me, I wasn't trying it out for him.

"Relax, Griffin. I'm not trying to convert you," he laughed when I was reluctant to leave the car.

We walked down a staircase that smelled like sour mop into a small classroom where about a dozen people were sitting on folding chairs in a circle. It was clear this was some kind of support group. I froze.

"You don't have to share anything," Mr. Rothman assured me. "But just being here might be good for you. The art is helping, but you need more, son. Please give it a chance."

Turned out, it was a support group for families and friends of victims of abuse. I knew there were groups for the actual victims, but I had no idea there was somewhere for those on the periphery.

Everyone introduced themselves the way they always do on TV. Then some people told their stories. One girl talked about her sister, who was in an abusive relationship for a few years, but was too afraid to leave, and how she herself went to bed every night terrified of what she'd hear in the morning. An older man talked about his son who was so ashamed his boyfriend was hitting him, he hid it until the boyfriend busted his jaw and he had to have it wired shut. I listened intently, feeling relieved there were other people dealing with this, but guilty for being happy these people were feeling the same pain as me.

I went back each Wednesday night. Mr. Rothman was right. The meetings were good for me. I hadn't shared in the month I'd been going, but being around people who understood was enough for the time being. Between the meetings and the sculpting, I was maintaining control.

One Wednesday, I arrived about ten minutes early. People were talking in groups, as if they knew one another. It surprised me. I assumed everyone did what I did. Got there when it started and left as soon as it was over.

There was a woman I didn't recognize, maybe in her late-twenties, chatting over coffee with a bunch of regulars. Though I'd never seen her before, it was obviously not her first time. She was much too at home.

When our group leader arrived, we all sat and introduced ourselves. A few people shared their stories. Then the new woman spoke.

"Hi, I'm Taylor," she said.

"Griffin?"

It takes me a second to realize it's Frankie's voice I'm hearing, not Taylor's.

"Griffin, are you okay?"

"What?" I must have zoned out.

"I said those women are lucky," she repeats.

I shake my head. "You have it backwards, Frankie. The entire thing."

Chapter Ten

Frankie

Just a tiny bit closer. If I can manage to move in one more centimeter, it will be mine. The perfect shot. I have to be at work in an hour, but I want to take this last picture, go home, and play with it before I have to be there.

"Can I ask what you're taking?" an unfamiliar voice asks.

"You can ask," I say without directing my attention toward the voice. If I move even an inch, I might lose it. "But I may not answer."

The stranger laughs. "Okay, then, what are you taking?"

"A spider." Got it. It should be exactly the way I wanted. I stand and check it out to be sure.

"A spider? Any particular spider, or one of many?"

I glance up, irritated at his mocking tone. He's slightly older, with light hair and a slim physique. But it's his smug face and obnoxious aura of confidence that throw me.

"A very specific spider." I call up the picture, zoom in a little and show him what I got. You can see the top portion of the spider on its web. The web itself appears to be a thick rope and the spider resembles a monster more than an insect. Shadowy effects will make the whole thing very menacing. "See?"

The obnoxious stranger gives the usual, "Hmm," that I've become accustomed to when people think my pictures are weird. I'm about to pull the camera away, when he adds to the monosyllabic sound effect. "This is very interesting. You've got some potential here."

Potential? That's a word I haven't heard about my pictures before. I'll take potential. Potential's good.

"Yeah?" I say. "Are you an expert?" Something about him still rubs me wrong, and I'm being ruder than necessary.

"Something like that." He holds out a hand for me to shake. "Scott Hannah, freelance writer in search of a talented photographer. Nice to meet you."

I shake his hand. "Francesca Moore, nice to meet you, too."

"So, Francesca Moore. Are there any other shots you'd like to show me?"

Is this how it happens in New York? You get discovered while hunched over the steps of some dirty apartment building on a random downtown street to get a picture of an ugly bug? If so, that's pretty damn cool.

"I've got tons." I select a few of the pictures I think best show my style and Scott Hannah makes a small but positive comment after each one. He takes a step away from me when I finish.

"I'm in need of some photographers to help me with a book I'm writing. Does that sound like something you'd be interested in?"

I fidget, adjusting the small skirt and tight blouse I'm wearing. I wish I were dressed more professionally. Who knew I would have a job interview in the middle of Varick Street?

"Um, yeah, that sounds good." Ugh, bad answer, Frankie. I should have said something along the lines of *Please, tell me more about your book?* or *What are you hoping to find in a photographer?* Instead, I all but swallow my tongue. Scott Hannah seems unfazed, though.

"Great. Give me your cell number and I'll call to arrange a meeting where I can see your work on actual paper, not a tiny screen."

I rattle off the digits of my phone number, even though I'm so excited to at the possibility of having a photography job I can barely remember them. He plugs them into his cell before sticking it back in his jacket pocket. "Okay, Francesca, expect to hear from me in the next day or so." Then, just before he turns to walk away, he winks at me. This guy's too cocky for my liking, but if he's going to pay me, he can wink all he wants.

I practically skip all the way home, before panic sets in. I don't have any actual printed pictures. All my photos are either on my camera or in the computer. I'll have to pick out a few of my best, order them, and pray they get delivered before this Scott Hannah wants to have a meeting.

I fly to my bed with my computer on my lap and scroll through the pictures. Suddenly, they all look like shit, and I can't believe anyone would ever pay a dime for them. The lighting is off, the focus isn't sharp, and what the hell am I even taking pictures of anyway— garbage?

Okay, Frankie. Take a step back. You're just freaking out because this is the first opportunity you've ever had to do something real with your life. No need to get all self-doubty. But of course you're going to get that way because all you've ever been told is how you're too impetuous and not serious enough about anything. Even this photography thing was done on a whim. So what makes you think you can make anything of it?

"Who are you talking to?" Sarah stands in my doorway.

Why do I keep leaving it open? Where do I think I live? Idiot, I chastise myself again and scrunch my nose in embarrassment. "Myself? It's a thing I do when I'm nervous."

"Well, it sounded like you were being pretty hard on yourself. I didn't think you were like that." Sarah makes her way into my apartment and sits on my bed.

"I'm generally not. Just when I'm reminding myself what my parents think of my life choices." I direct my attention back to the computer.

"What are you doing?" Sarah asks.

"I met someone today. A writer. He said he wants photographers to help with a book he's working on and we kind of set up a tentative interview for him to view my work. But he expects to see it on paper, which I don't have. I need to get some pictures printed before the meeting, which means if I don't pick some this minute, I'm going to be thinking about it all night at work, and I won't be able to concentrate on any of the customers' orders. Then I'll get fired, and I won't have any job because my photography career won't work because I didn't get the prints in time. I won't have any money to pay rent. But it's all for the best anyway because this whole thing is probably just my latest hobby, and as soon as it doesn't pan out, I'll move on like I always do." I pause to take a breath.

Sarah's eyebrows are raised into her bangs and mouth is puckered. "Wow," she says. "Th-that's a lot of words."

"Sorry," I say, more embarrassed. "I tend to blather when I'm nervous, too."

"I can see that." Sarah nods. She closes the laptop. I'm about to protest but she puts her hand up to stop my words. "Why don't you go to work? When you come home, you and I can go through the pictures together. We'll choose the best ones to order."

Her suggestion calms me.

"You're not going out tonight?" I ask.

"I don't think so. Griffin mentioned something earlier in the week about getting together, but then he said a client needed to change an appointment to tonight. So I doubt it."

A ridiculous feeling of envy sweeps over me when she mentions Griffin. It's silly really. I know they're close. And she did say they made the plans earlier in the week, which probably means they made them before Griffin came over the other night to see if I'd like to "take a chance on him."

He was so comfortable with me that night. He told me about his sculptures and his friends. I told him about my perfect sister and my life in Buffalo before I came here. And every so often we'd kiss for a while. Beautiful, slow, weighty kisses that spoke volumes without words and aim straight for the heart. Then we'd talk again. We nodded off somewhere around three.

The way he kept watching me through the darkness was both unnerving and electrifying. It's like he wants to know every one of my thoughts. Like he can hear them just by homing in on me, the way, for me, zooming in on a picture strips away my subject's protective outer layer. If that's the case, it's going to be a problem for me because my thoughts are even nuttier than my actions, and I think I already like him a little too much for my own good.

I expected him to make up some excuse to escape in the morning, but he didn't.

Then I did something a little questionable. I felt all gross from being up half the night before and I wanted to shower. I went straight into the bathroom. I didn't realize I hadn't brought any clothes with me until I was already soaked. So I wrapped myself in a towel and traipsed out there trying not to act uncomfortable. When I had to bend over to pick a pair of panties out of a small bin in my closet, I wasn't sure if I wanted to cover up more or give him a show. I know he wants to take things slow, and that's fine, but there's nothing wrong with throwing out a little temptation, is there? It's all in good fun.

I was surprised by his invitation to go furniture shopping. And when I realized he was paying for that woman's stuff out of his own pocket, I almost disintegrated in the store. I mean, who does that? But I could tell he didn't want to discuss it. I may not be the best at reading people in general, but I can tell this guy doesn't appreciate how amazing he is.

As soon as we left the store, he changed. I should have kept my mouth shut. I shouldn't have brought up Taylor. But I didn't know my simple statement would take him away and bring him somewhere deep in thought, unreachable. After we walked for about a minute, he said he had to get to the warehouse to sculpt.

That was three days ago, and I haven't seen him since.

He did text me yesterday to say hi but didn't mention anything about getting together. So when Sarah tells me they had tentative plans, it hurts a little, even though I know it shouldn't.

"That would be great, Sarah. I'd really appreciate it." I hope the brief sadness, whizzing through my veins like kids on a water slide, doesn't show on the outside. If it does, she doesn't acknowledge it.

"No problem. Now get to work so that whole stream of consciousness thing doesn't come true."

****

When I get back from work, Sarah's not home. She teaches art classes to children and teenagers at a private extracurricular art school and her last class ends at eight. That means she went out, after all. Did she forget about me or just blow me off? I'm not sure, but the thought that she may be with Griffin fills every crevice of my brain, even though I do my best to dig it out with a mental shovel.

I'm not going to worry about it. I'm going to pick out my pictures, with or without Sarah's help, and place this order. I pull my computer onto my lap on the couch and wait a few seconds for it to boot up.

There's a tap on the door and it opens a second later. Sarah's frame fills the doorway. "Sorry I'm late. I had to run out and pick something up."

Griffin walks in behind her. "Hey, you." He waits in the doorway.

I'm not sure why he's being hesitant. I'm not one of those controlling girls who freaks out if she doesn't get a text every few hours. Even though I do kind of wish he'd called today. But hey, I'm busy. I have other things going on, too.

"Hey, you." I smile.

Sarah sprawls on my bed, leaving only the couch next to me open for Griffin to sit on, which he does. "So let's take a look at those pictures," Sarah says.

"No client tonight?" I ask Griffin in a voice as casual as I can muster. He shakes his head but offers no explanation.

We wade through a bunch of my shots, and while we're inspecting them, I add a couple more effects here and there. We pick half a dozen to order. I think that should be sufficient, but since I've got no point of reference, I don't know for sure. As soon as I've completed the order, Sarah yawns. It's so fake I almost laugh.

"Well, I'm exhausted. Those damn kids were so annoying today. I hate my Friday classes."

I stand to put my computer away, unsure of whether Griffin is leaving or not.

I don't know if Sarah forced him to come. She gets right behind me. "He wants to be here, Frankie. He just needs a little shove every now and again." She disappears from my apartment.

I sit next to Griffin. "How was your day?" I ask. It's such a lame question, but I know he could sit here in silence forever.

I can't.

"I'm sorry I haven't called."

"You don't have to call me every day, Griffin. We just started dating. We're not married."

"You don't want me to?" His expression is somber.

"I didn't say that." I chuckle, embarrassed that yes,

we just started seeing each other, but I'd love to hear from him every day.

"Because I want to. I want to call you every day. I like talking to you."

"Then why didn't you?"

He breathes his usual contemplative sigh. With any other guy, it would be that he forgot or just didn't feel like calling. With Griffin, there's always something more.

"I hate the word complicated. It's so overused. People say it when they want to get out of answering questions, don't you think?"

I nod but have no idea where's he's going with this.

"My life is complicated. Really, my thoughts are complicated. I think that's more accurate. The other night...I haven't felt that close to a person, maybe ever. For me, it was amazing. I didn't want my time with you to end, which is why I asked you to come shopping with me. But when you mentioned Taylor, it brought a memory from my past. That happens all the time. Everything causes me to flash back to things I don't want to think about because for me, my past is my present, since it's still happening. And then I start to sizzle. When I feel like exploding, I run to my warehouse. It's my outlet. It's the only place I can let go of the anger. My mother and her life will always be my burden. I'll never walk away from her, and it will never stop making me furious. I don't want to subject you to that, yet the idea of letting you go when I just found you brings me right back to the dark place. It's not fair to you, and I just don't know what to do."

I'm quiet for a minute, taking in everything. My

heart swells at how honest he is. He tortures himself, but is more worried about how it will affect me than what it does to him.

He reads my silence wrong and starts to get up. "This is too much to ask. My life shouldn't become your problem, too, Frankie. I'm sorry I even asked you to be on board with this."

"Griffin." I take his hand, pulling him back onto the couch. "Stop apologizing. It's not too much. That's not what I was thinking. I was thinking that maybe instead of always feeling like you have to run away every time you're pulled into a memory, you could tell me about it."

He shakes his head. "You don't want that."

"You'd be surprised at the things I want." I lean in and brush my lips against his. We kiss for a minute, but our lips never part. The kiss is gentle and warm and just a little sad.

"So we're okay? Even though I blew in here the other night, woke you up to tell you how unstable I am, kissed you the entire night, freaked out over a simple statement you made and then didn't call for three days? It's not exactly a great beginning to a relationship."

I laugh. "You're not unstable. And yes, we're okay." I snuggle a little closer on the couch, and he puts his arm around me. It doesn't feel like we're as new as we are. We're too comfortable. But I'm afraid that's just me jumping in again. I know with Griffin things will be bumpy. Lucky for me, I've never been afraid of a few rocky roads.

"You really want to hear about these things when they pop into my head? Because it's fucking mayhem in there sometimes." He's doubtful.

"I want to know *you* and whatever comes with that."

He tightens his arms around me and nuzzles his face in my neck. "Well, what do you want to know?" He's smiling into my skin and his beard tickles.

"Hmmm." I think for a few seconds, as I squirm around. "Okay, I know. What's the story behind your favorite sculpture?"

Chapter Eleven

Griffin

"My favorite sculpture," I repeat, trying to determine which one that would be. "Well, what are the criteria?"

"What do you mean, criteria?" she asks.

I rub my cheek into her once more, because it's making her itch and squirm against me, which I'm enjoying more than I should if I want to continue this conversation. "You know…" I clear my throat in an attempt to disguise what her body is doing to mine. "Like, favorite piece based on best art or favorite piece based on best story behind the art?"

"Uh, best story, I guess."

My head teems with great stories. I take a while to scan through them but Frankie grows impatient.

"How about the first one, Griffin? The first one you did at Holly's."

That one's easy. "Vera."

"Vera?" Frankie asks.

"That was her name." I smile. I'll never forget her.

When I met Taylor in group, and learned about Holly's House, I knew immediately that I wanted to work there but for a long time, I had no idea what I could offer. Then one afternoon in college, Sarah was driving me crazy. She was bored and nagging me to do something with her. When she suggested I sculpt her, I said no way, I didn't do real people, only imaginary ones. But she kept pestering me, so I finally gave in. Once I was working on it, she couldn't sit still and she kept complaining, so I told her to leave. But before she left, I asked her to give me a story to hold onto, so I could visualize something about her as I worked. She shared a memory about her older brother. So, I created a sculpture of a little girl on her brother's lap holding hands. She was very moved by it. It gave me the idea of how I could volunteer at Holly's.

When I met up with Taylor again, she seemed older, in a good way. More professional. She sized me up when I got there. I looked different too, maybe not in a good way. Last time she saw me I was a clean-shaven, neatly dressed teen. This time, I was a hairy, tatted-up, not so pressed, young man. Whether she wondered what brought about the change in my appearance or not, she didn't ask. She just brought me into the sitting room and motioned toward the couch. She sat beside me.

"First off," she said, "I want to thank you for volunteering your time."

"I'm happy to do it. It just took me a while to get here," I said.

"Yes." She nodded. "Well, I'm glad you're here now. Second, I want to tell you a little about how things work. The women here need their privacy. They need their anonymity. And above all else, they need to know they are unequivocally safe. I love your idea about sculpting them. Many of these women have had to leave their homes in a rush, bringing nothing with them. No possessions. The clothes on their backs—coats if they're lucky. This way they can have something that belongs to them. The fact that it's something sentimental makes it even more wonderful."

I have to admit, I hadn't thought about that aspect of it at that point. I just thought it would be nice for them to see themselves through my eyes, instead of those of the assholes who beat on them.

"We need to set up ground rules, especially since you're a man—no offense. I'm not saying there's no domestic abuse between women, but that's not the majority of what we see here."

I nodded. No offense taken.

"The sculptures will be done on a voluntary basis, naturally. You will meet with the women here in the sitting room. Access to the rest of the house is for guests only. Please do not ask our guests any personal information. What they choose to share with you is their business, but I don't want anyone thinking they're having a piece of art done and then feeling like they're being interrogated. Even if you mean well, personal questions can come off as intimidating. Especially to those in a fragile state, as people in this transitional stage of their lives often are."

"I understand."

"I explained what you are offering to my guests and a couple of them showed an interest. We did a lottery of sorts to see who would be your first guinea pig." Taylor smiled. "The winner of the lottery is a woman named Vera. She's ready to join us whenever we're all set."

"Ready when you are," I said.

Taylor rose to get Vera, but stopped in her tracks. "Oh, and Griffin, no physical contact."

Again, I nodded.

Taylor disappeared for a minute and returned with a woman.

I expected to be prepared for what I saw. After all, I'd been a witness to it my entire life. But when Vera walked in the sitting room, bile rose in my throat.

The girl couldn't have been more than eighteen or nineteen. She was covered in cuts and bruises. Judging by the scabbing, they'd been healing for a while. Her lip was still swollen though, and I wondered how bad it was to begin with. I couldn't remember ever seeing my mother that battered.

For a second, I was thankful.

My expression must have given me away, because there was a warning in Taylor's face. It told me if I didn't get it together in a hurry, I'd be out. I composed myself, gave Vera a muted smile and introduced myself. I almost stuck my hand out for her to shake, but I remembered Taylor's words and left it by my side.

"I'm Vera." The girl sat on the couch. Taylor took the opposite end, opened a book, and pretended to read it. I didn't know she'd be staying, but it made sense. She wanted to watch me, to make sure I was doing the right thing. She probably wanted to make sure Vera was comfortable, too. I liked how protective she was.

I was glad someone was.

I sat in a nearby armchair and thought for a minute. I brought some of my art supplies with me and intended to sculpt her the way I did Sarah. But Taylor said no personal questions. Asking her to tell me something no one else knew was out of the question. But how personal was personal?

I could have done a sculpture of her as she was, but

it was hard to even tell what she looked like with all of the marks on her face. I wouldn't be able to capture her outer beauty that way. And if I didn't ask her anything, I wouldn't be able to capture her inner beauty, either. I was stuck.

"We can start anytime, Griffin," Taylor prompted. I guess I didn't realize how long I'd been sitting there without saying a word.

I took a large piece of clay from my supply bag and found there was no table to work on, and nothing with which I could moisten the clay. I hadn't thought through the logistics of this. It would turn out to be a disaster unless I found a way to rectify these issues.

I took a chance.

"Can you tell me about something you enjoy?" I asked.

Taylor shot me a glower from behind her book without lifting her head. She wanted to know where I was going with this.

"Um, let me think." Vera tilted her head. "I guess I like to dance."

"What kind of dance?" I asked.

"Like, club dancing," she answered.

I got up. I picked the largest hardcover I could find from one of the shelves, sat and put the clay on it, on my lap. There was no way I could do it there, but at least it gave the appearance I was doing something other than violating one of Taylor's rules. I worked the clay, not forming anything.

"Do you go to clubs often?"

"Griffin." Taylor's voice was stern. She didn't like this at all.

"I'm trying to get a visual. I can't create a statue of

her sitting on this couch."

Taylor took me in for a few seconds before nodding and going back to the imaginary page in her book.

"I used to." Vera paused. She probably hadn't been clubbing in a while. She looked dejected, and I felt bad for asking, but she quickly composed herself. "I used to love clubs. The loud music, all the sweaty people. I never even minded getting wet from the occasional spilled drink. But the dancing was the best. I used to dance until like four in the morning. I didn't even have a curfew." She smiled as she discussed more of this memory and I knew exactly what I would create.

"You will again," I said, risking Taylor throwing me out. Instead, she peered over her book at me with a grin so tiny I almost missed it.

But I didn't.

My intention may have been to sculpt while I was at Holly's, but that plan wasn't feasible. I explained to Vera that I'd have to do it back at school, and I'd return with it in a few days.

The sculpture turned out well, but it wasn't as powerful as it could have been if I'd been working while talking to her. Then I could have captured her expressions and some of her body language. As it was, I worked entirely from memory. I had to figure out a way for the models to come to me in the future.

When I returned to Holly's to deliver Vera's piece, Taylor was more at ease. "I didn't know what you were doing," she confessed. "Especially after I specifically said no personal questions. But I think I get it."

"I can't sculpt them as they are now, Taylor. Who would want a memento of their lowest moments? I want to give them a vision of who they were and can be again. Or someone new they want to be. I want them to have proof that there's more to them than this. I want to show them they are still beautiful and no one can take that away. I can only do that if I talk to them and get a sense of who they are. I promise I won't ask anything that makes them uncomfortable."

She watched me for a minute before going to get Vera. "Where did you come from, Griffin Stone?"

I waited in the sitting room again but noticed its charm for the first time. I liked it there. I wished my mother would.

Vera called to me and I turned. Her cuts and lip were slightly improved, even though it had only been four days. I took the armchair so she didn't have to sit next to me on the couch, but she sat at the close end, near the chair. I handed her the bag with the sculpture.

She pulled out the figure of a girl dancing. Her clothes swayed around her, one of her legs appeared to be in motion and her arms were raised. She was energetic. Happy. Free.

Vera ran her hand over the image. "Wow. This is fantastic. It's just like how I used to be. Griffin, how did you do this?"

"You did it. You lived it and you described it. I just listened."

Her ear to ear smile was toothy. "Thank you. I love it. I'm going to keep it forever to remind myself to dance. On the inside and the outside. Never stop dancing, right?" She got up from the couch and hugged me. I didn't hug her back, because I wasn't sure where the line was. Besides, I didn't need her to thank me or hug me. I just wanted her to be happy.

"I love it, Griffin. I love it so much."

On my way out, I noticed a plaque mounted to the wall. I ran my fingers over the inspirational words, digesting each one. For the first time I could remember, I did something meaningful.

"Thank you, Taylor," I said as I left.

"Shouldn't I be thanking you, Griffin?"

"No," I answered. "I need this much more than they do."

****

We've shifted on the couch. I'm on my back and Frankie is lying halfway on me with our legs intertwined. She's rubbing my chest and stomach, over my T-shirt.

"But where did you do the sculptures if you were still in college?"

"Well, it was an art school. People were free to work wherever a free inch of space could be found. My roommates and I used the suite in our dorm room for our projects."

"When did you find a way to get the women to come to you?"

"Not until I graduated. I had to find a place of my own, but I knew I couldn't work out of my apartment, because there was no way I could ask those women to be alone with me. I decided to find somewhere to set up shop first, then get a place to live nearby. A guy I was in school with heard about the warehouse and asked if I wanted to split the space with him."

"And Taylor didn't have a problem with you meeting them there?"

Frankie is so curious. I love the interest she's taking in this, and I'm surprised how natural it is for me to talk to her about it. But this is the easy stuff, I guess. The harder stuff will come later.

"They're free to come and go however they like. But Taylor insists the initial meeting always takes place at Holly's. That way, each person can decide if she's comfortable enough with me to go to the warehouse. I'll still do it if they don't want to go there. It just turns out so much better when I can do at least part of the work with them in front of me."

"Mmm." Her sound is hazy. She's falling asleep on my chest. As much as I'm enjoying having her lie on me, part of me wishes she'd stay awake and we could spend the night the same way we did last time, taking turns talking and kissing. I'm also still somewhat affected by the way her hips wiggled into me when I tickled her a few minutes ago, so maybe I'd like to do a bit more than that. But she must be tired from work and the excitement of a potential job.

I stroke her hair and whisper in her ear. "Frankie, you're falling asleep. Do you want to move to the bed?"

"That depends," she answers, groggy. "Are you going to let me lie on you like this if we move or are you going to leave? Because if you're leaving, I'd just as soon stay here."

I smile, even though I know she can't see me. "I'll stay, and you can lie however you want."

"Deal." She yawns, but doesn't budge. Seconds later, her hand stops moving on my chest and her breathing turns velvety. She's asleep. I try to fall asleep too, because I don't want to wake her and because having her sleep on me is the most content and relaxed I've been in quite some time. Unfortunately, it's not the most comfortable I've been, and sleep evades me. After a while, my leg starts twitching because the couch is narrow and most of her weight is on me. I have to get up. I try to jostle her as little as possible as I slide out from under her. She mumbles something unintelligible, and I whisper that it's time to move.

She stands with her eyes almost completely shut and stumbles toward her bed, which is just feet away. She has no idea where she is. I'm sure she doesn't even realize I'm still here because she's rubbing her face and scratching everywhere as she walks. She'd probably be embarrassed if she knew I was witnessing this. Then again, it *is* Frankie, so who knows.

If I want to, I can tuck her in, leave a note that I'll call tomorrow and get out of here. But there's no way I'm doing that. She's the most adorable creature, walking like she's out of it, and the only thing I want to do is climb next to her and pull her close. I don't normally do sleepovers, and this will be our second already, most likely setting a precedent, but it's what I want to do, and I won't let my father win. I follow Frankie into bed.

She sleeps like the dead, with her head on my chest almost the entire time. I hardly sleep for the first half of the night, because I'm loving watching her lie on me, and loving the feel of her hair through my fingers. I nod off periodically, but then I wake for a while and watch her some more. I also spend the night rationalizing to myself all the reasons it's okay for me to be with her, even though, down the line, I can't imagine us having a relationship any different than my parents'.

But I have to try. That's the last thing I think before falling into a deep sleep.

I wake to tiny kisses on my neck.

"Are you going to sleep all day?" She nibbles on me. Man, her mouth feels amazing against my skin. I can't help craving more, but I drive the thought away for now.

Her hair is wet, hanging down her back, and her teeth are brushed.

"You showered already?" I ask.

"Well, I tried to wait until you woke up, but I was still wearing my work clothes and I felt gross, so yeah, I did. But I'm happy to get back into bed," she teases, eyes twinkling inches from mine. She's making it difficult to hold back, and I know I'm about to give in a little. I pull her face in and we kiss for a while, before her cell rings.

She reaches over me to grab it. "Hello?" She squeezes my arm when the person on the other end speaks. "Hi! How are you?" Pause. "No, of course I'm still interested... Yes, that should be fine...Okay, great, I'll meet you there."

She hangs up and screeches at such a high pitch I think my eardrum bursts. She sits on top of me. "Guess who that was?" She's bucking up and down on my legs with excitement she can't contain.

"Hmmm, who could it be?" I put my finger to my mouth to pretend I'm thinking.

"Griffin!"

I smile wide. "The freelancer?"

"Of course! He wants me to meet with him next week. Oh God!" Her hands fly into her hair. "What if he doesn't like the pictures?" She starts to climb off of me, but I seize her hips. "What if..."

"He will, Frankie. Don't worry, he will."

She stops squirming and glances at my hands on

her. "Yeah?" She leans into me, not trying to climb off anymore. The shine on her face changes to one less chaste, and I can tell it's no longer about the book. It's about me. About us. About this moment. I smile as I realize I might have the same gleam.

"Yeah." I pull her close, and I spend the next hour congratulating her on her anticipated success.

Chapter Twelve

Frankie

"I need to do something," I tell Sarah and Griffin. I'm bouncing off the walls. I don't know how I'm going to wait a full week to meet with this man. "I'm freaking out. I need to find a way to expend some of this nervous energy."

Griffin comes up behind me, squeezes my shoulders, and whispers in my ear. His rich voice sends a chill down my back. "I thought that's what we were just doing."

I blush. It's true. Though we weren't having sex, Griffin did manage to find one or two ways to relieve some of my tension this morning. And I found out something; aside from being an amazing kisser and staring at me in ways that make me feel completely exposed, Griffin is *really* good at relieving tension. This morning, he said, was all about me. I dip my head to try to hide my embarrassed smile as I think about the moments we just shared.

"Hey, you two, I'm happy for you and all, but you're not invisible and just because you whisper doesn't mean I can't figure out the general context. If you need to say something I don't want to hear, keep it downstairs." Sarah's voice may be sharp, but she's winking at Griffin. She's busting his balls.

He grins slyly at her and puts his mouth back by my ear. "Can't wait to expend more nervous energy later."

I shiver. Okay, now I'm in a full body-blush. I'm glad I'm dressed so no one can notice.

I just learned something else about Griffin.

He's spiteful.

I like it.

I pull from his grasp because otherwise I might drag him right back to my place. And we did come up here to share my news with Sarah, so we should be more considerate. "I'm serious. I want to do something. What do you guys think?"

"It's Saturday," Sarah replies. "My busiest day with classes. I've got to be there in an hour. I'm out."

I turn to Griffin. "Do you have to work?" Or has he had enough of me for one day? These unplanned dates of ours do tend to last a while. I don't know what to expect from him, yet. I'm happy to give him all the space he needs as he tries to figure out how to handle his mixed emotions about getting involved with me. But with that comes with a side of confusion and uncertainty about how much I should ask for.

He could have easily left after I fell asleep last night. I was so tired I wouldn't have even known he was gone. But he stayed and held me all night, dressed and everything, which I found incredibly sweet. When I woke up and saw how we were lying, my heart did a little jig. I'm sure he wasn't that comfortable with me on him, but he had his arms on me anyway—one around my back and the other draped on me, with my hair in his hand, like he fell asleep stroking it.

It was an image I won't soon forget.

Griffin's so different from the other guys I've dated. He likes to talk between kisses, about things that are important, not space-filling conversations so he can get a little further with me. And when I talk, he hears everything I say.

This morning, he asked about Randy, and I told the whole story, down to my tendency to jump into situations. He was quiet when I talked, though his pupils grew much larger, giving his eyes a smoky appearance. When I discussed my whimsical nature, he told me there was nothing wrong with going where the wind blows, as long as you know when it's time to resist the wind, when it's trying to take you away from somewhere you want to be. I didn't know if that was his way of asking me to stick around, but I'd like to think so.

"I have to work on something, but I can do it later. What did you have in mind?"

"Something physical," I say.

Griffin raises one mischievous eyebrow and Sarah grunts from the other side of the room.

"Uy, get your minds out of the gutter, both of you. I meant something outdoorsy or sportsy. That kind of physical."

Griffin chuckles. "I'm not really an outdoorsy kind of guy."

Then how did he get so ripped, I'd like to know. But since I don't think Sarah would, I keep that question to myself.

"Well, how about we do an indoor outdoorsy activity that will use up all my nervous energy?"

"Such as?" Griffin grimaces, like he's afraid what I might suggest.

"Rock climbing."

****

I've never done it before. I've been wanting to try it for a while. His expression tells me he hasn't done it either, but he's doing it anyway. For me.

Standing in front of the highest indoor rock climbing wall in the city, I kind of want to kick everybody off. The waves and curves have vibrant pegs stuck throughout, giving little blasts of life to an otherwise drab wall. What an amazing shot it would be if I could get it from the right angle.

We pay for our hour of climbing and get hooked into these harness-type things. The straps surround Griffin's thighs, right at the crotch.

"Be careful," I rib him. "I haven't had a chance to explore there yet, and it would be a shame if it was damaged before I got to it."

Griffin chokes on his own saliva. Now it's his turn to be embarrassed. Serves him right, making me blush in front of Sarah.

We start to climb. This is much harder than I thought. I keep losing my grip and falling off, getting suspended in the air by my cord. I try over and over, but only make it about one peg higher each time. I get annoyed when a kid who can't be older than ten stealthily passes me. But then I spot Griffin, swinging in the air, and laugh out loud.

"How's it going over there?" I call to him.

He shoots me a nasty glare. "This is what you wanted to do?"

"Oh, come on. We have forty-five minutes left. First one to the top gets a special treat later."

His face contorts, but definitely not from anger.

With a determination I haven't yet seen in him, he climbs, one peg after the other, a tight grip on each. Not to be outdone, I pick up my pace. Over the course of the hour, we both make a lot of progress, but Griffin reaches the top before I do. If I'm being honest, I might not have been trying as hard as I could have. Maybe the idea of giving him a special treat was more enticing to me than reaching the top of the wall.

When our time is up, we get out of the harnesses and leave. As soon as we step out of the faux cave and into the light, Griffin stops. He stands toe to toe with me. "Thank you," he says.

"For what?"

"For today. I had fun. I don't usually leave everything behind and do something that's just…fun."

"And don't forget your special surprise later," I tease.

He rests his forehead against mine. "I don't give a damn about any of that, Frankie. I just want to be with you."

But I do. We spend the rest of the day together, talking, walking, and eating. In the evening, Griffin brings me to his apartment for the first time. After he tells a funny story about a terrible band Sarah brought him to hear in college, and how he fell asleep in the middle of a loud, crowded bar, I deliver on my promise. When my name spills from Griffin's lips, I know I'm in trouble, because the sounds of him losing himself to me bring me too much happiness. And as I fall asleep next to him, in that same position with my head resting on his chest, butterflies do a mambo in my stomach. Because I realize not only am I jumping in headfirst with this one, but I've got an anchor tied around my neck to boot.

****

Griffin's fingers in my hair and lips on my eyelids lull me out of a contented sleep. I think I was dreaming about him. Or maybe I was thinking about him as I was waking up. Either way, I'm happy he's the first thing I see today.

"Morning, you," he says.

"Morning, you."

"So, yesterday we did something you wanted. How about today you come with me to do something I want?"

"Sure," I answer, without caring in the slightest where we're going.

"I have to get some work done downstairs this morning. I kind of neglected it yesterday." He smiles. "Do you have to work today?"

I shake my head. "Not until tonight. I have to be in at seven."

"Would you want to hang around while I work? Or I could meet up with you later. Unless you're sick of me."

So, I'm not the only one who's afraid of presuming too much. "Nope, not yet," I tease. Never, I think. "Just let me go home and change. I'll be back in a little bit."

I gather my clothes and give him a long, deep kiss goodbye. When I walk into the living room, I'm careful about where I step. The edges of the floor are cluttered with sculptures. The small, one-bedroom apartment has little furniture. In the living room, he's got a couch and table and nothing else. While the floor is almost naked of furniture, the walls are fully clothed. Pictures of various sizes and styles are splayed everywhere. "These are beautiful," I say as I walk along the perimeter of the room, examining each one. "Whose are they?"

"Kaitlyn's." He points at a wall with a few sketches and paintings. "The rest are Sarah's. She gives me all the ones she thinks are junk."

"These are her throwaways?" I call over my shoulder.

"Yeah." He laughs. "Can you picture the ones she likes?"

"She's so talented." I wish I had the kind of talent these guys do.

"Yeah, she is. Too bad hardly anyone knows it. She lacks the confidence to do anything with them, but she enjoys teaching painting. So I guess it's okay."

I kiss him goodbye and tell him I'll be back soon.

****

I'm not proud of the way I fly home and shower so I can get back to Griffin's. I consider packing an overnight bag just in case, but immediately reprimand myself. Too soon, Frankie. And much too forward. The last couple of nights were spontaneous. Take a step back.

My cell rings, and I get a girly flutter thinking Griffin forgot to tell me something. But it's not him. It's my sister. "Hi Gab," I answer while applying just enough makeup to give me a glow. Maybe I'll tell her about Griffin this time.

"Hey, how's it going?" She sounds strange. Not like she's calling to check up on me.

"Good. What's up?" I don't mean to cut her off, but…well, yes I do. I've got somewhere to be.

"So, I have a couple of days off from school two weeks from now. Would it be okay if I came to visit then?"

"Of course. For how long?"

"I don't know, two or three days?"

"Sure," I answer. Two or three days. That's a lot of information to have to spin before it reaches my parents.

"Okay, Frankie. I'm gonna go. Text me your address. I'll see you then."

No game of twenty questions? No probing into my life? Odd. Oh well, I'll deal with it in two weeks. Right now I need to finish getting ready.

****

Griffin's text said to meet him in the warehouse instead of his apartment. I expect to find him alone behind the divider, but before I reach it, I hear another voice. A guy's voice.

"Who is she?" the voice, higher than Griffin's, asks.

Griffin chuckles. "Someone with a boatload of crazy."

"Yeah? How many times have you gotten together with her?"

"A couple. Enough to know she's a handful. I'll be relieved when she comes, and I can show her we're done."

I stop dead in my tracks. Is he talking about me? How could he be? But who else could he be saying this about? It's got to be me.

I'm crushed. No, crushed isn't a strong enough word. I cannot believe those words just came out of his mouth. And I can't believe how much they hurt.

I consider leaving before he knows I'm here. I'm grateful I wore ballerina flats so they didn't make any noise. But of course I won't just go quietly. That's not my style. I reveal myself from behind the divider and Griffin smiles.

"Hey, you."

Hey you? After what he just said? I say nothing. He walks over to me and dabs my lips with his, leaving space between our bodies. I don't kiss him back.

"Are you okay?" he asks.

I still don't answer. Then I discover the reason for the space between us. Griffin's holding a statue of a woman. She's happy. And confused. And filled with...oh...a boatload of crazy.

"This is the woman you were talking about?" I ask.

"What?" He looks down, then at me. His grin mocks me and tells me he knows exactly what I thought. He reaches an arm around my waist. "Antonio, I'd like you to meet Frankie."

"Nice to meet you." Antonio tips his head.

"Antonio works there." Griffin points to the space behind the other divider. He places the statue back on the table and turns to me. "My client, the one I was just talking about," he specifies with a smirk, "will be here tomorrow to pick this up. I finished it this morning."

"Got it." I'd like to shrink down to nothing right now. I feel foolish about how easily my mind freaked, and I'm embarrassed Griffin picked up on it.

"You going with Griffin to get some ink?" Antonio asks me.

I want to kiss him for changing the subject.

"I hadn't told her yet." Griffin winces.

"Is that the fun thing?" I ask.

He nods.

"Cool. Let's go."

We take the train to the Lower East Side where we walk into a small tattoo parlor.

"Griffin, my man!" He is greeted by a thin guy with detailed tattoos all over, and I mean all over. Up his neck, behind his ears, even on his bald scalp. Griffin slaps his hand. "What are we doing today?"

Griffin takes a slip of paper out of his jeans pocket, unfolds it, and hands it over. The guy approves. "I've got an appointment coming in now. A small piece. I can do you right afterwards."

We sit on a couch and wait.

"So…" Griffin rubs my leg over my leggings. "You thought I was talking about you back there?"

I lower my head. He picks up my chin and repeats the words he said once before. "Don't deny me, Frankie." Now, I know what he means. He reads eyes. When he can't see mine, he feels like I'm concealing myself from him. I guess I am.

"I might have thought that."

"There's something you need to know about me. I don't lie. I hated having to do it when I was younger, and I don't do it any more. If I tell you how I feel, it's for real." He gives me a soft, closed kiss. "And I can tell you, I love doing that."

All better.

"So what tattoo are you getting?"

"Remember how you told me you've got a lot of *things*, and I'd have to put in the time to find them out?"

I love that he remembers our conversations so well. "Yeah?"

"Well, I've got a bunch of things, too. I wanted to share one of them with you today."

Uh-oh, I think I'm about to sink deeper.

"Every time I do a sculpture of a woman at Holly's, I get a small tattoo of something that reminds me of her. That way, I won't forget her years from now. I had plenty of tattoos before, but those were for different reasons. The ones on my arms, their initial purpose was pissing my father off. Then I kind of got addicted and got a bunch more, for art's sake. But these mean a lot more to me than most of the others. These I have just for me, where the rest of the world doesn't usually see."

Griffin's body is his own personal memorial of the women he's helped. Unbelievable.

I noticed a number of tattoos on his chest and back last night, but I appreciated them as an entire collage. Now I want to get home so I can inspect every single one.

"So what are you getting today?"

"I'm doing April's, the woman I was visiting at Holly's the day I met you. It's been a hard one for me, because every time I think of something that reminds me of her, I can't decide if it's about her or you, since you came in right afterward and you've occupied my thoughts since then. I've had trouble separating it in my mind. So I'm going to get something that fits you both. April spoke to me about how she and her daughter prayed to the moon every night. April promised her that one day they'd follow the moon together, just the two of them, free to go wherever it brought them. And you, Frankie, you're my light in a night of darkness. You are my moon."

Too soon, too soon, too soon. It's too soon for me to be falling for this guy. He'll cut and run when he feels like he's becoming his father, and I'm going to be left. We're new, casual. It's too soon to be falling.

But there's nothing casual about what he's saying. And I know it's true, because he doesn't lie. He speaks only what he feels.

He holds out the unfolded paper. An iridescent crescent moon surrounded by shades of black and gray and dark blue. The night sky.

I beg my throat not to close up as I ask my next question. "Where are you getting it?" If he says over his heart, I'll love it, even though it will be a little bit cliché. I wouldn't mind being his cliché.

But he reaches around his back and puts a finger by his shoulder blade.

"That'll be...oh hell, Griffin, what am I even supposed to say to that?" I reach for his face and give him a kiss that's much too private for this very public place.

"You're up, my friend." The tattoo-headed guy interrupts my kiss, which is probably a good thing, considering.

Chapter Thirteen

Griffin

"Can you do this for me?" I pass Sarah the salve so she can apply it to my tattoo. With the number of tats I have, I usually don't even notice the itching that comes with them as they heal, but for some reason this one's driving me crazy. Would serve me right if it got infected. What's wrong with me? Saying things to Frankie like *you're my moon*? It's like the day I decided to do this, the sagacious, deliberate Griffin was replaced by a guy who says whatever the hell he's feeling at the moment. And unfortunately, with Frankie, I'm feeling much more than I want to be.

The furniture I bought for April set me back a little more than I expected, and I've got a waiting list of clients. Even though I hate to take on too much at once because I fear the quality of my work will decrease, I need the money, so I booked appointments back to back and haven't seen Frankie since I got the tattoo. We've been texting every day, though, and talking every night. I didn't intend to enter into something where I was in contact with a woman daily, but when I'm with her, it's like I have some relief from being me. From being so heavy all the time. Somehow, she lightens me and when she's gone, the weight is almost harder to carry than it was before because now I know how it feels to have it lifted.

I'm going to see her tonight, and I hate that I'm acutely aware of how many hours stand between now and then.

"It's a little red, Griffin." Sarah finishes rubbing in the salve.

"It'll be okay." I pull my shirt over my head. "Just needs to heal."

"Maybe it's angry because you spoke about it to the person who inspired it."

I cringe. "Frankie didn't inspire it." No way can I have gotten a tattoo for a girl I just started seeing. None of my tattoos are for women I've dated, even though I'm sheathed in them. "It was inspired by April. It's her tattoo."

"I know, but it had a dual meaning. And you told her that."

I frown, but she smiles.

"Keep moving forward, Griffin. You're doing great."

I shake my head. "It's moving too fast. I'm making it move too fast, but when I'm with her I don't know how to stop it."

"That's because the real you doesn't do halfway. You know that. All the others were time fillers. This is the first time I've seen you be yourself with a girl."

"That's what I'm afraid of."

"What's it going to take? What the hell is it going to take?" Sarah's getting frustrated with me. I understand why. She's watched me do this to myself for years. I'm frustrated with myself.

"If I knew the answer to that, my life would be much easier."

I head down to the warehouse, one of my few places of refuge. The woman who was supposed to pick up her statue the other day...the crazy one Frankie heard me talking about...has blown me off a few days in a row and is supposed to come soon. Even when she does show, she's chronically late. And extremely strange.

She's had me do two sculptures so far, insisting her two parrots, Nanny and Poppy, be included. I know people love their pets like family, but these birds were dressed like her grandparents, from whom she insists they are reincarnated. That's a little odd, even for me. But one person's odd is another person's eccentric, and this eccentric pays well, as do the many friends she refers my way.

Four hours later, I'm working on another client's piece when she arrives in a red and white-checkered jumper so busy I get a little dizzy. Nanny and Poppy sit on either shoulder wearing the same clothes, except Poppy is wearing a matching cap. She offers no apology for keeping me waiting. She just floats in, praising the statue I couldn't help but make appear insane, and shrieks about how I captured her "essence" perfectly. Essence. Yeah, that's it.

As she flitters away, she mentions another client she's sending. I give her a wholehearted thank you and calculate how much furniture that will buy for the next woman at Holly's.

"Interesting outfit." Frankie's voice sends a jolt down my spine. We're not supposed to meet for another three hours. I break out in an ear-to-ear grin, which feels pretty good.

"Yeah, she's a trend setter, that one," I joke.

Frankie comes behind the table, puts her arms around my neck and plants a chaste kiss on my lips. I don't think I realized quite how much I've missed her this week until this very second. I put my hands on her waist and kiss her back. Her waist is tiny in my hands. I want under her shirt so I can experience just how small, soft and receptive it is to my fingers. But I know once I'm under there, no way I'm stopping at her waist.

"That's one trend I'll let pass me by."

"Oh yeah? Well, she's the woman I was talking about when you thought I was talking about you."

Frankie blushes and lets out a small giggle. For a while, I couldn't stand the sound of giggling, but coming from her lips, I think I'm learning to love it again. "What are you doing here? I thought we were meeting at seven."

"Yeah, well, I told you I do whatever pops into my head. And my head told me to come early and see if you wanted to get a few drinks before we went out. I knew you might still be working, but I decided to surprise you anyway. I figured everyone loves surprises, right?"

My body grows cold at the word and I tighten my hands on her waist. "I hate surprises." I didn't mean to say it aloud, and even if I'd meant to say it, I would never have intentionally said it in the tone that just came out. Stinging, disdainful, bitter.

Frankie drops her arms from my neck and all traces of happiness disappear from her face. She thinks I'm saying I didn't want her to come. She backs away. "Oh. Sorry. I just thought... You know what, I shouldn't have come without calling. I'm sorry, we had plans at a certain time, and I should have stuck to them."

She starts to walk around the table and for a split second all I can think is how I need to get my hands on the clay in front of me. This very second. Knead the memory away, let it seep from my mind, down my neck, through my fingers, into the clay. It's almost like a drug for me. It's my escape.

But then it hits me like a sledgehammer. I don't want the clay to be my only escape. I don't want Frankie to walk out, leaving me alone to work this out with my hands. I want to work this out with her. I want this to work, period.

I lean across the table and grab her wrist before she can get any farther. "I didn't mean that the way it sounded."

She freezes, waiting for more of an explanation.

"Please, stay. I'm sorry. That wasn't about you. I'm happy you're here. Really, really happy."

Her sparkle returns, and she lets me guide her by the hand to my side of the table. "Yeah?"

"Yeah."

"What was it about?" She's close to me again, and I let out a breath. I run my hands up her back, over her sweater, relieved to have my hands on her instead of a statue.

"The slightest things people say make me think of my parents and set me off. It's not normal, Frankie."

She presses up to me and puts her palms on my cheeks. Her thumbs trace my nose, my lips, my chin under my stubble. "What's normal?" She's calm and quiet. "Nobody's normal, Griffin. Everybody's got their things that make them flawed. They're different for everyone. Come to think of it, I guess by definition, since everyone is flawed, then everyone *is* normal.

Because that would mean being flawed is the norm. We're all just trying to figure out how to deal with our own things in order to get by. But it's a lot easier to do if we do it together."

"Together," I say.

She nods. "Together."

"And the fact that the word *surprises* almost sent me into a spiraling rage?"

"Normally flawed." She nods. "Are you in a spiraling rage now?" She pecks my lips.

"No, but that's because I'm holding onto you."

"Then just keep holding on and tell my why."

"Why?" I scoff. "There's always one reason why."

"What surprise did he give you?"

"Not me." I shake my head. "Her."

I had the trifecta. Peace, quiet, and a perfect little joint one of my friends at school gave me, in return for the twenty I had in my pocket. I hadn't smoked in about a month, and my mouth was salivating as I walked into my house. With my parents at work, cutting my last two classes, smoking this baby and forgetting all the fighting that went on last week was all I could think about. I even took a couple of hits in the bathroom at school before I left to come home, which may not have been the smartest thing to do. But I was feeling so good I didn't really give a flying fuck.

I went up to my room to enjoy the rest of it. With each delicious inhale, life seemed a little less shitty, almost good, in fact. I rested my head against my pillow and appreciated the buzz. The sound of tires seemed far away, until I heard a car door open. One of my parents was home.

Fear rushed into me. Not only was I cutting school,

but I was completely high. Getting out of the house before he or she could realize I was there might have been the only choice. I opened my window to let out the scent. I sneaked out of my room and listened from the top of the stairs.

It was both of them.

"What was so important you had to drag me out of work?" My mother wasn't annoyed. If anything, she was being coy. I peeked over the banister. I felt invisible. Maybe I am, I thought with a small chuckle.

My father closed the door with his foot and moved within an inch of her, grabbing her waist. "I love you."

"I know." She smiled.

"No. You don't know. I love you so much I ache when you're not by my side." He kissed her and she put her arms around him.

I wanted to leave. I wanted to fly out of the house. But if I moved, the stairs might have creaked and then I'd be busted. Ditching school. Baked. I decided to stay put.

My father pulled away and revealed two small bags from inside his jacket.

"I got you a surprise. And I got one for myself, too."

"More surprises?" My mother swooned at him with adoration and I disliked her a little more than the day before. "Evan, you know you don't have to do all this for me."

"I love giving you surprises. If I could, I'd give them to you every day. Because I love you. And because I want to make up for the other stuff."

"Hush." My mother put two fingers up to his lips. "I know you're trying. I don't need the surprises."

"I am. I'm trying so hard. But surprising you makes you happy and seeing you happy makes me happy."

He pulled a jewelry box out of the first bag. He opened it and revealed what I thought, from the stairs, was a very expensive diamond bracelet. My mother covered her mouth with a hand. "My God, Evan."

Then he opened the other bag. "This one is my gift." He revealed his charming, toothy smile that melted my mother and sent me straight to hell. He pulled out a sexy nightgown. I had to hold back my vomit. Don't know if it was from what I was witnessing or the pot, but I thought I was seconds away from yacking.

"You're everything to me, Cindy. I couldn't live without you. I'd fucking kill myself. I really would. You know that, right?"

"Don't even say that, Evan. You'll never have to live without me."

"Promise. Promise you'll never leave me. Promise you'll keep letting me give you surprises forever. No matter what." He kissed her and pulled him against her. Finally, she came up for air.

"I promise," she barely got out before his mouth was on hers again.

"No one will ever love you the way I do. Tell me you know that."

"I know that." More deep, nauseating kisses.

"No one will ever make you feel the way I can. Tell me."

"No one, Evan. Only you." They were kissing and petting, and I was holding in vomit. My father pulled back. He whispered to her, but unfortunately, I must have gained the power of supersonic hearing, because his raspy voice was clear. "Wear only these two things for me. Nothing else." He held up the bracelet and the nightgown. My mother took them from his hands and went into the bathroom. It was my chance to escape. All I needed to do was sneak back into my room.

But my head wasn't working right, and all I could think was that I wanted to go downstairs and scream at the top of my lungs. At him, for being a monster that hides who he really is behind good looks, a charismatic personality, and romantic gestures. And at her. How could she be this easily manipulated? How could she brush off all the bad, for these brief moments of happiness? How could she love him, want him, after what he does to her? How could she be so stupid?

And at myself. I wanted to scream at myself until I was hoarse. Until I used up the last of my voice, and I could never make a sound again. How could I stand by and watch this day in, day out? Why couldn't I be stronger and force her to leave? And how, God, please tell me how in the world, could I blame my mother so much for the life I was living, when she was the fucking victim?

Now Frankie understands why I don't like surprises, but I omit the way I feel about my mother.

Indefinitely.

Chapter Fourteen

Frankie

Pictures in portfolio binder? Check. Camera? Check. Heavy dose of deodorant? Double check.

I'm meeting Scott Hannah at some trendy hotel bar in Midtown. I don't know the place, but Sarah says anyone who's anyone goes there. It's appealing online, but one drink there might cost all the tips I made last night. I sure hope he's buying.

I inhale and exhale countless times, trying to steady myself before I head to the subway. I can't stop sweating and between that and the fact that I'm sure it's going to be muggy underground, I'm praying I don't wilt before I get to the hotel.

Time to pull it together, Frankie. Don't panic. So what if this is the first real opportunity in your entire life to make anything of yourself? Don't screw it up.

"Are you doing that thing where you talk to yourself again?" Sarah calls from her living room. I wish I would realize when I was doing it. It would make life less embarrassing.

"Yeah, can't help it." I check my reflection in Sarah's full-length mirror. She was nice enough to lend me an outfit for the interview, since I had nothing appropriate.

"Well, you might want to try giving yourself

uplifting pep talks instead of always mentioning what a screw-up you are." She stands in her doorway.

"Old habits die hard. I don't really think *I'm* a screw-up. I just have a tendency to screw things up. See the distinction?"

She shakes her head. "Not really. Here, try this." Sarah reaches to a shelf and hands me a necklace. I go to grab it but am distracted by the other objects on the shelf. A picture and a statue of two children.

"Griffin told me he sculpted you." I nod in its direction.

"Yeah," Sarah answers. "A long time ago."

It's incredible, but I don't need to tell her. I'm sure she knows. Griffin undersold this piece when he described it to me.

Shocker.

"Has Griffin sculpted anyone else I know?"

Sarah starts playing with her phone. "Um." She pauses for too long. She doesn't want to answer. "Kaitlyn, I think."

Kaitlyn. That girl he used to date. I've heard about her. Her guy, Jackson, is the one who gives Griffin furniture sometimes.

So, he's sculpted Sarah and he's sculpted Kaitlyn. But the one time Sarah mentioned sculpting me, daggers nearly shot from his eyes, and neither of them has brought it up since. I've been in the warehouse numerous times and not once has Griffin made any reference to wanting to sculpt me. Even when we were sharing intimate moments. That would be the perfect time, I would think. Is it because he's closer to them than me? I mean, Sarah I understand, but I thought he and Kaitlyn were just a casual thing. Was he sleeping with her? Is that why he sculpted her? He hasn't slept with me yet, so that theory could hold water. But if that's the case, has he slept with Sarah? Envy fills me before I can stop it from seeping in. I search Sarah for any confirmation my theory is correct, but she doesn't give anything away. She continues to scroll through something on her phone. I try to shake the thoughts out of my head. Things have been going very well with Griffin. Don't overthink.

With her attention still on her phone, Sarah speaks. "Don't do what you're doing."

"What am I doing?" I know full well what I'm doing, but she doesn't.

"You're going through all the possible reasons in your head why he's done us and not you."

Damn.

"But why? Why won't he sculpt me even though he did you and Kaitlyn? Is it because we haven't slept together?"

Sarah barks a laugh that's accompanied by spit. "You think we've slept together?"

"I don't know."

Her laughter disappears and is replaced by a sober face. "No, Frankie, we haven't. We've never even kissed. At all. And for the record, he never slept with Kaitlyn either. Griffin generally doesn't sleep with the girls he cares about. Just the ones he doesn't think he'll get attached to." She pauses. "I'm guessing there will be an exception, though."

"So he cared about Kaitlyn, then?" I ask, missing her exception line for a moment.

"He cared about her, yes, but more as a friend. Nothing like the way he cares about you."

I know she said they've never kissed, but I have to know if they've ever wanted to, so I can put these little thoughts that peck at my brain to rest.

"And you?"

She stops what she's doing and gives me her undivided attention. "Griffin loves me. And I love him. I'd kill for him. But not for a second have we even shared a moment that's been more than one between friends. Not ever. Trust me, Frankie, he's never cared about anyone the way he cares about you."

I must have doubt written all over me.

She tosses her phone aside. "What?" she asks.

"Nothing. Things are good. It's just…he's not…"

"What?"

How much can I say to her? She's Griffin's best friend. Her loyalty is with him. On the other hand, no one knows him better than Sarah. If I want information, she's the go to person.

"I think there are things he's not ready to share with me yet."

"You're concerned because he's not having sex with you." Her blunt answer makes me shudder with discomfort, but I'm grateful I don't have to say it.

"I know it hasn't been that long, and I'm not in any rush, but if he cares about me the way you say he does, the way I care about him…I mean, if there's a reason. If something's preventing him…"

She laughs, misunderstanding. "Nothing's preventing him. Griffin's just fine."

I blush. I didn't mean like *that*. I'm perfectly aware from the time we've spent together there's nothing physically wrong with him. Nothing at all.

"I meant emotionally," I say.

"I knew what you meant," she snorts. "I'm just messing with you."

Oh. She didn't misunderstand. I turn even redder.

"Anyway, if there's a reason…"

She sighs now. "You know the reason, Frankie."

"He's afraid once we cross that threshold, he's going to feel like I'm committed to him and that's when all the bad stuff will come out." I repeat his words almost verbatim.

"Yep." She frowns.

"But…"

She puts her hand up to stop me. "You don't have to tell me, Frankie. If there's anyone who knows how great he is and wants him to be happy, it's me. But it's hard not to believe you're a certain way when you've been told it all your life.

I know how that is. Makes me wonder, did my parents call me flighty because I always was, or do I behave that way because it's expected of me? Was it a self-fulfilling prophecy? And if so, will it be for Griffin?

"It's a catch-22," Sarah says. "He's afraid of what will happen if he's in a serious long-term relationship, but the only way he can see it'll be okay is for him to be in one."

I take a minute to think about her words.

"Has Griffin told you how we met?" Sarah interrupts my thoughts.

I shake my head.

"No, I guess he wouldn't." She sits up and backs into her pillows, making herself comfortable. "In high school, Griffin didn't know me, but I knew him. Or at least I knew *of* him. He had a reputation around school as a loose cannon. He got in fights a lot. Cut school all the time. There was some speculation about whether or not he was into drugs. He wasn't the kind of guy people wanted to get close to because they never knew what was coming. He didn't seem to care. Kept to himself. This was before he discovered art and Mr. Rothman and now I know what was going on with him, but at the time I didn't. No one did."

Griffin has mentioned Mr. Rothman. He speaks of him with so much love. Now Sarah's bringing him up, too. I'm curious to know how he came to be in Griffin's life.

Sarah continues. "So when he approached me for the first time, I was taken aback, to say the least. He came right up to me and stared...you know, the way he does. He started asking me all these weird questions. Was I okay; was I safe? Did I need any help? My boyfriend at the time was a real asshole. I didn't know it at first, not for about four months. From the beginning, he would insult me and tell me how lucky I was to be with him because he was handsome and popular and I wasn't. I knew he wasn't nice, but I felt he was right. I was lucky to be with someone everyone wanted, and I didn't think he was dangerous. After that, I found out the hard way, with his fists, but by then I was nervous to leave. He was friends with everyone in the school. They all thought he was the shit and I was nothing. Plus he had a temper. I was afraid of what would happen if I broke up with him. I didn't know where to turn.

"My brother was away at college, and we always fought anyway, so I felt weird to call him about it. So I stuck it out. Figured he'd get tired of me and move on and it would all be a bad memory. But he wasn't getting tired of me. In fact, if anything, he was getting more possessive. At first, when he was physical, he did it in private. But then he got bolder. The day Griffin approached me, he'd gotten right in my space in the hallway. My back was against the lockers, and he was hovering over me so close he spat in my face as he yelled. He didn't touch me that day, but I guess his behavior was obvious enough to draw the attention of anyone who wanted to see it. Most people didn't. Most people just walked right on by. But Griffin saw it.

"When he asked me those questions, I wanted to tell him everything. Here was a guy who noticed what was happening. And even had the decency to check if I was okay. But I was also confused. Griffin had a worse reputation than the guy I was with. You know what they say...the devil you know is better than the one you don't. How could I trust this stranger? What if he made things worse for me? So I got defensive. I think I told him to mind his own business or something, I don't remember. I left him and cried because I felt like I might have walked away from the one person who could help me, but was too scared to take the chance.

"Griffin didn't approach me again for about a week, but he kept watching me. I pretended not to notice, but inside I was thankful. My boyfriend was in a lousy mood one afternoon. His basketball coach had ridden him pretty hard, and he needed to take it out on someone. I knew who that someone was going to be, and I was terrified to let him drive me home. But I was more afraid of what would happen if I didn't. I guess I hesitated when he asked me to get in his car, because he grabbed my wrist and twisted. His hand was wrapped so tight I knew I'd have marks, but in that moment I knew if I got in that car, I'd be in trouble. I tried to pull it away, but he was too strong. There was no way.

"Within seconds, Griffin was standing behind me. 'Ready to go, Sarah?' he asked. I didn't even know he knew my name. Anyway, as soon as he spoke, my boyfriend let go of my wrist. 'Go where?' my boyfriend asked, dumbfounded. Griffin said we had a project to work on for history class. We didn't have any classes together, but my boyfriend couldn't know that offhand. He was seething, but Griffin stood his ground. I told him I had to do this project, and I'd call him later. He said no, I needed to go home with him. Griffin said my name again. He told Griffin to mind his own fucking business. Instead of addressing my boyfriend again, or continuing the charade of having a project to work on, Griffin turned to me and said, 'Sarah, you don't have to go with him'. Something about the way he said it made me know right away that he was going to help me and everything would be okay if I went with him. I told my boyfriend I was going to do the project, and he was fuming. He wasn't going to make a public scene, but he said he'd see me later. It was a veiled threat.

"Griffin took me to a diner. He asked me nothing. He just spoke for an hour straight about how I deserved better, how things would only get worse going forward and how if I left, he'd protect me. He had no reason to do this, but it was obvious he meant it. When I broke up with my boyfriend that night, Griffin came with me. Griffin told him if he came after me, he'd have Griffin to deal with. The guy looked like he was going to pop a blood vessel in his forehead. His expression scared the hell out of me, but he said something about me being a stupid whore and not worth the trouble, and fine, Griffin could have his sloppy seconds. Griffin took me home and made sure I locked the door before he left. I'd never been so relieved in my life. I felt free. Griffin told me he'd see me at school the next day. It was the first time I looked forward to going to school in a while, even though I was nervous about seeing my ex there. But I had an ally and that was enough to give me hope."

Sarah pauses for a second here. She goes to get a bottle of water before she sits back on her bed and takes a long slug. "Early the next morning, I was walking to the bus stop to go to school, when my ex grabbed from behind. He pulled me into his car and locked the doors with a touch of a button. No one was around. He emitted pure hatred, and terror I'd never felt zipped through me. I tried to open the door, but like I said, he'd locked it. He jerked me by the back of the hair and started screaming in my ear. Who did I think I was? Bringing a guy to his house to break up with him? He called me every disgusting name you could think of. And then he punched me, hard, in the stomach while his other hand was still clutching my hair, holding me upright. He punched me again and I thought, this is it, he's going to kill me. But then glass smashed and my hair was released from his grip. I hunched over in pain, but heard yelling. The car door was opening and my ex was getting pulled out."

She pauses again to take another sip and makes sure I'm paying attention. How could I not be? "Griffin beat the shit out of him, Frankie. Really, really bad. He was protecting me, but I had to protect him, too. I jumped in his way to get him to stop pounding on the guy because I was afraid of what would happen to

Griffin if I didn't. He finally backed away, but told the guy if he ever came near me again, he'd put him in the hospital, if he even made it there. My ex left me alone after that. No one witnessed the fight and my ex never reported it, probably because he knew I could bring charges against him. Griffin asked if I wanted to have the guy arrested. He encouraged it, and said he'd be happy to spend a little time in juvie if it meant this guy would, too. But I didn't want that. I just wanted it over with. Later, Griffin told me as soon as he got home that first night, he realized my ex might come after me in the morning, so he decided to meet me at my house. Thank God he did."

Her story is finished, and she seems exhausted to have relived it.

"I'm very sorry you went through that, Sarah."

"Don't. That's not why I told you. It's so you can understand him a little better. Griffin's not only been a witness to violence his entire life. He's been involved in his share of it, too. Every time he gets mixed up in something physical, he thinks that's proof he's got a proclivity for violence, even if it's for a good reason. To people like us it doesn't seem rational. But to someone with his past, it makes perfect sense. Don't give up on him, Frankie. You may be the only one who can get through that fucked-up head of his and prove to him that he's a good guy, through and through. Don't walk away when he gets all twisted up with self-loathing and pushes you away because he thinks he's too much like his pig father to deserve anything good."

I shake my head. "I won't. I'm not going to." I've seen that in him before. "So there's nothing I can do except wait?"

"I didn't say that." She gives an evil grin. "I'm sure you've got some irresistible moves up your sleeve. He'll come around. Eventually." She stands by her door. "Besides, you need to get to your interview. Don't clog up your head with bullshit." She puts her hand on her door, which lets me know it's time for me to go. And she's right. I have more important things to focus on right now.

****

The hotel is even swankier than I expected. I'm way underdressed in Sarah's conservative black slacks and white blouse. I find Scott Hannah sitting at the bar, sipping a martini.

"Hello, Mr. Hannah." I pull up the stool next to him.

"Oh Lord, Francesca, please call me Scott."

"Okay, then, Scott, call me Frankie."

"I like that." He smiles. "It fits you better." He asks what I'd like, then orders my pinot grigio.

We talk for a while as we sip our drinks. He asks some questions about me. Where I'm from, how long I've been in New York. What brought me here? I hate to think it's obvious that I'm new to the city, but I guess it is. It's going pretty well. He doesn't offer much up about himself, but I suppose that's standard in an interview. He acts impressed as he thumbs through my pictures.

"These are even better printed out, Frankie. You do very nice work."

"Thank you." I'm demure, but wish I could stand up and cheer.

"So let me tell you a little bit about what I'm doing. I'm putting together a book of Manhattan's hotel bars, like this one. Comparing and contrasting the cultures, discussing the allure of each one. I'd like to have pictures to accompany them, but I want them from unique points of view. Not something you can see if you walk in off the street. I need someone with a different perspective to take them for me. Sound like something you'd be interested in?"

"Yes!" I jump, then admonish myself for sounding too desperate. It mustn't bother him, though.

"Great." He finishes his third martini. "I'll text the address of each hotel the day before I want to go there. Sometimes we'll do two in a night. You're free at night?" he presumes with the same cocky air that was a little off-putting the first time I met him.

"Well, I waitress, but I'll try to make it work."

"Wonderful." He gets up and staggers a tiny bit. "And when we go out, I'll want to be inconspicuous, to get good shots. So don't dress like you're going to a convention." He takes his time perusing my body in a way that makes me want to cross my arms. "Wear something like you were wearing when we met on the street that day. You know, that cute little skirt? It'll put people more at ease when they see you with a camera around your neck." He throws some cash on the bar and walks out, leaving me a little uncertain about what just happened.

What was I wearing that day? Oh, I remember. I'd been out with Griffin. I had on a short black skirt with black stockings and a snug off-the-shoulder top. And this guy remembers that?

Whatever. He wants me to dress more like I'm hanging at the bar than working at it. I get it. No problem, even though I think a huge camera around my neck would be more obvious to people than a pair of slacks.

I head straight to Sam's Tavern and change into my work uniform. I'm in a terrific mood and am extra friendly to the customers, which seems to translate to better tips. Who would have thought?

My heart skips a beat when fingers clutch my hips, a voice rumbles in my ear, and the most heavenly scent envelops me. "Hey, you." I turn and Griffin's hands stay on my hips.

"Hey, you."

"How did it go?" He wasn't supposed to meet me here. I was going call him when I got home and tell him all about the interview. It's not the first time he's come here unannounced. For someone who hates surprises, he sure shows up unexpectedly a lot. But I'm not the one who says she hates surprises. I love them.

"I think it went well. He liked the pictures and offered me a job."

Griffin smiles, but I can't see the dimples because his hair has grown long and straggly again. I miss them.

"That's great, Frankie. I'm so proud of you." His focus on my lips says he wants to kiss me, but I'm at work, so he refrains.

"Thanks." I wish we were alone and I was supposed to see him tonight. But I know he doesn't want to spend every single night together. As it is, we were together the last three nights in a row.

I tell him everything Scott said about the book.

"When do you start?" he asks.

"Um, I'm not sure. He said he'll text me."

"Okay," he says. "What days are you going to be working?"

"It's kind of up in the air."

"Well, I'm sure it will be great."

A customer clears her throat, signaling that I'm ignoring her, and Griffin lets go of my waist. He leans into me before he leaves. "I know we said we're taking a night off, but I don't like the idea of sleeping without you. Want to come over after work? You can tell me more about the job."

As if I need an excuse to spend the night with him. "Of course." I hope this isn't the second man I've sounded desperate to today. Except with Griffin, I don't think I care. I'm not afraid to let him know I want to see him every day. "But I'll have to go home and pick up some clothes first."

"Don't bother." He grins.

And I melt.

****

Gabby should be here any minute. Her train arrived a little while ago, and I've been pacing ever since. I've got everything planned. I'm going to preempt any and all questions by spewing as much information as I can as soon as she walks in. I'm going to tell her about my photography job. I'm going to tell her about the great new guy I'm seeing. I'm going to tell her about the waitressing job that keeps me afloat. Hopefully, that will be all that gets reported to my parents. Not the fact that there's probably a hooker on my front steps or that the guy I'm with is terrified he's going to beat the crap out of me one day or that I have no specifics about the job I took. Which didn't even occur to me initially.

It hit me once Griffin started asking questions about it after my interview the other day. His questions weren't meant to make me second-guess myself, but when I didn't know the answers to any of them, that's exactly what happened. The question he didn't ask, but that I thought of afterwards, was what is Scott Hannah paying me? How did I not ask that question? I jumped at the opportunity, not stopping for a second to think it through. Typical Frankie.

The doorbell rings, and I practically leap to the door. Even though I hate hearing my parents' patronizing statements after Gabby reports to them, I do love hanging out with my sister and I haven't seen her in months. Besides, I'm a grown woman. My parents' disappointment shouldn't bother me any more.

I squeeze the life out of Gabby when she walks in the apartment.

"How are you? I've missed you," I say, which is true.

"Me, too," she says as I usher her inside.

"What can I get you? You must be starved."

"I'm fine. Maybe just some water."

We sit in on my couch, and I start running off at the mouth. I don't think I stop talking for an hour straight. But it's not preemptive. I'm enjoying sharing my life with her. It's been a long time since I girl-talked with someone. I mean, Sarah and I chat, but she's Griffin's person not mine, so there's a limit to what I can say to her.

I pull out the photos I showed Scott and flip through, describing what each one is and how I captured the shot. When I reach the last one, I close the binder.

"They're really great, Fransister."

Fransister—Gabby's childhood nickname for me. When she was little, she thought Francesca was pronounced *fransistuh*. These days, she only uses it when she's sad. I stop talking to find her eyes filled to the brim with tears. One escapes, and I can't believe I rambled on for so long without noticing she's upset. "What's wrong, Gabby?"

She puts her head in both hands and shakes it.

"What is it? You know you can tell me anything."

She doesn't pick up her head, but I can understand her muffled words. "Mitchell left me."

Oh no. She's been with him for what, four years, or so. She must be devastated.

"I'm so sorry, Gab."

She shakes her head. "It's my fault."

"No, I'm sure it's not."

"No, Frankie, it is. Last semester, I was, I don't know, bored. I can't explain it any other way. We'd fallen into a rut, staying in and watching TV." She wipes her wet hands on her jeans. "This guy from one of my classes had been flirting for a while. One night I went out with girlfriends while Mitchell stayed home. The guy was there, being all funny and whatever. And I-I…"

She can't finish her sentence. She doesn't need to. I know what she did.

"I'm so stupid. How could I have done this?"

"People make mistakes. You made a mistake."

"It gets worse. I hadn't told Mitchell. I was sorry and ashamed and I figured if I forgot about it, it would be like it never happened. Then, about a month ago, I started having some burning so I went to the doctor. They tested me and they said I had gonorrhea."

The words hang suspended in the air. I almost ask her to repeat herself, because I don't believe it, but it

149

was hard enough for her to say the first time. She's full-on sobbing now and I wrap my arms around her.

"Oh, Gabby."

"Until then, I had no symptoms, but it had been a bunch of months since I'd been with that guy, so I'd had it for a while without knowing. The doctor said because it was left untreated, it was pretty bad. There's a good chance I might not ever be able to get pregnant."

I don't even know what to say. I know how much she wants to have a family someday. I feel terrible. Plus I want to scream at her. If she got gonorrhea, she probably had sex with this strange guy without using a condom. I mean, even though they're not one hundred percent effective, chances are she wasn't using one.

"I had to tell Mitchell, because there was a good chance I gave it to him. Which I did. You had to see his face, Frankie. He despises me." She leans into her hands again and makes the saddest sounds I've ever heard. After letting it out for a few minutes, she sits up, with soaked cheeks. "I always thought Mitchell and I would have tons of kids. Now I don't have him and I might not even be able to have them."

"You don't know for sure, Gabby. They have all sorts of ways to help women get pregnant. And you don't need to worry about that for years."

"It's not just that." Her words are full of despair and my heart aches for her. "All our friends were his friends. Or their girlfriends. He was my whole life. Now all our friends have chosen him because they all know what I did. I have no one. I can't believe I screwed everything up like this. I can't even get out of bed most days. I'm going to fail everything this semester. I'll never get into med school now. I tried to apologize to him a million times. But he won't call me back or return my texts. I'm never going to get him back." Her face is covered in wet streaks of makeup and her words come between chokes.

I can't believe her wonderful relationship crumbled like this. I was right. Nothing is ever all beautiful or all ugly. Everything's layered. Sometimes you have to peel away the bad to find the good. Unfortunately, sometimes it's the other way around.

She wipes her nose with her sleeve and sniffles. "We were amazing together and now our life is ruined. How could I do this to him? What was I thinking? I love him so much…" Her voice trails off, and she sobs some more. I hold her tight and let her cry.

"Don't worry," I say. "Everything's not as bad as it seems. It'll get better. You just need some time to work it out." I know these words are as empty as they sound, but they're the best I can come up with on short notice. I hold her and rock her, the way I did when we were little and she got hurt. "Maybe you'll stay here for a while."

She lets out a snicker and pulls away to give a small wave around. "Here, Frankie? Really?" It's her first indication she noticed where I'm living.

I chuckle. "Well, maybe not here. But it will get better. I promise."

Chapter Fifteen

Griffin

"What's she going to do?" I ask Frankie after a few grueling days of not seeing her.

I knew something was wrong when she was texting me over the weekend. Normally, her texts ramble on so much talking on the phone would be quicker. Each of this weekend's texts was brief and evasive, and it took her a while to respond to mine. If I didn't know her sister was there, I would have thought she was pissed at me for something.

"Well, there's really nothing she can do. Just give it time. She's on her way home now to tell my parents about the breakup. She's going to try to take incompletes for her courses. Maybe she can finish them next semester. I offered to go back with her, for moral support, but she said she didn't want to disrupt my life or make me take off work. She just feels so alone. My heart's breaking for her." Frankie pouts.

"Is there anything I can do?"

"What you're doing right now is perfect."

Rubbing her. That's what I'm doing. She's lying facedown on my bed, the way I love her to be when I'm massaging her, from the base of her neck to the soles of her feet. I'm incredibly happy to have my hands on her again. As awful as it was being without her, when she mentioned the possibility of going to Buffalo with Gabby, I felt a stab in my chest at the thought of going longer without seeing her. I was relieved when she said she wasn't going home after all. I'd never tell her that. Those are the kind of thoughts that could get us both in trouble.

"So what did you do while I was preoccupied?" she asks. "Were you alone the entire time?"

I think this is her way of asking if I am seeing anyone else. We haven't had that conversation yet and she hasn't put me on the spot. In light of what happened to her sister, it makes sense. But trying to take things slow doesn't mean I want to see other people. Besides, I'm doing a terrible job of taking things slow with Frankie. I have no desire to so much as look at another woman. And I'm ashamed of how even the thought of her seeing anyone else makes my temperature rise.

"Are you trying to ask me something?"

She turns underneath me to face me. "Are you trying not to answer something, Griffin?" She's being coy, but I can tell she wants a specific answer to her vague question.

"No."

"No, you weren't alone or no, you're not trying to not answer something?"

"No, I have no idea what you're saying right now," I tease.

"Griffin," she sighs, frustrated. "Yes or no?"

I kiss the lips I've been denied for too many days. They're fuller and downier than they were three days ago. Or maybe they only seem that way because I've been yearning for them. "No, I'm not avoiding a question, and yes, I was alone. Well, not alone, alone, but alone the way you mean."

"What way do I mean?"

"Frankie. Ask me what you really want to ask me."

She inhales and there's a good possibility she's going to turn blue, because she holds in the breath for so long. Then she asks the question that's been on her mind as she exhales. "Are you seeing other women, or do you want to be, because we've never discussed it so you're not doing anything wrong if you are. I should just know if you are because then I'd—"

I cut her off with a long, deep kiss and only stop kissing her because I know she's waiting for my answer. "I'm not seeing anyone else. I don't want to be seeing anyone else. And if you are or you do, then we have a problem because as hard as I'm trying to not feel possessive over you, I'm failing miserably."

My answer causes exactly the outcome I intended. A broad, uneven smile, every contour of which I've memorized. Frankie tugs a little at my beard and pulls me down to her. "I'm not and I don't. More than you know." We don't speak any more for a while, because we're too busy enjoying each other, now that we know there's no one else. In truth, I think we've both known that all along.

****

I can't stop touching her. Technically, it's not that I can't as much as I just don't want to. We're each lying on our sides, facing each other. Her hand caresses every inch of the side of my face, slowly, affectionately as I run my palm up and down the curve of her hip.

"I love looking at you," she says. "I see something else in your face every time I'm this close to it. Sometimes I just want to keep staring at you so I can find a new chisel, or a line I've never noticed before. Does that sound creepy?"

I laugh. I find myself laughing a lot more lately. "Maybe, but it's a good kind of creepy. I've known you were strange since I saw you sprawled on the sidewalk in Washington Square."

"Hey." She tickles my jaw with her fingertips. "I told you, I wanted to get a certain angle."

"Maybe that was an excuse." I pull on her leg and drape it over my hip. "Maybe you have some weird fetish about getting dirty in public places."

She lets out a laugh that sounds more like a chicken's cackle than a sound emanating from a human being. It causes me to burst out with unexpected laughter, which in turn makes her hysterical. She rests her forehead into my shoulder while her back convulses. I pull her closer to me, loving the feeling coursing throughout her body. Sometimes, simply touching her makes things seem more blithe.

Our laughter subsides, and morphs into a series of fun kisses, which turn into deeper, more affectionate ones, which eventually turn into, well…just more.

Afterwards, we lie in the same position we started, face to face. I like lying this way the best. It gives me a full view of every bend of her body. She's stroking my cheek again, but this time, her fingers trace my lips as well.

"You have a beautiful mouth," she tells me.

"So do you." I feather my lips to hers for a second.

"No, but I mean, the shape of your lips, your teeth, your smile. You have the most amazing smile. I wish I could see more of it."

"I've been smiling a lot more since you came

around."

She blushes. "Good, I'm glad. But that's not what I meant. I meant sometimes I think you keep yourself hidden. Don't get me wrong, I'm crazy for you any way you are, but when you've got light scruff, with your hair pushed back like you are tonight, and I can see all of you, it's like you're here, open for me, not shoved somewhere for no one to find. And these dimples. When they're revealed, it means I did something that makes you happy. It's like a gift. I bet I sound weird again, right?"

"No. You don't." But I no longer want to have this conversation. I kiss her forehead and turn to the other direction, giving her my back. In all likelihood, I insulted her and I didn't mean to, but I had to turn away. When the bed dips, I'm afraid she's going to leave. I don't want that. I just spent three of the longest days without her. But I need a second to my own thoughts. Then I can turn back around and be with her again.

Instead of leaving, she climbs over me, and lies down, facing me from the other side. "Now you're the one denying access, Griffin." She throws my words back at me.

"What?"

"I said something that bothered you, though I don't know what it was, and you got lost somewhere in your head. Don't do it. Talk to me." She places her hand in my hair and runs her fingers through it, pushing it back. "Talk to me."

I shiver. "It's nothing. It's stupid."

"It's not stupid if it made you retreat into yourself and took you away from me. Was it about your dimples? Or your smile? Because I think that's the last thing I said."

Her fingers are sublime against my scalp. I close my eyes. It brings her closer and pushes the memory farther, so maybe I can talk to her about it without losing my cool.

"Do you have a favorite day?" I ask her.

"Like Saturday?"

"Of the year."

Mine used to be Thanksgiving. My mother goes all out every year, cooking the most succulent dishes. It's not just the food that always made me enjoy the day, though. It's the day itself. My father loves Thanksgiving. He loves carving the turkey at the head of the table in front of the entire family, while they praise his precision in slicing. He loves watching my mother saunter around in her holiday apron, which shows a turkey from behind and says, "Kiss my giblets." He loves watching football with his brothers while my mother divvies out a smorgasbord of pies.

Thanksgiving had always been my one day. My one day a year when I wasn't worried, because he's happy and relaxed, and when he's happy and relaxed, my mother is safe.

My first year away at college, I was pretty busy. I didn't have much time or energy to take care of myself. Laundry took a backseat to whatever project I was working on, and shaving took a backseat to laundry. Still does, I guess. I didn't even realize how much scruff I'd grown until I got home.

My father asked me what was all over my face as soon as I walked in the door. I ignored him. Even he couldn't diminish how happy the smells of turkey, potatoes, and pie made me.

Instead, I asked where my mother was. He said she was upstairs resting. She'd been working all day and he said he'd hold down the fort until company arrived. It was very big of him.

He asked how school was, and I mumbled something under my breath. He wanted me to sit with him, and pretend we had some kind of relationship. Maybe he was deluded and really thought we did. I don't know.

When I refused, saying I didn't feel like talking, he insisted. By his tone, I knew if I didn't, not only would he ruin my day, but my mother's as well. So I sat.

"You need to grow up, Griffin," he spat at me. "You're in college now, but you're still carrying around that same baby shit you were when you lived here. Life isn't perfect. People aren't perfect. I'm not. Your mother's not. Even you, though you sit in constant judgment of me, are not. You need to get over it and move on. Your mother can. She's happy with me and I'm happy with her, and whatever we have between us is our business, not yours. Grow the hell up, and start acting like a man instead of a petulant child."

Heat shot through my body at lightning speed. "Act like a man—like you?" I shouted. "What should I do, go pick some amazing woman who's full of life and beat it out of her until she can't even recognize herself any more, until she can't even differentiate between love and pain? Is that what a man does, Dad? Is that what I should do?"

My father stood, and I was sure this was the first time he was going to punch me. Instead, he broke into a smile. An evil, condescending, terrifying smile. "You think you're so different from me?" He hovered over me. His tone was sinister, as if he was trying to cut through my skin with nothing but his voice. "You think you're better? That this blood of mine doesn't run through your veins? I have news for you, Griffin. We are the same. Everything you feel…the depths of your rage, your heat…you think that's yours alone? It comes from me. Everything you are, everything you have, everything you will be comes from me. Get up."

He yanked my arm and pulled me by the elbow into the bathroom. I didn't know what he was going to do to me, but I was prepared to protect myself, especially after the words he just said. He grabbed the back of my head and forced me to face the mirror.

"Look at yourself, Griffin. And look at me. Everything about you comes from me. We are the same. You may deny it now. You may put yourself on a pedestal, thinking you're above being human, but just know that the fire inside you, that's my fire. That passion, it's mine. And when you have an uncontrollable desire to love, to hurt, to possess a woman, it's from me. Nothing is yours alone. Even this face." He snagged my chin between his strong fingers. I tried to yank it away from his grasp, but he held on too tight. "It's mine. And there's nothing you can do about it. You can try to mask it in this mess of hair and clothes and tattoos you have going on, but know that every time a woman falls in love with that face, every time she says she can't resist you because of it, every time she needs you and can't walk away from you…it's because of me. It's because you are me. We. Are. The. Same." He released my chin with a shove and left the bathroom.

"Griffin, I didn't know," Frankie says, still holding me. Her gentle touch calms me from my memory as well as any clay ever has. "I didn't mean I wanted you to change for me. I love seeing your face, that's all I meant. Keep it any way you want. Seriously."

"It's not really that I want to keep myself this way. I've just been trying to not be him for such a long time, I don't know how to be any other way."

"He even took your one day from you." She sighs. Her lips stroke my beard, and I pull her even closer. It's getting to the point where all I want to do is lie in bed with her and hold her. Well, not *just* hold her.

If I didn't have my sculptures to center me, I'd be having a lot harder a time letting her go when it's time. I don't like feeling this way. It scares me. But the thought of not having her, not feeling this way, going back to how I was before her, is scarier.

My phone rings. I'll check who it is, and if it's not an absolute emergency, I won't move from this spot. I won't break our connection. But Taylor's number comes up and since I have no outstanding appointments at Holly's, it can't be good. "Hey, what's up?"

"Griffin, can you please come here? I need your help."

****

I race to Holly's House as quickly as humanly possible. I've never heard panic in Taylor's voice before. I didn't even waste time asking what was wrong. I just grabbed my wallet and left. Frankie wanted to come, but I didn't know what I was in store for me when I got here, so I told her to wait at my place and promised I'd let her know something as soon as possible.

Taylor buzzes me in after checking me out on the camera, but the buzzer only goes off for a split second and I miss it. I have to ask her to do it again. This time I'm prepared, and I get the door open before the buzzing stops.

"What's the matter?" I approach her desk.

"Come in here." She ushers me into the sitting room and slides the pocket door closed. I never even knew it was there. She whispers, "We have a problem. I didn't know who else to call."

"What is it?"

"There's a woman here. She came in, oh, maybe a month and a half ago. Maybe more. I can't remember now. Doesn't matter. Anyway, she was very messed up. Escaped at the end of bad episode in her home, after her husband passed out. We rushed her to the emergency room. She had him arrested, but he's out on bail. She's been hiding here, afraid to even go outside because she didn't want him to find her. But he did. I don't know how. He's been circling the block. We have an order of protection, but the judge only gave it to us for one hundred feet. I called the police, but they said that because he hasn't actually done anything and hasn't violated the order, there's nothing they can do.

"This man isn't stable, Griffin. I'm afraid he's going to try to get in here when we open the door for someone. I'm sorry for calling you and making this your problem, but I didn't know what else to do."

"No." I shake my head. "I told you. You call me anytime, for any reason." I walk to the front of the building and move the blinds aside to peek through. There's no one suspicious in view, but I'm not naïve enough to think that means he isn't there. "I don't see anyone, but let me stay a while in case he comes back."

"Thank you." She puts a shaky hand on my shoulder. "I don't really know what you can do, but having you here makes me feel a thousand times more relaxed."

I pull up a chair by the window so I can periodically check whether this asshole is passing by. Taylor told me he's driving a navy convertible. His car will be easy to spot. She talks to me from behind her desk, where she has a view of the window too, and it occurs to me this is the longest we've ever spoken. She tells me about her husband, which surprises me. I didn't realize she was married. She doesn't wear a ring. She asks a little about my life, and I tell her about Frankie, which reminds me I haven't checked in with her. I'm sure she's worried. I pull out my cell to call, but it's dead. Damn, I forgot to charge it. I'm about to ask Taylor if I can use her landline, when she bellows. "Griffin, that's his car!"

Sure enough, a blue convertible creeps past. The driver turns toward the house, and I want to run outside and pummel this asshole to the ground. Just the fact that he's spying over here is an intrusion into this haven. But I control myself. Getting arrested won't help anyone.

"Is he back?" A woman walks up behind us. She appears to be in her late forties and she's got slight discolorations all over her face and neck.

"He just drove by," Taylor tells the woman. "This is Griffin. He's going to watch out for us."

"Thank you." She lowers her head.

I hate being thanked for something any decent person would do. I nod.

"Do you mind if I go lie down? This is all making me very nervous," she says.

"Of course not. Go, rest," Taylor says.

The woman leaves.

"I hate this, Griffin." Fury and fear radiate from Taylor for the first time since I've known her. She's normally very levelheaded. "Why won't the police do anything? What will it take? He has to kill her, or someone else before they'll intervene? It's so frustrating I want to break something."

I know how she feels. There were so many times I wished they'd arrest my father. But without my mother admitting he did anything to her, there was nothing they could do.

Taylor's experience with frustration is even more haunting than my own. I learned this the first day I saw her at the support group meeting. After she introduced herself, Taylor told us a story about her mother, Holly, who remarried when Taylor was fourteen. Taylor described her abusive stepfather, how he hit her once in a while, but focused on her mom most of the time. Her mom begged her not to tell, saying then Taylor would get taken away, so Taylor kept her mother's secret. The final time he pushed her down the stairs and broke her neck, killing her instantly.

Her stepfather went to jail, and Taylor went to live with her father. But she never got over the guilt for not telling anyone before it was too late. She majored in business and right after she graduated college, opened Holly's House, with her mother's life insurance money to help her start off.

As soon as Taylor finished her story, I knew I had to speak to her and have a connection with this incredible place. If I could help one person, even if wasn't my own mother, I would have a purpose.

"Excuse me." I approached Taylor after the meeting. "My name is Griffin." I held out my hand.

"Hello." Her handshake was firm and confident.

"I was hoping…" I didn't know what to say. "Your story…it was…"

She waited, patiently. I'm sure I wasn't the first person to tell her she had a moving past. "I'd like to help at the place where you work." I sounded like an ignorant child.

She gave me a patronizing smile and a tilt of her head. "In what way?"

In what way? I had no idea. In that second, I felt foolish. I was just a high school student. What could I possibly do for those women? "I don't know, any way I can. I'd just really like to help."

I must have sounded more serious that time, because her expression changed to one of understanding. "Well, Griffin, we can always use extra help. I'll give you my number. If you think of some creative way to lend your services, whether it's now or in the future, give me a call."

I knew there was something I could do. It just took me a while to figure out what that something was.

Evening falls outside, and I start to think the husband may have left. He hasn't driven by in hours. That's the problem. These psychos are unpredictable. I could leave now and he'll show up again in the middle of the night, planning God knows what. And even if he does show up, what am I going to do? Actually, I know exactly what I'll do. It's best not to think about it.

The buzzer goes off and causes us both to jump.

Would he have the nerve to ring the bell? Taylor studies the screen behind her desk, that shows someone standing in front of the security camera. "It's not him. It's a woman. I think I know her." She frowns, trying to place the person outside. "Yes?" she calls through the intercom.

"Hi, it's Frankie Moore. I'm looking for Griffin. Is he here?"

What is she doing here? I told her to stay at my place. I don't want her involved in this.

"Yeah, Frankie, he's here. Come…" Taylor's voice stops mid-sentence and her hand, that was about to buzz Frankie in, freezes in the air. "My God, Griffin. Look."

I go behind Taylor's desk. My heart stops beating in my chest at the picture on the screen. A step behind Frankie is a man. His back is to the camera and we can't make out his face, but there's no question about his identity.

"Buzz her in," I direct Taylor, my eyes glued to the screen.

"I can't."

"Buzz her in, Taylor. I'll block the entrance."

"Griffin," Taylor pleads. "You know I can't do that."

"For Christ's sake, Taylor, open the fucking door!" My voice is booming and I probably scared any of the women in hearing range, but if she doesn't let Frankie in and get her away from that man, I'm going to completely lose it. I reach around her to press the button myself, but she blocks my way with defiance, knowing there's no way I'll push past her.

"Griffin…" She smooths her tone, trying to get me to regain my composure. "I'll call the police. He violated the order. They'll come now."

"Not soon enough." I'm panicking. Frankie's studying the security camera, no doubt wondering what's taking so long.

"Taylor?" she calls.

"Just a sec," Taylor sings to Frankie. Then she addresses me. "He won't do anything to her. He has no reason to. He doesn't know her."

"You don't know that." I dart to the door to open it manually.

"Griffin!" Taylor dials the phone. The door flies open. The man turns around and takes a step next to Frankie. It is the man from the car. No doubt about it.

He tries to walk past me, but I block his entrance.

"Excuse me," he says.

I don't move a millimeter.

"Step aside, friend," he says, but there's no hint of friendship in his voice. I'm hoping Frankie will sneak down the steps, without him noticing.

"No can do, *friend*." We remain in a locked standoff. His mouth distorts. In a matter of seconds this could escalate into something ugly. I don't care for me. I haven't been in a fight since high school, but I certainly wouldn't shy away from one, for the right cause. I just need Frankie to move away from this first.

She opens her mouth, and I've never wished more for mental telepathy, to beg her not to speak or draw attention to herself.

"Griffin, what are you…"

She doesn't have a chance to finish her sentence before the man realizes there's a connection between us. Before I can blink, he's got his fist wrapped around the ponytail at the back of her head and a small pocketknife pressed against her throat. "I don't want any trouble. Let me by so I can get my wife and everything will be fine."

I can't move. I can't think. I can't even breathe. Let him by, my head screams. Every nerve inside me tells me the same thing. Protect Frankie at all costs. But I can't. There's got to be a way to protect both women.

"She's not here," I answer, stalling for time while I figure out what to do.

"Don't fucking lie to me!" He presses the knife into Frankie's neck just a touch. Just enough to produce a tiny nick on her neck. She inhales.

I see nothing but red. I lunge to grab Frankie. The man shoves her away from him and pushes past me to get inside. I have less than a second to assess the situation and decide what to do. Frankie tumbles down the stairs. I'm pulled to her, but I know, even though she might be hurt, she's safe.

"I'll be right there!"

I fly inside after this guy. My rage is unleashed; I'm going to flatten him into the ground.

I catch up to him as he grabs Taylor by the arm, wielding his knife. "Tell me where she is!"

I take hold of the back of his collar and yank. He stumbles back a step and I punch the back of his skull, because it's all I can reach. Intense pain shoots through my hand and up my arm. I think I might have broken it.

He grabs his head and curses. He turns to me. I'm clutching my hand and he uses it to his advantage, crushing my hand with both of his. The sheer agony drops me to my knees. Thinking I'm no longer a threat, he turns to go find his wife. I ignore the pounding and wrap my uninjured hand around his ankle. He kicks back, but I hold fast. He does it again, harder. This time, his foot collides with the top of my head and everything goes black.

Women are screaming and sirens are blaring but all that registers is I need to stop him. It's my fault he's even inside.

"Griffin, Griffin, can you hear me?" It's the voice that's danced in my dreams for a while now. I lift my lids and there she is. "Can you see me?"

"Yeah, Frankie, and I've never been happier about it." I try to sit up.

"Don't move." She places her hands on my chest. "They want to check you out."

When I can focus, I find myself lying on my back in the entryway of Holly's, with my head in Frankie's lap. "Where's the guy?" I ask, nervous about what happened in the time I lost.

Taylor answers. "The police caught him before he got inside. Thanks to you."

I tip my head to see her. "I'm sorry, Taylor. I couldn't leave her out there."

"I know." She smiles. "I'm sure I would have done the same in your position."

I can't believe she's not furious. I put every woman in Holly's in danger. Everything comes rushing back and I remember he threw Frankie down the stairs. This time I do jolt up. My head pounds.

"What about you? Are you okay?"

"I'm fine. Just a little banged up."

I touch the small bandage on her neck and am reminded about my wounded hand by the instant, intense throbbing. I curse under my breath.

"They'll check that out for you. And your head,"

Frankie says.

I shake my head. All I want to do is get home and hold her. I can't believe how close that asshole came to hurting her. "I'll be fine." I flex my fingers and wince. "See? Nothing's broken. And I know what to watch for in case of concussion." Unfortunately, I've been on concussion patrol before and am too familiar with the signs. "All they'll do is tell me to make sure I'm not nauseous, or dizzy, etc. etc. And they'll tell me not to sleep right away."

"Well, I still think you should have them check you, but I can help with the staying awake part."

I don't know if she meant that how it sounded, but I've never longed for her as much as I do this second. I almost exploded when that guy had his hands on her. I would have torn him apart if he didn't have a knife to her throat. For a moment, I felt handcuffed, as I've so often been with my own mother. I think that's the worst feeling in the world.

I have to remind myself she's not my mother and she's not in any danger now. I can't hold back from her any more. I have to touch her, to know she's real and she's all right. But it's more than that. As close as we've been, as much as we've explored each other in almost every way, I haven't been able to cross that final line, to completely become each other's. But right now, my fear of the future is displaced by my overwhelming need to erase this feeling, to envelop her and give her everything I am. And there's only one way to do that.

Chapter Sixteen

Frankie

"Come home with me?" Griffin eases his way up to his feet. His hands run down my arms, and he flinches when he threads his bruised fingers with mine. But he doesn't let go. His eyes search me. They stop on my neck for a second.

"I'm fine," I reassure him.

"I'm just checking." He frowns.

When we get to his place, I grab some ice from the freezer and hold it on his swollen knuckles. His face gnarls, and I assume it's from the cold. "I'm sorry, but it'll help with the swelling."

"It doesn't bother me. I was just thinking."

"About?"

"Frankie, when he had you like that, I wanted to rip him into a thousand pieces and yet I couldn't move because I was petrified of what would happen if I did." Anguish oozes from each of his syllables.

"I know. I'm sorry I came. You told me to wait here. I should have listened. I put everyone in danger."

"No, don't apologize. He was the one who did something wrong, not you. You were concerned about me. I know that. But I-I've been helpless so many times in my life, incapable of saving my mother, of getting her to leave, getting her to understand I can take care of her and she doesn't need him. That feeling tortures me, and it came back again when he had you. I never want to feel that way again." He removes the ice from his knuckles and runs both hands through my hair. "And from the second I woke up in your lap, all I could think is I need to show you...I need to show you..." His voice trails and I want to ask him what he needs to show me. But he lays me backwards onto his bed, and his mouth is on mine, and he's kissing me in a way he's never kissed me before. It's slow and intense, but sensual and searching and as he gathers me into him I can tell tonight is going to be different.

I know what's been holding him back and I get it. And honestly, all the build-up has been wonderful and sexy and satisfying, so even though I've wanted him like I've never wanted anyone else, it hasn't felt like something was missing. Except I knew that until we did have sex, it meant he wasn't ready to take the risk.

But now, in this moment, I understand why he's been reluctant. Because as we link together. Griffin is giving me all of himself. He's pouring his soul into me. In every torturously slow touch, every deliberate kiss, every penetrating look, he is surrendering every bit of himself, and it's exactly the same for me. Any thoughts of self-preservation are abandoned. It's almost too much to take. My chest aches for more of him, even though he's as close as he can be. I have to stop every so often to catch my breath, so I'm not completely overwhelmed by the way we're opening ourselves to each other.

I'm filled with mixed emotions as I soar higher than I've ever been. On the one hand, I've never experienced such an intense emotional and physical reaction at the same time. On the other hand, it means this experience is coming to an end and there's no way we can go back to being our individual selves. Not when we've just melded together as one. I can't imagine ever letting go of him and before either of us has even had a chance to compose ourselves, I'm dreading the inevitable moment when we'll have to separate.

But when it's over, when we've given and taken all we have, Griffin doesn't let go. Not even for a second as he rolls us onto our sides and we face each other. One of his hands is pinned under me, holding my waist and the injured hand is caressing my shoulder. Either he can read my mind, or he's desperate to remain tied to me, too.

He puts his forehead against mine and sighs. "I'm scared to death, Frankie."

"Why?" I ask, confused. That's not the post-first-sex comment I was expecting.

"This. What's happening with us. What *just* happened with us. This is far more than I ever wanted to feel for anyone. You make me forget who I am and where I come from. You make me think it's possible to share this incredible, all-consuming connection with you and there will be no repercussions."

"So isn't that a good thing?"

"Right now, yes. Right now it's more incredible than anything I could imagine. While we were together just now, I had the most overpowering feeling that you're mine and I'm yours and I would never be able to let you go. And while that sounds romantic now, what happens tomorrow, or next week, or next year? What happens in five years when I can't keep my past from surfacing and repeating itself, when I'm too possessive to let you go and you're in too deep to walk away?"

His words take me by surprise.

"You're thinking five years from now with me?" I mock, trying to downplay his horrible view of his future.

"Frankie." He's despondent, not picking up my carefree tone. "When I look at you, I think forever."

****

"Was it every day?" I ask Griffin.

After he said that to me about *thinking forever*, we made love again. We had to. It was the only way to relieve our chests from the agonizing swell of emotions inside them. And it was the only way I could tell Griffin how I feel without speaking the words out loud.

I love him. I'm confident of it. Before, I thought I was in the middle of falling. But when I saw his distress when that lunatic grabbed my hair, my first thought was of his pain. If that's not a sign, I don't know what is. It wasn't the most opportune time to realize I'm in love, but it happened all the same.

I'm going to tell him as soon as I think he can handle it. Right now, even though he all but told me he loves me too—I mean, forever is a long time with someone you don't love—I don't think he's ready to hear the words. So for now, I'll keep showing him and one day we'll get there. Eventually, I'll find a way to help him see how extraordinary he is and maybe he can let go of some of the fear.

I'm sitting between Griffin's legs, leaning into his chest. His arms are wrapped around my stomach, and we're all covered up, as he talks about his parents. I think that's the only time he's not staring into me. It must be hard enough for him to dig into his own soul, without being distracted by mine at the same time.

"No." He sighs. His fingers trail a path over my stomach as he speaks. His hands are never idle when we're together. They're always tracing me, grazing me, stroking me in some way.

I enjoy these touches of his as much as the sexy ones. They might be even more intimate and revealing.

"For long periods of time…six months, a year, maybe more, he wouldn't hit her at all. Things would be good between them. Sweet even. But I was always on edge, waiting for the next blow to come. Because it always did. Something bad would happen at work, or some guy would pay too much attention to my mother. Or something random would trigger him. Then he'd come home and take it out on her."

"And no one ever asked questions?"

"For the most part, people look the other way. They don't want to get involved. It's possible people have tried to help my mother, but that's not something she'd admit to me. She won't accept help anyway. Social services did come to the house once, right after I got assigned detention with Roth."

"Wait, you sat detention with Mr. Rothman?"

He laughs. "Yeah. Best punishment of my life."

I shake my head, confused. He adores that man. How could he have met him in detention?

He kisses my temple. "I got into a lot of fights in high school, for obvious reasons. They threatened me with expulsion if I got in another one. So naturally, I punched a kid in the jaw. Got called into a meeting with the principal, who was furious. I waited for him to pull the trigger and kick me out for good. Not that that's what I wanted. God knows I didn't want to sit home with my parents, but at that point I just didn't give a shit what happened. But when my parents walked in and my mother removed her sunglasses, my principal's demeanor changed. He assigned me to detention for a month, which was cake to me. I'd done detention plenty of times. As soon as they left, he asked me if my father hit me too, or just her. No matter how much makeup my mother wore, she couldn't disguise the bruise across her cheekbone.

"I was shocked. No one ever asked me that before. My first instinct was to act like I didn't know what he was talking about, like I'd been trained to do for years. But for some reason, I didn't want to. Screw my father. Why should I lie for him? Or for her, for that matter? Screw both of them. So I told him my father only hit her. I thought he was satisfied with my answer, but I guess not, because social services came right after that. Anyway, he brought me down to the other side of the school to sit detention with this art teacher I'd never met. Mr. Rothman's classroom was filled with huge heavy wooden tables and a few backless stools scattered here and there. And it smelled strange. I'd never been around art supplies before.

"I didn't know what to make of this guy. His graying mustache and jeans had faint white marks all over them. And he was all smiles. Not at all what you'd expect when you're sitting detention."

There's such admiration in the way Griffin talks about this man. Even if I'd never heard Griffin speak of him until now, his devotion for Mr. Rothman would be obvious.

"The first thing he did was ask if I'd ever worked

with clay before. I felt like I was in some alternate universe. I had no clue what was happening. When I mustered up a no, he gave me a block of clay and showed me how to knead it. I just stood like a statue and asked him if he knew I was there for detention. He said he knew, but worked on his own clay. I decided to roll with it. I watched his fingers for a second, noticing how he pushed on the clay with the pads of them, before using his palms. I copied his movements, surprised at the texture of the clay. It was hard and smooth but almost chalky at the same time. I ran my thumbs over it, but I didn't use enough force, and it didn't really move. So I applied more pressure, and that time the clay shifted. I started using the rest of my fingers, feeling the clay indenting beneath them. As I pushed harder with my palms, the hunk of clay became more malleable, and I liked the way it got softer under my touch. I picked it up and pressed it between my palms, folding it into itself over and over. I didn't want to stop. Kneading that clay took all my focus. I forgot about Mr. Rothman, the kid I punched, my asshole parents. There were just me and this clay, which was getting more pliant every moment. I have no idea how long I worked with it, but before I knew it, Mr. Rothman said it was time to go.

"I went back the next day and the next and the next. I was looking forward to something, for maybe the first time in my life. Each day, Mr. Rothman taught me a new skill about sculpting and let me experiment with it for the rest of the hour. And each day, while I was working, he told me an anecdotal story about his grown kids, his wife, his cat. On the fifth day, his story changed. He told me he was fifteen when he started painting. I continued molding, not paying much attention. Then he told me he'd run out of the house after a pretty bad beating from his stepfather.

"My hands stopped, frozen on the sculpture, not daring to move. I didn't breathe. Either he didn't notice or didn't care. He simply went on with his story, working by my side on his own piece. He told me how he went to his community center looking for a fight, but found an easel instead. He painted a picture to kill some time, which a volunteer at the center complimented. He said the painting was actually pretty awful, but it didn't matter. He'd escaped his reality for a while. He had control over this, over something, and it was cathartic. He said until that moment, his abuse owned him. Painting was the only thing that set him free.

"He was quiet then, maybe waiting for me to say something. Or maybe letting me digest what he just told me. Finally, he said one last thing. 'You have a choice, Griffin. You can let what he does to your mother own you and destroy you. Or you can try to find a healthy outlet for your anger.' Not to sound hokey, Frankie, but Mr. Rothman saved me from myself. God only knows the shit I would have gotten into if it hadn't been for him."

I'm all chills inside. I'm so thankful for this man, whom I've never met. "I kind of love him, Griffin."

"Yeah. Me, too. Of course, when social services came my mother denied anything was wrong. When they asked me questions, my mother was in the room. Without making a sound, she pled with me, as usual, not to tell. So as always, I said everything was fine. They didn't dig too deep, probably because I wasn't the one he was suspected of hitting. I think they were just concerned with the physical safety of the minor. I remember some kind of investigation after one of our hospital visits too, but it's fuzzy. My mother tried to shield me from anything she could. Nothing ever came of any of it, anyway. Everything always stayed the same."

The room goes quiet, and I'm not sure if I should ask any more questions. I don't want to upset him, but he brought it up and I think he wants to talk about it. Maybe it's good for him.

"Did you ever fight…" My words fade off because I'm treading lightly. This might not be the best question.

"Did I fight him?"

I nod, wishing I'd kept my mouth shut. His hand grows tense over my belly button.

"Over the years, there were times when I tried. I threatened to call the police. I yelled at him. One time, I even tried to step in. But it was always the same. She'd cry, beg me not to get involved. She told me I'd only hurt her if I interfered. *I'd* hurt her. Is that unbelievable? I was the one taking care of her afterwards every time. I was the one getting ice, feeding her painkillers, bandaging her. I was the one sitting with her at the hospital, where she made up some bullshit stories of how she was so clumsy. I did everything for her, but she told me I was the one who would hurt her. Fucking unbelievable. The day I almost fought him back, she grabbed me with both hands and screamed that if I loved her, I wouldn't ruin her life by fighting him. That we were her boys, the two loves of her life, and she couldn't bear it if we fought. And didn't I love her enough to do that for her?"

His voice cracks, and his arms grow tighter around me as he finishes reliving his past. I think he's had enough reminiscing for one day. I try to turn so I can kiss him or do anything to make him smile and alleviate some of the hurt, but he holds me in place.

"That's why I'm so afraid for you, Frankie. Don't you see? I won't be able to take it if one day you're asking someone if they love you enough to let me hurt you. It would destroy me."

This time, I'm forceful enough to ease his arms off of me and turn into him. "You will *never* hurt me. You need to believe in yourself the way I believe in you."

"Frankie, statistics don't lie. They say…"

"Griffin, I don't want to hear any more about statistics. If you don't want to be with me, fine. But if you do, stop trying to force me away by quoting some damn numbers. You are not a statistic."

"Don't want to be with you?" His laugh is harsh. "How can you even ask that after today?"

"Then stop saying this stuff. I don't believe it now, and I never will. You're kind and giving and introspective. You'd never allow yourself to turn into that."

"Just remember the promise you made."

Ugh, the promise to leave him. I sigh. "Yeah, yeah, I remember. Can we be done with this now? Because I'd much rather talk about something that will make you happy." To make sure Griffin doesn't have a concussion, we stay awake talking into the night about lighter topics. Only then does it occur to me that maybe tonight's activities weren't as restful as they should have been. But Griffin doesn't seem any worse for wear.

****

Griffin's got a client coming this morning so he went downstairs before I was fully awake. He told me to stay as long as I want, but said he wouldn't be back for a long time because the first meeting with a new client always takes the longest.

Making myself some toast, I begin to reflect on yesterday and how crazy and violent that guy was. Last night, I was distracted. It didn't sink in until today, now that I'm alone.

That guy could have hurt me, big time. I don't even want to think about what he would have done to his poor wife if he'd reached her. Never having witnessed violence, stories about it always seemed sad but distant at the same time. I never gave much thought about what it would be like before I stepped foot in Holly's. Now I'm aware of it all the time.

It makes me wonder about what Griffin's been saying. About his father. About himself. About the statistics. Am I being naïve, assuming he'd never turn into that? No, if refuse to believe it. Not the Griffin I know.

But how many women think that and then end up in dangerous situations?

With guilt poking at my psyche, I turn on Griffin's computer. I just want to see for myself. How bad are the statistics? As it boots up, I'm nervous. Maybe I don't want to see. But it's not better to stick my head in the sand. I have to know what they say, while keeping in mind that what I told Griffin is true. He is not a statistic.

As soon as I read the first article, I'm sorry I did. They talk about the adverse effects of domestic violence on children, even those who are not abused themselves. They say they're likely to do poorly in school, get into fights, do drugs, suffer from depression or other mental illness, become unemployed or homeless. They talk about their anger at both parents, their guilt at feeling angry toward the victim. They discuss how much more probable it is that they will become perpetrators of domestic abuse than people who did not witness it.

It's not good.

Each article brings me more grief for the victims, and for the children who grow up in those households. And when I think of Griffin sitting here the same way I am now, reading about what could become of him, I want to cry. I'm sad for him, furious for him. I want to protect him from the hurt, but I know I can't. I want to take on the world for him to alleviate some of his pain.

The one thing I'm not, though, is afraid of him. I know what it says here. And from what he's told me, many of these things are consistent with what he's experienced. But whether I'm just being silly Frankie or not, I believe in him. He is aware enough of what could happen not to let it happen. I want to run downstairs and grab him, tell him I've read it all. Tell him this is not his destiny. Tell him I have faith in him. Tell him I love him.

But he's with a client. Besides, I've had this conversation with him enough to know what I say isn't going to make a difference. He's got to see it for himself. Together, we have to find a way to make him believe it.

I shut down the computer and gather my stuff. Scott Hannah wants to see me tonight. Even though

Griffin told me to hang out if I want, I'd rather get home. I've got to take my clothes to the laundromat, my most hated New York City domestic chore, and run a couple other errands before I meet him at the hotel. Plus, I'll need to allot some time for freaking out and talking to myself before I get there. It's my first time taking pictures for him, and I want them to turn out great.

The day drags as my clothes spin in the machine. I fold them on the long table in the middle of the laundromat and put aside the ones I'm going to wear tonight: a short gray skirt similar to the one I was wearing when I met Scott. And a sheer black top with a black cami underneath, which will go great with my sky-high strappy sandals that crisscross all the way up my calf. I want to make sure I don't look like I'm an interview candidate again. I'll bring an oversized purse and stick my camera in there. That way, I'll blend in as much as possible, which is what Scott wants.

It's five thirty when I arrive at the hotel. The bar is downstairs, underground, but the hotel itself is so posh I'm almost afraid to venture down the steps. Though I'm dressed well, I'm nowhere near the rest of the model material walking downstairs. Sucking in a breath and reminding myself I'm here to work anyway, not pick up guys, I make my way downstairs where Scott sips another martini. A glass of pinot grigio sits next to him on the bar, and for a second I'm flattered that he remembered my drink. Even though it's not really my drink. I'm actually much more of a draft beer kind of girl, but wine seemed like a more professional choice.

He inspects my outfit as I approach and smiles. I guess he thinks I'm in more suitable attire today.

"Francesca. So good to see you again."

"Good to be seen." I pull up a stool. "So, what do we do?"

He chuckles as if I cracked some hilarious joke. "Anxious much?"

I shrug.

"Relax." He pushes the base of my wineglass toward me with the tips of his fingers. "This is the happy hour crowd. Let's let them get settled in before we start snapping pictures around them, okay?"

"Right." I'm coming off tense, when he wants to chill with a drink before we start. I need to get used to this. I take a sip of my wine and before I know it, Scott and I are talking as if we're friends. He asks a lot of questions, but it doesn't feel like an interview. While I talk, he nods and gives the occasional *un-huh, right* to show he's listening. Most of the conversation is about photography, with a few questions about me scattered in between. What do I like to do? How did I start taking pictures?

When I ask about the book, Scott answers, but gives no more than the question requires. He may not trust me enough yet to divulge the entire project. And why would he? He doesn't know me from a hole in the wall.

After our third drink, happy hour is coming to a close.

"Why don't you snap a few shots now, before the place clears out? Then we'll come back, when the evening crowd shows up."

When I take out my camera and ask what he wants me to take, he shakes his head. "Use your vision. For now, take whatever you see. In between sessions, we'll review your shots and we'll move from there."

I take a few general shots around the bar, careful not to target anyone specifically. Around seven thirty, there's a definite lull.

"Okay." Scott pays the check and rises from his stool. "Let's get out of here, grab something to eat and come back in a couple of hours."

It sounds more like a direction than I like, in that cocky way of his. But why not? We both have to eat.

We walk a couple of blocks before we get to a fusion restaurant Scott likes. While we eat, he scrolls through my pictures. Now feels like as good as time as any to broach the topic of money.

"So, Scott, do you generally pay your photographers as you go or when the book comes out?"

Not acknowledging my question, Scott suddenly scowls at the camera. "Man, Frankie, these aren't anything like the ones you were taking on the street. What happened to your vision?"

I'm a little stunned. He told me to take whatever I saw, without giving any guidance and now he's criticizing. I get defensive. "You said to take whatever I wanted. What's wrong with them?"

"What's wrong with them? I could have taken these myself. They're bland. The Francesca I saw on the street had no problem getting down in the trenches. That's what I want from you." He hands the camera back to me with care. "Can you do that for me when we go back? Can you take pictures of what I can't see?"

"Yes." I'm definite. I can do that. That's what I do.

We have more drinks with dinner, but I stop at the second glass of wine. I'm afraid I won't be able to focus on the pictures if I have more, but Scott has no such fear. He drinks until he pays the check, and then as soon as we get back to the hotel bar, he orders another glass of wine for me, and a martini for himself.

"I better not." I wave off the bartender.

"Come on. It'll loosen you up and the pictures won't come out as...stiff."

It might be my imagination, but I could swear he licked his lips right before he grinned that last word. It's probably just the drinks.

I observe the people around the bar to get ideas for out-of-the-box pictures.

"What if I—"

"Don't ask me," Scott says. "Do it."

It would be cool to take people's legs underneath their tables. Though they don't realize it, how they're sitting reveals a lot. Even the parts of them that are hidden. Some people are relaxed, with their legs draped. Others are tight, crossed at the ankle. And as it gets later, certain legs inch closer to others, trying to be subtle. These could make an interesting series of shots. But how do I get them without making a spectacle of myself?

I pull out the camera, trying to be discreet. I pretend to drop a napkin on the floor, which is not as discreet as I'm going for, but I can't think of any other excuse for crouching that low. I take a couple of shots I hope will be interesting when a hand cinches my hip. A little lower than my hip, actually. I freeze.

"I'll act like I'm helping you find something," Scott whispers in my ear, with the side of his leg resting against mine. "It'll buy time."

"Okay." I'm a little uncomfortable, but it makes sense, I guess. We could be searching for something now. Still, I hustle to take the shots, and get to my feet. "I think I got some good ones."

"Good. That's enough for tonight."

On the way out, an idea comes to me. "What if we did a series of hands on the bar, too? See if they're fidgety or relaxed, playing with phones or straws. Things like that."

"I love it. Save it for next week." He offers to take me home, but I decline. It's not necessary. He hails me a cab and holds the door. "Oh, and Frankie?" he says as I pull my leg into the cab.

"Yeah?"

"Wear these sandals next week. They make you blend in the crowd."

Chapter Seventeen

Griffin

My father could sell veal to a vegan. I don't think I've ever heard a person say no to him. When he turns on the charm and flashes his smile, no one is immune to the enchantment that is Evan Stone.

Except, of course, for me.

That's actually how my parents met. My father is in sales. Years ago, before he discovered the depth of his talent, he sold office supplies. Unlike most salesmen who conduct business online or at least over the phone, he pitched his clients in person. It doesn't take a genius to figure out why.

My mother did billing and managerial work for an insurance company. When her assistant, without explanation, switched suppliers from a company they'd used for years, to a new, more expensive company, my mother demanded to know why. The assistant couldn't come up with a good reason, so my mother took matters into her own hands. She tried to cancel the order over the phone, but the very persuasive salesman coerced her to take a meeting with him beforehand. He might not have had all his physical advantages over the phone, but he was still alluring enough to get her to agree.

By the end of the meeting, my mother's company not only had a new supplier, but an order that included three times more ink than they'd ever got before. And my mother had a date with the most captivating man she'd ever met.

My father's days of selling office supplies are long gone. Now, he sells advertising space on TV. Naturally, he's the head of his sales team. He conducts team meetings every Monday night. Coincidentally, the only day of the week I'm free for dinner is Monday. While I don't see my mother on a scheduled basis, I almost never have dinner with her any other day of the week.

This particular Monday is pretty sticky for early June. My mother's got all the windows open and the air is thick and heavy. I scratch at my beard and think I could use a shave.

That's interesting. I can't remember ever thinking that before.

"Why don't you turn on the air?" I ask as I reach over my mother to take a taste of the stir-fry she's cooking. "Yum."

"The air conditioner is broken." She swats at my hand. It's our ritual. I sneak tastes of her food while she cooks, and she pretends it annoys her.

"So, why don't you get it fixed?" I place a couple of plates and napkins on the kitchen table.

She shrugs. "You know your father. He doesn't want a repairman here alone with me. He'll take a day off soon so the guy can come."

I frown but refuse to let it set me off. I'm in a good mood. Business is busy, I just helped a woman at Holly's get settled into a new place and Frankie...well, and then there's Frankie. I can't believe how well things are going with her.

I was partially right when I was afraid Frankie

would make me look at things another way, reliving parts of my past. But when I discuss them with her, I don't feel exhausted or gutted the way I do when I talk about my parents to Sarah or Mr. Rothman. I'm soothed and at ease, as if she took a bad part of me away. I find myself wanting to share with her, because she balances me. I don't know how she does it, but just thinking about her makes me happy in ways I've never been.

"What?" my mother asks.

"What, what?" I reply.

"Well, (a) you've got on a goofy smile, which is fabulous to see, by the way, and (b) you didn't jump at the opportunity to make a nasty crack about your father. What's up with you?"

"Nothing." I take the salad from her and bring it to the table. We sit together and I dish us out some chicken and vegetables.

"Don't tell me nothing. You think you're the only one in this family who can read people?"

I try to change the subject. "Everything's been okay?" I ask, though I already know it has. Things calmed down after our last trip to the hospital.

"Yes, Griffin." She rolls her eyes, as if she's the child and I'm the pestering parent. "I'm fine. Now tell me what's making you smile."

"I'm not."

"Well, then…" She taps her chin in feigned thought. "I'd say maybe you're getting lucky, but I've known that was happening since I found a condom wrapper in your room when you were in high school, and that never seemed to lighten you any."

"Mom!"

She laughs. "It's not my fault, Griffin. You're the

one who left it there. I didn't mind, though. It meant you were being careful."

I shake my head, mortified. I will not engage in this conversation.

"So it can't just be sex. Is it a girl, though? It's that girl you brought over, isn't it? The one you insisted I show my bruise?"

I don't answer.

"I figured you must have been into her if you brought her here, but I was afraid to ask, especially after that whole interaction."

Again, I don't answer, but my face must reveal the truth.

"It is," she goggles. "And she knows?"

About us. About my father. About my potential.

"Yes."

"And she doesn't care?"

"Not so far."

"Are you in love with her?"

I nod once. I may not be ready to utter the words aloud yet, but that doesn't mean I'm unaware of my feelings.

My mother is delighted. "What's she like?"

I crunch on my broccoli, searching for a simple answer to the question. But there isn't one, because Frankie is anything but simple. A million adjectives tangle in my mind at once. But only one thought emerges. "She's just like you."

My mother's eyes glass over, and she speaks the words I've been dreading since I knew this thing between Frankie and me was real.

"I want to meet her."

I haven't introduced a girl to my parents since high

school, and even that was an accident. They were out at some party for the night, so I figured I'd have my own party at home. Having free rein of my house with the girl I was dating had me all kinds of excited. I should have been more romantic than dragging her right up to my bedroom, but I was seventeen and a gorgeous girl was half-naked in my bed. I could be romantic later.

Then they barged through the front door downstairs, fighting. In my frenzy to get into my room, I hadn't closed the door. We could hear everything. I got dressed and flew downstairs to let them know we had company before anything bad happened. My parents were stunned. I never brought anyone home. But my announcement achieved the desired effect. They stopped yelling.

The girl followed me downstairs, and I knew in that split second I had to break up with her. At the sight of my father, her mouth broke into a wide, mesmerized grin. And when he flashed his dimples, giving her his devastating smile and talking about how all Stone men are a handful, she sighed out loud.

After my father led my mother upstairs by linked fingertips, the girl swooned at me. "Is that how you're going to be one day? All possessive and smoldery?" she asked, attention fixed on the empty stairs my father just climbed. "He did say you're exactly alike." She sucked in her lip in an attempt to be seductive, while her middle finger grazed my chest.

She wanted me to be like him. She had no idea what she was asking for. It would have been better if she'd heard how that fight would play out.

She leaned in to kiss me but I pulled back. I ushered her out of my house before she had a chance to ask what was wrong. I broke up with her the next day. And I never made the mistake of letting them meet a girl again.

****

I don't trust Scott Hannah.

I'm working on a very intricate part of my latest sculpture. A man is presenting a family heirloom to the woman he loves, on his knees, imploring her to understand what she means to him. This heirloom was more significant than any other piece in my client's story, and the delicate links on the pocket watch need to lie just right as they hang from the man's hand.

I'm trying to stay in the zone, but every word Frankie tells me about her last few meetings with Hannah has me more concerned.

I searched him online as soon as she started working for him. Or with him. I'm not even sure which it is, because as far as I can tell, she hasn't discussed whether he's paying her or she's got a stake in the sales of his book. I tried to ask enough questions to encourage her to get more information, but when I sounded more like an interrogator than I intended, I stopped.

The guy's got a few books out. They're all similar in style to the one he described to Frankie. One compared different parks throughout the boroughs and who went to them. Another highlighted various nightclubs.

The credibility of the books themselves isn't what's making me apprehensive. It's the fact that for each of Hannah's five books, he credits a different photographer. All women and all unknowns when he found them.

192

So what I want to know is, why can't he hold on to one photographer, and why doesn't he hire professionals?

And why the hell, each time they go out for a photo shoot, does he find a reason to put his fucking hands on my girl?

I'm sure Frankie isn't telling me about these interactions to make me jealous. I think she's just relaying her day to me without censoring herself. Unfortunately, when she tells me things like, *I think Scott was more comfortable with the way I dressed this time because he asked me to wear my sandals again next week,* it kind of makes me want to put my fist through the guy's throat. Because I saw her in those sandals. And when I did, photography was the furthest thing from my mind.

But jealousy is the absolute last thing I want to feel in this relationship. Jealousy leads to possessive rage, which leads to worse. Even questioning Frankie about his motives feels out of line because it would be like implying the only reason she got the job is because Hannah wants to get in her pants. I don't want to travel down that unsupportive road, so I let her talk, making one mental note after the other to watch her back.

Because I do not trust Scott Hannah.

"Tonight was occupied by the women's accessories. Some of these women went all out, half a dozen bracelets, big chunky earrings, bag to match. Others were much more subtle. The night crowd wore more bling than the happy hour crowd, which is to be expected, I guess."

She goes on for a little while about accessories, which makes it easier to keep my attention on the job at hand. Her voice soothes me in my warehouse, but this is not a conversation I need to have both ears on.

"I was able to capture some of the textures of the necklaces too, even though I wasn't getting too close to the women. When I zoomed in, you could see how smooth some pieces were compared to the rough texture of others. Made me want to reach over and touch a couple of women's necks." She laughs at herself.

"That would have made for a more interesting picture," I joke, finessing the connection between two links.

"Yeah, I bet," she quips. "Sometimes I wonder if Scott knows what I'm talking about. I was explaining to him about the textures. I tried to show him in the pictures, but he still didn't get it. He said he's more of a tactile learner. He needed to feel my pendant to understand."

I squash the last three links I just worked on in my fist. Hanging between her breasts is a chain. And attached to that chain, about two inches below, is a pendant.

"Fuck," I mutter.

"Crap, Griffin, am I distracting you? Should I go?"

I can't stay quiet about this any longer. "You don't see a problem with this?"

"With what?" she asks, but her candid, contrite expression tell me she knows exactly what I'm talking about.

"Frankie…" I hate that I'm about to break my rule and be the jealous boyfriend, but this isn't even about me. It's about how he's treating her. Why doesn't she see it? I open my mouth, but she speaks.

"It's weird, right?"

I'm grateful she said it first. "Yeah, it is."

"At first I thought I was being, I don't know, too stuffy or something, that it was no big deal. But if he's my boss, he shouldn't be needing to touch me this much. I'm not being overly sensitive, am I?"

"No."

"I don't know. Maybe it's just his way. Some people don't account for personal space."

"I think it's more than that."

"Well, we'll see, I guess. We're always in public. What's going to happen?"

I walk to the couch where she's been sitting for the past hour. "Do you want me to talk to him?"

She's alarmed. "No, Griffin, definitely not. This is my job. I'll deal with it myself."

There's really nothing else I can do. She's aware of the situation, and she's right, it's her job. She's got to do what she sees fit. That doesn't mean I'm comfortable with it, though.

She puts her hands on my cheeks. "Stop frowning." She brings her lips to the creases in my forehead. "You're going to get wrinkles. I can handle it, Griffin. I promise."

I sweep my lips across hers in acquiescence and head back behind my table to continue working, when her cell goes off. It's late. I don't know who would be calling her now. She walks behind the divider to take the call so she doesn't disturb me, but since they're just fancy accordion folders and not actual walls, I can still hear everything she's saying. "Hi, is everything okay…All right…Well, has she gone to class…In how long?…I don't know, she didn't answer my text yesterday…Okay, I'll call her in the morning…Love you too, Mom." She reemerges from behind the divider, distraught.

"What is it?" I ask.

"Gabby was supposed to make up some of those credits over the summer, but she's not even attending classes or doing the work. My mother said she's just sulking around. My mother doesn't know the whole story, of course. She only knows they broke up. Gabby was too embarrassed to tell the rest. I texted her yesterday to check in, but she didn't answer. I should have followed up." She shakes her head.

"Frankie, you've been texting her almost every day. Give yourself a break. You've been there for her. It's not like you're ignoring her."

"I know, but I wish I was actually, physically there, you know? It's not the same by text or even phone. My mother said she's asleep so I'll call her tomorrow."

"I'm sure just hearing your dulcet voice will cheer her up. Always works for me." I smile. It's getting to a point where sometimes I don't even recognize myself any more. Words like that never made it past my lips before. But I like this new, unrecognizable part of me. He's someone I might want to be.

She gets up from the couch and meanders to my table. "Somehow, I don't think my voice effects all people the same way it does you, Griffin. But do you know what would cheer me up?"

"What?" I move my body close to hers because I'm sure she's about to suggest something I like very much.

"If you'd make me into one of these." She touches the statue and my stomach sinks. That is not what I thought she was about to suggest.

I pull back and turn my face away. "Frankie, I can't."

"Why not?" It's the first time she's really gotten annoyed with me. "You can do everyone else. Why not me?"

"Who is everyone else?"

"Sarah. Kaitlyn. All your clients. all the women at Holly's. So why, Griffin?"

I told her about Sarah's statue, but no way did I think she'd know I did Kaitlyn's. The only reason I did it was because I wanted the practice. Shit.

"I just can't." I know she deserves an answer, but I don't know how to put it into words without sounding awful.

"That's not a reason. Is it because you don't think there's anything beneath the surface about me that you can find? I'm too one-dimensional?"

"What?" Where the hell did that come from? "No, of course not."

"Then what?"

"Frankie, I just can't do it. Can you leave it alone?"

She's mad now. She's never mad, and it's a little disconcerting.

"Yeah, Griffin, fine, I can leave it alone. I'm going home."

This is exactly what I didn't want. Why did she have to ask me to do this? "Don't leave, Frankie. It's late. Stay, please."

"No, I want to go."

"At least let me take you."

"No, I'm perfectly fine on my own." She picks up her bag and walks toward the divider, but as she's about to step beyond it, she turns. "Maybe I'll ask Scott to mold me into something. I'm sure he'd be more than happy to do it." She disappears behind the divider and I hammer the clay I was working on with the side of my fist, destroying about ten hours of work. I don't even give a damn.

I'm not mad about the crack she made about Scott. I know that was anger talking, and she'd never go behind my back. There was frustration in her eyes when she said that to me, not vengeance.

The reason I'm furious is that no matter how hard I try, I still can't just live my fucking life. I so badly want to be able to give Frankie what she's asking for, but the thought of sculpting her makes me want to crawl in a hole and never emerge.

Chapter Eighteen

Frankie

As soon as the words are out of my mouth, I want to shove them back in. How could I say that to him?

I know why I said it. I was angry and irrational and hurt. And surprised by my own thought that maybe he won't do it because he thinks I'm too shallow to be worth sculpting. Who knew I even thought that about myself? I had no idea until the words were tumbling out, accusing him of thinking too little of me. He's never once belittled me for being impulsive. But he was questioning whether or not I realized what Scott was doing.

I'm not stupid. Of course I realize it. The question is, what do I want to do about it?

The way I see it, I have a couple of choices. I can play along with it, pretend it's no big deal and there's nothing strange about the fact that he finds some excuse to touch me every time we go out. Or I can tell him it bothers me and ask him to stop doing it. In which case I might lose my job.

It's not like he's done anything blatant. He hasn't patted my ass or ogled my chest with his tongue hanging out. I mean, he did "accidentally" graze the back of his hand against the bottom of my breast when he went to touch the pendant, but it was nothing so egregious I could call him out on it. He's much more subtle than that. What's the harm in a few suggestive comments or a playful brush of the fingers here and there? I've never been one to make a mountain out of a molehill. Besides, he knows I have a boyfriend. He won't ask me out.

I think Griffin's lack of confidence that I could handle the situation, coupled with the fact that he still will not consider sculpting me when he does it for the rest of the world, set me off. As soon as I'm on the other side of the divider, I want to turn around and apologize, but something stops me. I think it's that I just don't understand why he won't do it, which means he's still holding back from me.

I bang on Sarah's door until it opens.

"Why won't Griffin sculpt me?" I demand from the doorway.

All the lights are out in her apartment, giving it a very bland, monochrome feel. She gives me her back and returns to bed, groggy. But when I barge into her room and flip on the light, she's not asleep any more.

"What?" She rubs her eyes with her palms and tries to adjust to the light. "Are you kidding me right now?"

"No, I'm not kidding. We're sleeping together, he confides these horrible stories about his family. He says the most beautiful things to me. Why the hell won't he sculpt me?"

"Why is this such a big deal, Frankie?"

I sit on the corner of her bed. She glowers but I don't care.

"You know it's a big deal. It means something, except I don't know what. Sculpting is his world. If he won't share it with me, there must be a bad reason."

She scoots up against her headboard and yawns. The clock on her nightstand reads one fifty-three. Oops. *I didn't realize it was that late.*

She rubs her nose and her face and tilts her head back into the headboard. "Griffin sees himself as a fragmented person, Frankie. Broken into bits. One part of him deals with his parents, directly. That part's the hardest to control. Then there's the part he gives me and Roth. He lets us in, and we're there to try to guide him through the first part. And then there's the part he shows the rest of the world. The quiet, mysterious guy people are intrigued by but don't understand. But then there's his sculpting, which is his own bit, a bit unto itself. It's just for him, to free himself.

"Yeah, but this part he can't give me is the biggest part of him, isn't it?"

"Well, you're missing something, Frankie. You're missing the new bit he never had before. You. He never thought he would allow himself to have what he has with you. Don't you understand? Once he gives you the sculpting bit of him—because that's what will happen when all is said and done—he's combining the pieces of himself. He's never done that before. I don't think he even knows how. I bet he's afraid he'll combust." She chuckles.

"Why the hell is this so complicated? Why can't he just sculpt whatever he sees in me and get it done?"

"Because, what he sees in you is him."

****

I shouldn't have said that. I didn't mean it. I'm so sorry.

I shoot off the text to Griffin as soon as I leave Sarah's apartment. I assume he'll either be pissed off at me or asleep, so I put the phone aside and hope he'll answer tomorrow. As soon as it touches my nightstand, the cell vibrates.

I know you didn't mean it and I get why you said it. I'm sorry I can't do what you're asking. Please know it's not because I don't care about you.

I understand. Or at least I'm trying to.

He sends another text. *Can I come over?*

You know it's like 2, right? You'll be waiting for a train forever.

I don't care, his text replies. *I hate the way you left here and nothing else will pacify me. I need to hold onto you. Can I come?*

Of course.

Within fifteen minutes, Griffin has jumped in a cab and is lying against me. We're both too tired to do anything, but he does exactly what he said; he spends the night with his arms wrapped around me and doesn't let go.

"My mother wants to meet you," he tells me the next morning. He's been kneading me for the past hour while I drifted in and out of sleep. I've been waiting for him to explain about last night, but he hasn't. He's remained silent, allowing his hands and his gentle kisses on the back of my neck to do the talking.

"What?" I'm a little taken aback by his words. He won't sculpt me, but his mother knows about me and he's talking about introducing us? I thought it would be a cold day in hell before he brought me to meet his parents.

"She told me a few weeks ago, but I've been putting it off. For obvious reasons." He waits for an answer.

I'm not sure what to say. I think this is his way of making up for last night, but he doesn't need to offer this to me. I spent the better part of last night awake, thinking.

He was so torn up when he got here. Our fight obviously affected him at least as much as it did me. And the way he wouldn't let go of me the entire night, like he was afraid I would disappear, tells me what his words don't. Griffin is even intense when he's asleep.

So during the night, I decided I need to let go of this sculpting thing. If and when he's ready, we'll do it. Until then, I'll have to be patient. At least that's what I'm telling myself this morning, with his hands rippling over every inch of me. The trouble is, patience has never been one of my things.

"You don't have to do that, Griffin. Really."

"I know. I want to. I want you to meet her. And more importantly, I want her to meet you. It's time."

I notice he doesn't say anything about his father. That doesn't surprise me at all.

I roll over to face him. When I do, I inhale sharply. "You shaved."

"It was time for that, too. I figured we could try out this version of me for a while and see how we like it. What do you think?" He gives me a small, insecure smile.

What do I think? Holy Jesus, he's more gorgeous than ever. He's got the tiniest hint of scruff and I can see every bit of his sexy, chiseled face, along with his deep dimples, which are dancing for me. He's even cleaner now than when he sees clients. The sight of him makes my pulse race.

I'm careful about my reaction, though. He

associates his face with his father's, so this is a big step. Tomorrow, he may decide he can't tolerate his reflection. If I make a fuss about this and then he goes back to his beard, he'll think I don't find him attractive.

I cup his cheek in my palm and his short stubble tickles. "I love you every way."

I suck in, yanking my hand off him and trying to pull the words back from the air. I didn't mean to say that. I meant…I meant…oh God why do I have such a big mouth? "I mean, I love you every way you look." No! That's not what I meant either! I shake my head to stop the avalanche of idiotic words from falling any further. "I *mean*," I enunciate each word to get it right. "I love the way you look every way." I give a heavy sigh. Great save, Frankie. Way to make an awkward situation worse.

But Griffin is amused. He leans in and kisses me. "Good because I did it for you."

"I told you I didn't want you to change for me. I meant it."

He shakes his head. "No, I'm not changing my look for you, Frankie. I'm changing the way I look at things. And I shouldn't say I did it *for* you. Really, I did it *because* of you. That's more accurate."

I smile. I like the idea that he's changing the way he sees things because of me. I like it a lot. "When?" I ask.

"This morning, while you were asleep. You were out cold. Oh, but…" He squirms, flaunting those amazing dimples again, making my guts jiggle like Jell-O. "I used your razor and shaving cream. I think my skin smells like berries or something. Sorry."

I crack up. "You don't need to be sorry. I'm not the

one who shaved my face with a razor that's been God knows where."

He laughs and nuzzles me with his stubbly chin. "Well, it hasn't been anywhere that my face hasn't anyway."

For the next couple of hours, I take advantage of Griffin and his newly found, even more gorgeous self.

****

Can you be there at 8?

I haven't seen Scott since he played with my pendant a couple of weeks ago, and after knowing Griffin thinks his behavior is as questionable as I do, I'm not all that anxious to see him again. But I love the way my pictures have been coming out. They're very intricate and detailed and the fact that they're just parts, unattached to the whole subject, makes them seem like they hold secrets.

Taking these shots has given me more ideas for my own pictures too. After this, I plan to do series of subjects, instead of one shot here, one shot there. And, if things turn out the way I'd like them to, Scott's book will lead to more opportunities for me and I'll be able to say I've accomplished something. Hopefully.

I'm working the lunch shift today at Sam's but after that I've got nothing planned. I send a quick text to let Scott know that eight should be fine. We've been working on this project for a couple of months now, and he's got one or two more bars on his list, so things are coming together. I'm anxious to see what this is all going to be once it's finished.

Business is slow today. One of my tables is too busy Instagramming to pay their check and two other tables are nursing drinks so they don't have to leave, even though they're not ordering anything else. I don't bother giving them a polite nudge, since no one is waiting for a table, but I'd like it if they would go. That way, I don't have to keep going over and asking if they want anything else when I know the answer is no. I won't even make enough in tips today to pay for a cab ride to the bar. Guess I'll be taking the train again.

"Hey, you." Griffin squeezes my shoulders from behind. I spin around, smiling like a fool.

"Hey, you. What are you doing here? I thought you had work to do."

"I do. I just wanted to tell you I made plans to go to my mother's for dinner."

"Okay? You came all the way here for that? You could have texted me or called."

"I needed to see your expression when I told you, to read how you felt about it."

"And what do you see?" I ask.

He studies me. "Nothing, actually. I can't tell how you feel."

That's because I don't know how I feel. I'm glad he wants me to meet her, but he's so on edge whenever he talks about her. I don't know how it's going to go.

"I'm happy to meet her, Griffin."

"Okay, good." He pulls me into a corner for privacy, but there's no need. The place is dead. "Frankie, I need you to understand. Our relationship is…difficult. My mother's and mine, I mean. I don't ever introduce her to women, even if I tell her about them sometimes. I don't know how she's going to act, especially since you've already technically met her on two undesirable occasions." He flinches at the memories. "Now I kind of wish I hadn't dragged you to the house that day. But I had no idea this is how things would turn out. I meant to show you why we shouldn't be together." He takes my hand. "Didn't exactly work out the way I planned."

I rub his hand with my thumb. "I'm pretty thankful for that."

"Anyway, I'm just saying I don't know how she'll be. That's all."

"I'm not worried, Griffin. I'm sure she's fine."

He's unconvinced and shrugs. "Well, either way, we're going there on Monday, as long as you're free."

"Monday?" Strange day to make dinner plans.

"Yeah, Monday."

****

Scott's not at the bar when I get there, which is unusual. He's normally half a drink in by the time I arrive. I wait a few minutes, before checking my text to make sure I'm in the right place. As I call up our text history, another one comes through. *Meet me upstairs. I want to talk a little shop before we take pics tonight. Room 1216.*

Upstairs? In one of the hotel rooms? Red flags pop up everywhere. This isn't kosher. I shoot him a quick text back.

Why can't we talk down here? I'm already in the middle of a drink.

I haven't ordered anything yet, but I don't want it to sound like I don't trust him, even if I don't.

Too loud down there. You can bring it up. I'll wait here.

Since I don't see any way out of it, I order a glass of wine to back up my story, and trudge upstairs with my stomach in a ball of knots.

Scott smiles at me as he holds the hotel room door open for me. Once I'm inside, he leans against the door with one foot propped up against it.

"I think New York hotel rooms are the smallest in the world," he jokes.

I try to smile back, but I'm skittish. There's no good reason we need to talk here, and he must know I know that.

"Why don't you sit?" He motions to the bed, which takes up almost the entire room.

"I'm fine. Why are we up here, Scott?"

"I told you. We need to talk shop."

"Okay?"

"Can I see what you've got on the camera?"

I place my wineglass on a side table and I hand him the camera. He clicks through a few shots, then shuts off the camera. He turns it sideways, takes out the memory card and hands the camera back to me.

"We've got a nice slew of pictures here. Very good stuff, Frankie. I think we could produce something exceptional together. What you do you think?"

"That's what I'm hoping," I say.

"I'm well into writing about the hotels now, so it's time to discuss compensation."

This is where he's going to tell me how much he's paying me—why?

He doesn't move from the door. Just stands against it, appearing completely laid-back, which is the exact opposite of me right now.

"Being an amateur, I'm sure you understand things work a little differently."

Oh, here it is. He's going to tell me how little he's giving me and he didn't want me to make a scene in public.

"You're not going to try to screw me, are you, Scott?" I try to make it come off in gest, but I think I fall short.

He wears a sardonic smile I haven't seen on him before. Like he's stalking me and amused by it at the same time. But his body doesn't move at all. "Well, of sorts," he answers. His words knock the wind out of me. I was speaking figuratively, but he's speaking literally.

He wants me to sleep with him.

"The career of an unknown is an investment, of course. Now, I'm willing to invest in you by putting your work on the pages of my book, but you have to be willing to invest in yourself too. Are you willing to do that, Frankie?"

My mouth goes dry and my breathing becomes shallow. "Do what?" I manage to get out.

"Invest in yourself. Help me help you."

"By doing what exactly?" Spell it out for me, Scott. Do you have the nerve to say the disgusting thing you're suggesting?

"Come on, Frankie, you must realize that's the way it works. You scratch my back, I'll scratch yours. I give you full exposure. You give me..." He chuckles in a way that sends shivers down my spine. "The fully exposed you."

"What?" My jaw hangs open. I can't believe he's being so overt about this. I mean, I knew he might hit on me, and maybe even be pissed if I said no. But I didn't see this ultimatum coming.

Stupid.

He tilts his head to demean me. "Don't pretend to

be naïve. It's an insult to yourself. You've known where I was going with this for weeks. And you played along. Wearing anything I suggested, encouraging my off-color comments with laughter. You never pulled away and you kept coming back. I think you want this as much as I do."

"I wanted this job, not you."

"Ah, semantics. It's all rolled into one. I come with the job. No pun intended." He laughs again, but I don't. There's nothing funny here. "Lighten up, Frankie, this isn't a big deal. Happens all the time. This is the softer side of business."

"This is sexual harassment." I keep my voice firm and try not to show him how frightened I am right now.

"Well, maybe if I was your boss or something, but as far as I can tell, we're just two people working on a project together. No money or contracts have changed hands. Besides, even if you could prove it's sexual harassment, good luck getting work in this town after you've taken me to court for that. No one would touch you with a ten foot pole."

I want to cry. Or scream. Or belt him. How did I get myself into this situation? I followed my usual pattern of behavior and this time it bit me in the ass. Will I never learn?

Why would he go through all this trouble just to get me into bed? "Why didn't you just ask me out then, if this is all you wanted? Why did you pretend to like my work?"

"It's much more fun this way. It turns me on, like weeks of foreplay leading up to one explosive moment of release. And I do like your work. I'd never risk my career for a good lay. But as for why didn't I ask you out? Frankie, I don't want to *date* you." He doesn't need to continue with the follow-up sentence, because his meaning is perfectly clear, but he does anyway. "I want to *fuck* you."

I flinch.

"Oh come on, we're both grown-ups. It's not like I'm asking you to do something we both wouldn't enjoy. It's sex, for God's sake, not murder. It would stay between us. Trust me, I don't share my exploits with anyone."

Of course not. Because you blackmail them into sex.

He continues. "And it would be a shame if no one ever got to see all those wonderful pictures you took because you're being stubborn."

All my hard work. All the ideas I put behind those pictures. All the time I spent zooming, editing, working with the lighting, all for nothing if I don't do what he wants. But he stands to lose something, too.

"You'd give up your entire book just because I won't sleep with you?"

He jeers now, as if I'm the dumbest person in the world. I might not be far from it.

"Oh, sweetheart, if you won't do it, there's always someone right behind you who will. Trust me about that. I've got five published books to prove it. And this one will be published too, don't worry. What you have to decide is whether you want to be part of it, or if you're going to let someone else have what should be yours."

I've never been so frustrated. There's no way I'll touch even a hair on this man's head, but I've got no recourse. Those are my pictures. I took them and I want people to see them.

But no one ever will.

"I want my card back." At least I can have that. I stick out my firm hand, shocked that it's not trembling. His grin is conniving as he lifts the card between his pointer and middle fingers.

"Sure." He starts to lower his fingers into his jeans. My heart skips a beat. I'm not even going to get my card back. My jaw drops again. He guffaws now. "Aren't you just the most innocent thing? I'm just kidding, Frankie. Trying to ease the tension in here. I don't need to force you. Believe me." He holds out the card to me. I yank it from his fingers and take a step back.

"I'm leaving now. Get out of my way."

"No one's stopping you."

"You're blocking the door."

He pushes off the door with his foot and steps forward. Maybe three inches. I'll have to slither past him to get through, if I can even fit.

"Can you move more?"

His cocky smile disappears now. "Think this through before you walk out that door, Frankie. If you go, you're back to square one, just a waitress with no opportunities. If you stay, we could have a lot of fun for an hour or two, and your work can be seen by thousands. It could be the first step in a promising and successful career."

For a millionth of a second, I think about his words. Back to square one. Telling my parents I've fallen short again.

Just a waitress.

Just a waitress. That phrase knocks me back to

reality. I think of the conversation I had with Griffin when I first met him. *Just a waitress? What's wrong with that? What do you want to be?* Not a hooker, I can tell you that much.

Scott must notice me hesitate for a fraction of a second. His misreads the reason and steps toward me. He puts his hands on my hips and tries to pull me in, but I move back and pull a small can out of my back pocket.

"Get away from me!" I point it at him.

"What the hell is that?" he asks, shocked.

"Mace." In reality, it's a travel size can of hairspray. I had a feeling, after last time, that things might get weird tonight. I didn't have time to research where to buy mace, and then go pick some up. I figured hairspray would have the same effect if I had to threaten to spray it in his eyes.

He holds up his hands in surrender and backs away. "Jesus, Frankie, I told you I wasn't going to force you. That's not my style. But I think you're making a huge mistake here."

"My only mistake is still standing in this room. Now move the fuck out of my way before I blind you."

He shifts a few more inches. As I storm past and fling the door open, the silver camera card in my hand shines in the hallway light.

Is he kidding me?

I spin toward him and shove his chest with both hands as hard as I can. Because he's caught off-guard, he loses his balance and stumbles backward onto the bed. I hover over him.

"Give me back my card, asshole!" I fling the imposter card at his face.

"What are you talking about, Frankie?"

"My card is blue, dumbass." I kick him in the shin with all my might. He grabs his leg and groans. This man could easily overpower me, but my sudden change in demeanor has him confused. "Give it back or I swear to God I'll get it myself and I promise you won't like the way I do it!"

"Okay, okay. Calm down. Jeez." He reaches into his jeans once more and retrieves my navy card. I don't even want to think about what else is down there. Gross. My nails accidentally scratch his hand as I tear the card from him.

"Ow!"

Good.

But not enough.

"This I for the women who didn't get to say no." I aim my hairspray at his face and shoot. He screams that I'm crazy and covers his eyes. I don't know if I connect with my target or not, but as least I get some satisfaction.

Now it's enough.

I smack my full wineglass off the table onto his chest and bluster from the room, certain I'm the biggest failure alive.

Chapter Nineteen

Griffin

"I think you should start billing my insurance for therapy sessions." I take a slug of my beer.

"Would you stop? How many times do I have to tell you I'm not doing you any favors? I enjoy getting together with you, Griffin." Mr. Rothman sips his coffee. He doesn't drink. He suffered from his stepfather's indulgence too often to risk it.

"Yeah, Roth, but what do I ever do for you?"

"Relationships aren't always about what one person does for the other, you know. Sometimes, friends can just be friends because they find each other interesting. But for the record, every step you make toward a well-adjusted life makes me happy. That's what you do for me. And you pay it forward, helping others. That's what you do for me, too. Things don't have to be tit for tat, Griffin."

I shrug and play with my bottle. Even though I know he doesn't like praise any more than I do, I can't help feeling like I owe my sanity to the man sitting across from me.

"So what's got you all knotted up?"

I peel off part of the label. This bottle is wider than other beers I drink. If it were pinched in the center, it could be a shapely woman's body.

215

"I'm bringing Frankie to meet my mother." Mr. Rothman's face glows. I scowl at him. "Don't be so ecstatic about it. It could be a nightmare."

"How, Griffin? You're bringing the two women who love you together. That's a good thing, son."

At his words I stop mentally reshaping the bottle.

"Yes, I'm sure she loves you," he continues, as if I'd questioned him. "From what you've told me, it's obvious. All you have to do is accept it."

I brush off his statement. I already know Frankie loves me. She's not exactly a poker face. She's been good about giving me time and hasn't said it out loud, except for one slip she made the other day. That was an accident though, and I was more entertained by her tripping over herself than anything.

But that doesn't mean I can't read her. Knowing she feels that way about me brings me a joy I never thought possible, but it also almost paralyzes me with fear. Knowing I feel that way about her in return magnifies both of those emotions.

And yet, the idea of having her meet my mother introduces a whole new level of anxiety.

"Regardless, this could change everything, and I'm not ready for that."

"Change everything how?" He props his chin on his hands, which reminds me of the teacher in him.

"What if she…if she sees…" This is something I don't discuss, even with him. "Never mind. You know what, forget it." I down the rest of my beer.

"No, I won't. What if she sees what?"

A TV screen mounted on the bar wall plays some muted news channel. Closed caption words run across the bottom. I have no idea what they're saying but act as if they're the most engaging story I've ever read.

"Griffin."

I pretend not to hear him.

"If you want this to work, you've got to deal with whatever's making you this nervous."

I turn back to him. If I say the words aloud, even he might think less of me. Maybe I should gauge his reaction before I risk telling Frankie. A shiver runs through me.

"What if, when we're all together, Frankie can sense how I feel about her?"

"How you feel about her?"

I shake my head. "No."

After a fraction of a second, he understands. "Oh."

He's quiet for a couple of moments, deciding what to say next. "Why don't you tell me how you feel about your mother, Griffin?"

I open my mouth, but struggle to find my voice. I think this part bothers me more than the actual abuse. The way I feel about her. I realized it long ago, in the middle of the night, after one of the incidents. I was tending to her hurt wrist. It didn't appear damaged on the outside, but that didn't mean it's wasn't hurting on the inside. I knew that better than anyone.

I begged her to leave with me that night, but as always, she shut me down. The only thing she ever let me do was tend to her afterwards. It wasn't fair. And it made me furious. Worse than that. It made me wish she wasn't my mother.

She snuggled next to me that night, as she often did when she needed me to comfort her. She kissed my forehead before nodding off. "Sweet dreams, Griffin. I love you."

"I love you too, Mom," I answered, my response rote. But with great sadness in my heart, I realized what I felt for her was quite the opposite of love. The way I feel about her sickens me. Actually churns my stomach. It makes me so ashamed that it's impossible to accept any flattery that comes my way.

Hating my father makes sense. No one could blame me for that.

But her?

I can't bring myself to utter the words, not even to Roth. But I give him enough.

"Frankie thinks I'm this wonderful guy who helps people. She has this image of me as an altruistic human being, when really I'm just some asshole who's bitter that he had a less than perfect childhood, resents the victim for it, and spends his life trying to make up for it. What if she sees I'm not what she thinks and never views me the same way again?" There's a burning behind my eyes. I wish I had a huge mound of clay in front of me to absorb some of the emotions that are saturating my head and chest.

"Griffin, you are harder on yourself than any person should be. You are everything Frankie thinks you are. And you're entitled to your feelings. I get the guilt you carry about it, I do. But what you don't seem to understand is that you were a victim, too. Not the same way, but you were. And you're allowed to be angry about it. Because you had no control over it. None of it was your choice. Stop beating yourself up over every single emotion you have.

"And you know something else? Yes, there's a strong possibility Frankie will see your anger toward your mother. But she will also see the love you have for her. And the way you take care of her. A lot of men in your position wouldn't do what you do. They'd walk away. It's not their problem any more."

"I wish I could walk away," I confess.

He shakes his head. "It's not in you, Griffin. She'll see that, too."

My cell vibrates, and I take it out of my front pocket. A text from Frankie. *Are you home? Or at the warehouse?*

I tell her I'm out with Mr. Rothman.

Can you call whenever you get home?

I ask her if everything's okay.

Not really.

Mr. Rothman urges me to leave, offering to take care of the check. Within minutes, I'm flying up the stairs to my apartment, where I find Frankie sitting on the floor in front of my door crying. I kneel before her, taking her face in both of my hands. Her cheeks are soaked and her entire face is puffy, but she looks otherwise unharmed. I exhale a deep breath I didn't realize I'd been holding since 14th Street.

"What happened?"

"Can we go inside? I really have to pee." She laughs through her tears, which makes me feel a little better. If she's laughing, maybe it's not that bad.

As she retreats to the bathroom, I pace in front of my couch. How fucking long can she take in there? I need to know what happened.

Finally, she emerges. She's washed her face and though it remains blotchy, she's herself again. She sits on the couch, but I continue to pace.

"Griffin, can you sit? You're making me nervous." She pats the empty space next to her.

"I'm making *you* nervous? Frankie, I'm about to lose my goddamn mind here. Are you hurt?"

She shakes her head. Tears flow again and I sit next to her, taking both her hands. "Talk to me."

"I'm sick of being so stupid," she whimpers.

"What are you talking about?"

"Every decision I make is wrong. Everything I try to do turns out like shit. I'm so tired of it. I just want to make one choice that doesn't lead me toward disappointment. Is that too much to ask?"

"What happened?"

"You were right. About Scott. And I knew it. I knew something wasn't right. But I didn't care. I wanted to believe someone thought my work was good so much that I was willing to overlook what I knew was wrong."

At the mention of his name, my chest constricts. "What did he do?"

She tells me what happened in the hotel room and with each syllable, the red rushes in faster. Into my limbs, pooling at my core. It feels like hot lava, seeping through every canal in my body, waiting until her story is over to erupt out of me.

"He didn't even care about my photos. He probably saw some dumb girl leaning over in a tight skirt taking a picture of nothing important. I was an easy target. He does this all the time, apparently. He pretty much admitted all his other photographers had sex with him so they could be in his books."

I stand. I've got to go find this motherfucker and kill him. Luckily, I saved all the information about him. I pull my phone from my pocket and grab my keys.

"What are you doing?" she nearly shouts.

"I'm going to take care of this."

"No, you're not." She stands and grabs my arm. "That's not why I told you."

"Frankie, he needs to be taught a lesson."

"Griffin. Listen to me. I gave him my answer. He didn't attack me or anything. He's not a rapist. He's just a sleazy guy who gets off on his power and took advantage of a girl who was desperate for work. I don't want you to teach him a lesson. Please."

"Frankie, I have to take care of you."

She rubs the inside of my palm. "Sit down with me. I've got to explain something to you."

Her soft touch calms me immediately, even though I don't want it to. I want to stay heated and go after this guy. For her. But I sit. Also for her.

"It's important you pay close attention to what I'm about to tell you because I don't think it's something you're used to, okay?"

"Okay?"

"I'm crazy about you, Griffin. I'm happier with you than I've ever been with anyone and with every week that passes, I want to be with you more and more. But I don't want to be with you so you can protect me. I know that's what you do, but I don't need protection. I can take care of myself, even if I screw up along the way. I didn't tell you about tonight because I wanted you to protect me and *take care* of it. I told you about it because of all the people I have in my life—whether it's friends and family at home or anyone here—you're the one I wanted to share it with. You're the one I wanted to break down to about it. Not because I need you to make it better for me. Just because I want to be with you. Because you're amazing and talented and brilliant and good and because I love everything about you. So please, stop trying to protect me and just enjoy being with me."

I do enjoy being with her, more than she could possibly know. But to stop trying to protect her, when it's all I've ever done? Impossible. "I don't know how," I say.

"Well, then let me show you."

And she does.

Soon after, as we're lying together on my couch, I pull her tighter against my chest and though she's limp in my arms, I can tell it's not from what we just shared. She's feeling the effects of the day. She's defeated.

She's wrong, though. She does need me. Just not the way I planned to help her.

"You're not stupid, for the record. You just made a mistake." I stroke her long hair. It's wild against my skin, with unpredictable waves. Just like Frankie. My hands never tire of feeling every single surface and texture of her.

"I'm always making mistakes, Griffin. I think, yeah, that sounds like fun, I'll take a chance on it. I never stop to think anything through or consider the consequences of my actions. I'm twenty-three for God's sake, not thirteen. I should know better than this."

"Didn't you tell me you had no regrets? That you like living life and not settling?" I throw back her words from a conversation we had months ago, before I knew I would pine to be one of those things she jumped into with abandon.

"I don't know. I'm starting to think that's a flawed way of thinking."

"Normally flawed?" She brought me relief when she told me I was normal. Maybe I can do the same for her.

She lifts her head off of my chest to give me a soft, tired smile. I hate that her sad eyes are so swollen. Now they're gray moss on a cloudy day. No shining droplets today.

"Do you remember all the things people say?" she asks.

"Only certain people." I smile back.

She rests her head back on my bare chest and begins tracing each of my tattoos. "I can't believe you do this for all those women." Her fingers follow the lines of a cherry blossom on my ribcage. "Do you have any idea how incredible you are?"

I don't answer.

She sighs. "You don't, do you?" She stops mid-trace. "Can I see mine?"

I laugh at how blatant she is about it, when I specifically told her she was only part of the inspiration for the moon. In all honesty, even though I can't see it, I know it's there and it's a constant reminder of her. We sit up together and she grabs my T-shirt off the floor from our discarded pile of clothes. She slips it over her head as I give her my back. A single fingernail follows the lines of the moon and the sky around it. I suppress a shudder. How does just one of her nails have such a blistering effect on my body?

Then the same nail traces the tattoo parallel to hers. A faded sketch of a small, mustached man rescuing a child from drowning.

"I never noticed this one before. Is it for someone or is it just something you liked?" she asks.

"It's for someone." She doesn't follow up, but I know she's curious. "It's for Roth," I answer her silent question.

She finds the symbolism right away. "It's very powerful." Her voice flutters in my ear. "It's in the same exact spot as mine, on the other shoulder blade. You never struck me as the kind of guy who needs symmetry," she jokes.

"They're there for a reason."

"What significance are shoulder blades?"

I chuckle. "They're not on my shoulder blades, Frankie. They're on my lungs. Mr. Rothman taught me how to breathe years ago. You're the reason I keep doing it."

Chapter Twenty

Frankie

Griffin is positively green. He has been all day. And he's been sweating on and off for hours. If he weren't so damn gorgeous, he'd be downright disgusting. As it is, he's edging closer to average looking. I keep asking him if he's all right. I've put my lips to his forehead at least four times through the course of the day to check if he has a fever. But he doesn't. He's just clammy and green.

He says it's nerves about tonight. I don't understand why he's getting himself sick over me meeting his mother. I mean, I know he's uncomfortable about the whole thing with his father, but that's different. This shouldn't be so hard.

I have to admit, I'm nervous too, though nowhere near enough to vomit at any second. Griffin's mother knows he told me about their situation. It'll be like the elephant in the room the whole night. On the other hand, I know what a huge deal it is for Griffin, so as nervous as I am, I'm also thrilled about what this means.

Still, I've offered to cancel twice, since he seems miserable about it.

Sarah invited us to have a drink at her place before we went, no doubt because she knew he would be a basket case. I appreciate she's trying to help, but if Griffin's color is any indication, it's not working.

"Are you sure you want to go tonight?" I call through the bathroom door, giving him one last chance to bail. I don't know if he went in there to purge or to wash the sweat off, but he hasn't come out in about ten minutes. "We can tell her I'm not feeling well and postpone."

Sarah is sympathetic when I walk into her bedroom. "Don't worry about him. He'll be okay once it's over. Gotta break the seal sometime."

She's so nonchalant about everything with Griffin. She's been dealing with him for years, so his behavior never surprises her. Besides, she's not head over heels in love with the guy, so his actions don't affect her the same way they do me. I wish some of that would rub off on me.

I walk over to the sculpture on her shelf and stroke it. I wonder if she cherishes hers the way I would mine.

The bathroom door opens. "I told you I don't want to cancel. I'm fine."

He's standing in the doorway. He doesn't look fine. He looks like the dirt at the bottom of a puddle I photographed a few months ago.

His eyes follow my arm to the hand resting on Sarah's brother. Then they flick to my face. "I thought you were leaving that alone," he snaps at me in a tone I've never heard before.

"What?"

"The sculpture thing. Are we back on this, Frankie?"

"Huh? No, I…"

"Griffin." Sarah's gives a cautious warning. He

pushes his hand through his hair, which is wet with sweat at the tips.

"Never mind." He walks away and throws himself on the couch. One of his legs is bent at the knee, with his foot on a cushion. The other foot is touching the floor. His arm is slung over his face. I sit on the couch next to him.

"We don't have to do this if you're not ready, Griffin. I don't have to meet your mother if it's too soon in our relationship for you."

"It's not that."

I'm relieved at his words because the way I feel about him, I would have introduced him to my parents long ago if they lived here.

"Okay." I'm diffident, as if I'm trying to tame a lion. "Then what?"

He lowers his arm. "My parents just bring out the worst in me."

"Well, think of this as two women getting together who will probably want to share lots of embarrassing stories about you. And then when it's over, we'll come home and find a way to make you let go of some of this tension." I squeeze his quads, which are rock hard from equal parts of muscle and stress. I move my hands up his legs, but he pushes them away as he sits up.

"Let's just get this over with."

****

I recognize the house as soon as we turn the corner. The only difference between today and last time is today there is a BMW parked in the driveway. My fingers are linked with Griffin's and when he stops short, my arm yanks back behind me.

"You know what?" These are the first words out of

his mouth since we left the city. "I changed my mind. You were right. It's too soon. Let's go home."

Is he crazy? I turn to him, expecting his eyes to be searching mine for the answer they want. Instead, they're trained on the car by the house.

"What are you talking about? We can't cancel now."

"You said we didn't have to come, Frankie. You said if it was too soon, you'd understand."

"That was before. We were supposed to be here like twenty minutes ago. We can't not show up now."

It's bad enough all Griffin's hemming and hawing made us late. Now he wants to stand her up, too? This is a strange side of him I've never seen.

His feet don't venture any farther, and I'm afraid we're going to have some weird battle of wills in the middle of the sidewalk. It would be beyond rude to leave now, and after my first two non-introductions with his mother, I'm not agreeing to it.

Before I can figure out how to get him to consider this logically, a screen door creaks and Griffin's head snaps at the sound. His mood is black in an instant.

When Griffin's father strides out the door, I involuntarily suck in a gasp. Approaching us is possibly the most handsome man I've ever seen, especially in his sharp button-down shirt, slacks and designer shoes. He's almost Griffin's clone, except as he smiles to say hello, some soft lines surround his mouth and fiery brown eyes. His dark hair has the same slightly reddish tint as Griffin's but it's short, with not a single strand out of place, and it's laced with some gray. He's got Griffin's high cheekbones and deep dimples indenting his cheeks. These two could be twins born a couple of decades apart. If this is what Griffin will become in twenty-something years, I'd like to stick around to see it.

A small guttural sound spurts from Griffin, who practically has smoke coming out his ears, and two things occur to me. One: I cannot be thinking about how beautiful this man is. I have to hate him the way Griffin does, because, for God's sake, he's an abusive asshole. And two: even though he has explained it to me, I'm grasping for the first time why Griffin keeps his appearance the way he does. Morally, he is the polar opposite of his father, yet their physical features could make them identical. Griffin's personality suddenly makes a lot more sense to me and I'm sorry I ever asked him to shave.

"Frankie," his father says, exposing his dimples and revealing a smile matched in beauty only by his son's. "I'm so glad to be meeting you. I'm Evan." He extends his hand.

Griffin is absorbed by his father's manicured hand grasping mine. Definitely no tattoos on those knuckles.

He releases me and turns to Griffin. "Hello, my boy," he says, but doesn't reach for his hand. Maybe he knows Griffin won't shake it and doesn't want to make things awkward. Instead he gives Griffin a playful slap on the back.

Griffin straightens. "Why aren't you at work?" Griffin snaps at his father. Griffin's hands quiver and he crams them in his pockets.

"I was." His father ignores the tone. "But when your mother mentioned you were bringing a date for dinner, I decided to cut our meeting short. Doesn't happen every day. Why don't we go inside? Your mom said everything's almost ready." He tries to escort me by placing a hand on my spine. Griffin pulls me away and steps between us to walk.

Dinner should be interesting.

****

It turns out to be *very* interesting. Conversation between Griffin's parents flows with no effort. Their connection to each other reminds me of Griffin and me. Like he's not only hearing the words she's saying, but finding meaning in what she's not saying, too. There's an intensity in his gaze that she returns. If I didn't know better, I'd be envious of these two people.

There is something else there, too, though. I don't have Griffin's knack for reading people, but watching his mother tells me she feels more than just love for this man. I wouldn't call it fear exactly, but something I can't put my finger on.

Either way, it's hard to believe this is the same man who beats on his wife and leaves her broken. Aren't abusive husbands supposed to be scary, drunk, and domineering all the time? Because that's not what I'm seeing. It's hard to align my assumptions about abusers with the man I'm sitting across from right now. This man seems perfect. It makes me wonder how many men are walking around out there who come off as model husbands and boyfriends, when in fact they are anything but that. It also makes me see why Griffin's afraid of getting close to someone. If his father was an animal all the time, it would be obvious to Griffin that they're nothing alike. But if there's an intellectual, caring side of him one minute and the next he snaps, then it makes sense that Griffin would be afraid it might happen to him, too. It's confusing to me. How can someone switch gears so dramatically?

Evan Stone is nothing short of captivating the entire meal. He's witty, sarcastic, and incredibly friendly. He asks about my work, and when I put myself down, mocking what I'm trying to do, he builds me up, telling me I haven't bumped into my destiny yet. It'll happen, he encourages. Don't get frustrated. We discuss my family, and he wants to know about life in Buffalo. He shares an amusing story about when he went up to a Bulls college game and talks about some ridiculous situation he and his friends found themselves in. His delivery as he imitates his friend is hysterical, and I can't help but laugh. Griffin's mother almost cries. In spite of myself, I momentarily forget the situation and enjoy myself.

The only person who does not participate is Griffin.

In fact, as he and I help his mother clear the dishes and set up for dessert, he doesn't even acknowledge me.

"Hey, you." I rub his arm when we have a second alone. "Are you okay? Everything's going fine. You can relax."

He acts as if I didn't even speak to him when he brings a cake into the dining room.

After we help Griffin's mother rinse the dishes and load the dishwasher, we say our goodbyes. Griffin's mother says how nice it was to meet me. *Under different circumstances this time*, she whispers into my ear when her husband can't hear.

Evan Stone kisses me goodbye on the cheek. "What a wonderful way to spend an evening," he beams. "I hope we'll see a lot more of you, Frankie."

I open my mouth to tell him I had a nice time too, but Griffin interrupts. "You won't."

My jaw hangs, weighted down with the unspoken words that didn't make their way out.

"Griffin," his mother reprimands, but he turns away.

"Let's go," he says into the air, but it's obviously meant for me. I follow in shock.

****

He's silent on the train back to the city. As I sit next to him, stiffer than any of the statues he's molded, I repeat his two words over and over in my mind. *You won't.*

Did he say that because in the future he'll make sure his father isn't at dinner? Or did he say it because he's so angry at me for having a conversation with his father that he's done with me?

What was I supposed to do? Not talk to the man? This isn't my fault. It's unfair to blame me. I wouldn't be rude to his parents. Surely, he can see expecting I wouldn't speak to his father is irrational.

But there doesn't appear to be anything rational going on behind his frighteningly dark eyes right now. I wait until we exit the train and are on the platform before I say anything. "What did you mean by 'you won't'?" I ask as soon as the doors have closed and the train has pulled away.

Instead of answering, he makes a snide remark in a tone even colder than the one he used with me earlier. "You seemed to be enjoying yourself."

Ordinarily, that would be a good thing when you meet your boyfriend's parents. Not this time.

"I guess." I'm not sure what the appropriate

response is to this statement. I feel like he's baiting me, daring me to say the wrong thing.

"You liked him." He spits out the words as he walks up the subway steps leading to my street. He still doesn't look at me.

"Griffin, he was..." I start, as the warm night air hits our faces.

"I know how he is." He turns to me now. His voice is deep and gritty and booms for miles. People passing by glance for a second before minding their own business. Of all the things that happen on my block, this is probably the least exciting. "Don't you think I know how he is, Frankie? It's the reason she goes back for more. Over and over. He's a fucking prince, right?"

I don't know what to say. I know for sure anything that comes out of my mouth right now will be the wrong thing. "Griffin." I'm not sure of where I'm going. "You're overreacting. I didn't say any of that. I was just being polite. It's not so clear-cut. You're usually very perceptive, but I think you're too close to this. Like with your mother. I don't think you see everything that's there. I saw something in her...women stay for a lot of reasons—"

"Holy shit!" His hands fly into the air as he paces on the sidewalk. "Now you're going to defend her, too? You're going to tell me why she stays? I'm the one who lived there. I'm the one with the memories, not you. Don't you think I know what I lived with, Frankie?"

"I'm just saying you may not be the most objective right now." I want to stop talking. Everything I'm saying is making this worse. Every inch of his body is tense.

"This is just great! I hoped...I really thought of all

people, you'd understand. Even more than Sarah or Roth, it was important that you got it. That you could see him for what he is. But you reacted just like the rest of the world does. You got taken in by his looks and his fucking charm. And you're going to try to explain my mother to me. Just great." He's seething, pacing, clenching and unclenching his hands, running them through his hair frantically. I have no idea what to do. "Do you understand why it was so important, Frankie? Do you?"

"Griffin, I didn't even say anything about him," I plead. He needs to calm down.

"You didn't have to. I can see it all over your damn face. You fucking like him. Tell me I'm wrong."

I'm about to tell him the only parts of him I liked were the parts that made me think of Griffin, but I know it was all a façade and I know what's underneath. And of course I am the person who *does* understand. After everything he's shared with me, it would be impossible not to. Even though his father is beautiful on the outside, I know he's ugly on the inside. I get that. Looking closer is my thing. Of course I understand.

But I pause for too long and he interprets that as an acknowledgment that he's right.

"That's what I thought." But in that split second, he's lost his fury. Color has drained from him and he slouches. It's as if all the hope he had in the world has been sucked out of him. He turns his back and disappears down the steps into the subway.

****

I bawl as soon as I walk in my door, throwing myself on the couch with my purse in my lap. I rest my head on it while I cry. I go over all the things I should have told him, instead of the things I did say. *Of course I'm on your side. No, I didn't like him. I know he's an abusive monster, you're nothing like him.* But none of that came quickly enough.

Now that the floodgates are open, I let loose about everything. How he yelled at me. How things might be over between us because of one unscheduled meeting with his father. How he's probably not ready for this relationship if that's enough to end us, anyway. How I make horrible choices. How I have a dead end job with no prospects. I haven't even had the nerve to take a picture since the whole fiasco with Scott. What confidence I did have is gone. What am I even doing here? The negative energy just keeps on coming.

My forehead vibrates against my bag, and I dig through my mess of keys, makeup, and receipts to find my phone, hoping it's Griffin. Instead, my mother's picture fills the screen.

When it rains, the pouring is torrential.

Chapter Twenty-One

Griffin

"You need to calm down." Sarah clamps my shoulders between her hands, attempting to hold me in place, but I break free.

I continue pacing the warehouse, back and forth, my speed increasing with each lap. I can't even speak. All I can do is try in vain to control my breathing. I'm like a caged animal, rabid for a way out, except my cage lies deep within me.

"Griffin, I can't talk to you unless you calm down. Go behind your table and work the clay. It'll help."

She's wrong. It won't help. I know because while I was counting the minutes until she got here, I tried that. All I did was pound it with my fist and it didn't relax me in the least.

I called her as soon as I got off the train. She was out with friends, but left them as soon as she heard my voice. I must have sounded god-awful. I'm regretting calling though, because her presence here for the last hour is doing as little to calm me as the clay. If anything, it's annoying me more. But it's not her fault: it's mine. I should never have brought Frankie there.

Now everything is screwed up.

I wasn't prepared. All week, I planned out how that dinner would go. I lectured myself on ways to keep my emotions at bay, to put just the good part of my relationship with my mother on display. And after talking to Mr. Rothman, I felt like it might work. I hadn't even considered the possibility that he would be there. He's never home on Monday. I was anxious enough about the whole thing, but as soon as I saw his car in the driveway, any chance the evening would be tolerable disappeared.

The entire night is a blur. I remember him coming out to greet us, taking Frankie's hand. I remember him jabbering incessantly at dinner, showing Frankie what a first-rate guy he is. I remember Frankie smiling, laughing, being entertained. And I remember being irate. None of the smaller details registered.

"Stop!" Sarah yells, which surprises me and gets me to do just that. "Gather yourself so you can tell me what happened and we can fix it."

"It can't be fixed." My first words since she got here.

"Everything can be fixed. Start at the beginning."

I reel off whatever I can recall about the night, ending with the way I screamed at Frankie before leaving her on the street. I must have moved over to my table, because when my story is over, I find I'm forming some abstract object out of the gray mound in front of me.

I assume Sarah will be on my side. She's always on my side. She'll tell me I was right to be annoyed and then give me advice about how to cool down and make things better with Frankie. Instead, she reprimands me.

"You were completely out of line."

"What?"

"What did you expect her to do? She was in a no-win situation, Griffin. She couldn't very well be rude to your father, could she?"

"She didn't have to like him. Or defend her. I can't be with someone who likes him. You know that."

"You don't know if she liked him. All you know is she was polite to him and maybe she thought his stories were funny. Think about how uncomfortable she must have been, Griffin. You were ready to pop before you left here. She was doomed before you even stepped foot in that house."

"But she—"

"She nothing. You jumped on her about touching my sculpture when she didn't even say a word about it. You're obviously guilty about the fact that you can't do it for her. You snapped at her when she tried to let you out of the plans. I can't even imagine how tense the ride to your parents' house was. No matter what happened tonight, you were going to find an excuse to be pissed off, because you're scared of where this is going. I've watched you keep your distance from woman after woman over the years. And it never mattered because there wasn't a single one I thought could bring you to life. But this one can. This one *does*. You know it. And that's why you're sabotaging it now. This isn't just about Frankie not hating your father. It's about what it means if she can bring some peace into your life about him. You think you want to surround yourself with people who will keep fueling your anger by egging you on about him, but maybe that's not what you need. Maybe you need someone who will understand, but teach you to deal with it in a different way. And I'll tell you one thing, Griffin. If you throw this away now, you're a complete fool."

I'm surprised by the tough love, but Sarah's words slap me in the face. Even though I tried to convince myself I could pull off the evening, I was an explosion waiting to happen. I just didn't realize the blast was aimed at Frankie.

"I was really nasty to her."

"Yes."

"I said my parents wouldn't be seeing her again."

"Yep."

"I need to fix this."

"Yes, you do. Oh, and Griffin?"

"Yeah?"

"You're angrier than I've seen you in a long, long time. Did you..." She pauses. "Did you almost hit her?"

I'm appalled at the question. How could she even ask me that? "Of course not!" I snap.

She smirks. "What does that tell you?"

****

When Frankie doesn't answer her cell the first time I call, I hang up. I wasn't expecting her voicemail and I've got nothing rehearsed. Like some inexperienced high school kid, I spend the next hour asking Sarah for advice about what kind of message to leave. I'm not practiced in apologizing to women's cell phones, but I want to get this one right.

I'm humiliated as I go so far as to jot some notes to remind me what to say. It's absurd. I'm a straightforward guy. I say what I mean, and I mean what I say. But my mind is too garbled up, and if I try to leave an off-the-cuff message, I'm afraid I'll make things worse. I seem to lose all balanced thoughts when my parents are involved in a situation.

When I call back, I get her voicemail again. I was

hoping she'd answer this time, though I have no idea why she would. I leave an apologetic message, asking her to please call me back. I wait with my phone in my lap while Sarah watches me with pity.

"Give her time to be mad, Griffin. It doesn't mean the worst if she doesn't call you back right away."

I disagree. Frankie always calls back right away unless something is wrong. A quiet phone is definitely a bad sign.

Finally, I tell Sarah to leave.

"If you happen to run into her, you know, by pounding on her door, feel free to tell her how remorseful I am," I half joke. It's the first time I recall wanting someone to talk me up.

"Don't worry, Griffin. I'll talk to her. Try to keep it together in the meantime."

Easier said than done.

After Sarah leaves, I go upstairs. I don't want to work on anything, because it reminds me the whole sculpting thing was part of what set me off tonight. I'm sick of not doing the things I want because I'm afraid how they're going to affect me. If I want to sculpt her, I should sculpt her. Damn my father for making me second-guess all my actions. Damn him for making me so insecure about becoming like him that I can't live the way I want. Damn him to hell and back.

When I get upstairs, I flick on the TV, keeping my phone in my hand. I'm pathetic. I've been called many things in my life, but up to now, pathetic was not one of them.

When the cell vibrates, I nearly jump off the couch. But it's not her. It's Sarah.

"Griffin, I don't know how to tell you this…"

Her voice is tentative and cracking, and I don't like the sound of it at all.

"Just say whatever it is."

She's going to tell me Frankie's pissed and doesn't want to talk to me. Or maybe even see me any more. She's going to tell me I'm going to have to fight damn hard to get her back.

"Frankie didn't answer her door, so I used my spare key to get in, to make sure she was okay, ya know?" She waits for me to justify her breaking and entering.

"Yeah, and?"

"Frankie's not here. Neither is her toothbrush. Or makeup. Or hairdryer. Or any of her toiletries. I don't know about her clothes. There was stuff in her closet, but I don't know how much she had before. But her camera seems to be gone, too. I'm sorry, Griffin."

It takes me a moment to process what she's saying. She left? Just like that? Where would she go? My initial reaction is to think no way, nobody's going to take off over one fight, without telling anyone. But it's Frankie, and leaving spur of the moment is probably something she's accustomed to doing.

"We have to find her, Sarah. She can't just be gone. I need to fix this. She's got to give me a chance to fix it."

"Stay calm. I'm going to call her. Maybe she'll answer if it's me. I'll find out where she is, okay?"

"Okay."

She tells me to stay put and she'll call me as soon as she hears anything, but staying put is the last thing I want to do. I want to scour the city and make some grand gesture to get her back. I'll assure her I didn't mean what I said and show her I'm sorry. I've always hated grand gestures because of how many times my father made them.

I was livid after my father's biggest, emptiest one ever.

Their fight was different that time. Usually, my father got heated about something, hit her, and it was over. But that time, he called her names and said nasty things to her. Judging by how upset she was, his words hurt her more than his knuckles.

He tried to cheer her up. Begged for forgiveness. Brought her this whole pampering package, bath oils and shit. She said she forgave him, but he and I could both see she wasn't past it. For three days in a row, he brought stuff. He even came home with tickets to a show she'd been wanting to see. She thanked him and kissed him, but she was still melancholy.

The asshole was beside himself. I guess I should be thankful for that. I know other men don't even feel bad afterwards. They just blame their women for making them do it to them. At least he feels remorse.

Nothing was working. Then one morning, she said the words that shocked us both, words she'd never spoken before. She said she didn't know how much more she could take. Her words scared me. I thought he'd flip out. But instead he broke down and begged on his knees, not to say that.

Then he told the grandest lie ever uttered. He said he'd go to therapy.

I knew it was bullshit. Unfortunately, my mother didn't. She was overjoyed.

After two sessions, my father convinced my mother the therapist was a man-hating feminist who was trying to destroy their marriage and he never went again. My mother cried every day for a month after that, but she never let him see.

I swore to myself I'd never stoop to that level. I'd never rely on making a woman happy by making promises I might not live up to. But screw that. Just because my father did it and he's an asshole doesn't mean if I do it I'll disappoint Frankie, too. If I get the opportunity, I'm doing whatever I can to make this right.

When my phone rings in the morning and Sarah delivers her next bit of news, I'm not sure I'll ever get that opportunity.

"We have a little problem." Her voice is low, like she doesn't really want me to hear what she's saying.

"What is it?"

"So, I went back into her apartment this morning, to see if I could figure out where she might have gone. I rummaged around some more and tried calling her cell while I was in there. It rang. Her phone was stuck in her couch cushion."

I bury my head in my free hand. My only line of communication with her is broken. I have no idea where she is and no way to contact her. I groan into the phone.

"I'm sure when she realizes she doesn't have it, she'll come get it. She can't go long without a phone. I'll leave a note telling her I have it in case she comes home."

But I can't risk that. Once Sam's Tavern opens, I'm going there, finding out where she is and making the gesture I should have made months ago.

Chapter Twenty-Two

Frankie

I cannot believe I lost my cell. I don't even know if it's in my apartment or if it fell out of my bag somewhere on my way here. I called it this morning, but no one answered. Another wonderful move on my part.

"Do you want some coffee, Frankie?" my dad asks. It was a long bus ride in the middle of the night and I'm sure when I got here I looked like crap, between my crying episode and my forever-commute to Buffalo. I probably should have waited until morning to leave, but when my mother told me Gabby was so upset, I wanted to be home as soon as possible. I threw some things in a bag and jumped on the last available bus. Thank God I told my father which bus I was taking before I left my apartment, or without a cell in the middle of the night, I don't know how I would have contacted him to pick me up at the station.

"Yeah, thanks Dad."

He wraps an arm around me. "I'm glad you came. I think it'll be good for Gabby to see you here when she wakes up."

"How bad is she, really?"

He shrugs. "I've never seen her like this. She hasn't left her room in days and hasn't eaten anything I know of in at least a day. We're very worried about her."

"Okay." I nod. "As soon as she's awake, I'm going in."

He smiles. "Thanks, Frankie. So what's going on with you? Mom doesn't give me much."

"Probably because I don't give her much." I pull my mouth to the side in guilt. It's true I haven't shared a lot lately.

"I don't always blame you." he sighs. "So then, tell me. What's new?"

"Oh you know. Same old, same old."

He frowns. "Francesca Moore. There is nothing either the same or old in your life. Everything is always different and new when it comes to you. So please, give me something to go on."

I'm guarded because I don't feel like hearing I told you so, but my mother is the ringleader there. My father is just the quiet bystander. And I would like to lay out some of this burden.

"I don't know, Dad. Things aren't exactly going the way I thought they would."

"Things rarely do, honey. The best laid plans, and all that."

"Yeah, but I have no laid plans. Ya know?"

He laughs. "Yeah, I've noticed that's sometimes true."

"Thanks for the sometimes."

He kisses me on the head.

"That's never bothered you before. What's the problem?"

"I don't know. Every time I turn around, something I thought was going well turns to garbage. I'm not sure

I should have moved to New York. I don't know what I'm doing there. I'm thinking maybe it's time to come home." I'm surprised by my own words. I hadn't formulated the thought in my head yet, but saying it out loud feels like a relief. Maybe I should just give up and start over.

Again.

My father frowns. "Is that really what you want?"

"I don't know what I want." Well, that's not accurate. I know exactly what I want. I just don't know if I can have any of it.

"Frankie..." He sits back on the sofa to make himself comfortable. "When you said you were going to New York City with that guy, neither your mother nor I thought it was a good idea, right?"

"Right."

"But for me, it wasn't because you were going to try to make something of yourself in Manhattan. It was because I thought you were following the dream of some guy you hardly knew. But if you're there, trying to do something for yourself, don't give up before you've even gotten started. That's not the Frankie I know."

"Yeah, but I thought I had this cool job and it turned out the guy was a scammer. All I'm doing now is waitressing."

"So that one didn't work out. Don't run away because of one bad seed. You may find lots of them before finding a good one, but that doesn't mean you should stop hunting."

"But Dad, I'm always jumping into something new. Maybe it's time to just settle on one thing and stick with it, even if it's not something I love. I'm not getting any younger."

He laughs. "You have a lot of years left before you can use that expression. Now is the time to find what you love and keep pumping away until you do. Yes, you like to leap before you lock. Fine. But when you leap from one thing to the next, you don't run *from* things, Frankie, you run *toward* them. That's part of what makes you so special. Don't change that about yourself because of a few missteps. One of these days, you're going to leap into something worthwhile. Maybe you already have?" He lets the question hang out there, and I think he's referring to Griffin. Just because I haven't mentioned him doesn't mean Gabby hasn't.

I don't acknowledge his question. I'm still skeptical.

"Do you know what your name means?"

"What?"

"Francesca. Do you know what it means?"

"Um, isn't it some feminine version of an Italian name, like Franciscus or Francesco or something?"

"Yes, but it's a derivative of Francus, a freeman. Your name means free, Frankie. Somehow, from the second you were born, your mother and I knew you were going to be a free spirit. Francesca wasn't even supposed to be your name. It was supposed to be Lucy, after your grandmother, Lucille."

"Way to pick all the modern names, Dad."

He chuckles. "The point is, when we saw you, we changed to our second choice. We just felt it. Don't let your spirit be crushed by a couple of steps in the wrong direction. You're too unique for that."

I'm surprised by his advice. I never knew he approved of my path-less-taken behavior.

"Gabby's awake," my mother interrupts in a whisper. I nod and head to her room.

****

Gabby looks worse than I'd anticipated. Even worse than when she had mono in high school. Lying in bed, her hair is matted on one side and a rat's nest on the other. She's pale, her lips are all chapped, and her pajamas have to be at least three days old. So much for my perfect sister.

"What are you doing here?" she asks when I walk in without knocking.

"They called in the cavalry," I try to joke, but she doesn't laugh. "I thought things were a little better. You were going to try to make up some of the course work. What happened?"

"I don't know. When classes started, I was still too depressed to go. Then I fell too far behind and got overwhelmed and then when I finally dragged myself to campus to pick up the work I missed I ran into Mitchell. He was talking to another girl and I got crazy jealous. I acted like an idiot in front of them. I didn't even make it to class to pick up the stuff. A couple of days ago, I tried to call him again to leave another apology on his machine. But he answered this time. I spoke as fast as I could to get everything out. How I was sorry and it was a mistake and all of it."

She lowers her voice and asks me to close the door, which I do. "If he'd yelled at me, if he was mad at me and hurt, it would have been better. But he was calm when he told me he has no respect for the person I am now. He wishes me no harm but wants nothing to do with me, and every time he thinks about me, all he can picture is me letting another guy inside me unprotected, then bringing that disease back to him, and it disgusts him." She whimpers each word out. "This can't be the last thing he ever thinks of me, Frankie, it can't. Not after all these years. I can't take it. It hurts so bad."

I scoop her up but don't know what to say to make her feel better. She made a mistake. One mistake that changed everything. Sometimes things can't be fixed.

"I think you'll feel a little better if you take a shower," I offer.

"How's that going to help?" she cries.

"Well, for me, everything's worse when you're in bed obsessing over it. Let's get you up, showered and fed."

"I can't eat."

"You've got to, Gab. Even if it's just a little."

She lets me get her into the shower, where she spends enough time that it makes me nervous. When I knock on the door and she calls out, *yeah?*, I'm relieved.

She comes out, all cleaned up and smelling a lot fresher. I bet she hadn't showered in days. She allows my mother to make her some toast. "Having you here with me makes me feel a little better, Frankie. I'm not so alone, now."

"You're never alone." I smile at her. I may not have the right words, but at least my presence is useful. I call work and tell them I'm going to need a few more days off due to a family emergency.

****

Gabby and I spend the next few days doing sister stuff. At first, she doesn't want to leave her room, except to eat and shower. We talk. Mostly, she talks and cries about how upset she is and I listen. She's lost most of her friends in this breakup, so I'm all she has right now. I guess talking on the phone wasn't cutting it.

By the second day, I talk her into coming out of her room and watching some TV with my parents and me. By the third day, I know I have to find some words of wisdom, because she can't hide out forever. She wants me to give her hope Mitchell will forgive her and take her back, but I can't because it's clear that won't happen.

"Gab, I know this is hard to hear, but you have to find a way to function without him."

"I can't, Fransister," she answers.

"Of course you can. I know you don't want to, and I know it's hard because you're tormenting yourself over your mistake. But people make mistakes, Gabby. Nobody's perfect."

My words remind me of my conversation with Griffin from a while ago, and I get a stab of pain in my own chest, but I ignore it. Now is the time for Gabby's grief, not mine.

"Unfortunately, mistakes cause break-ups. Even with people who may have been right for each other. You're going to need to find a way to…" I don't want to say move on because those are the two words everyone dreads when they're lamenting a lost love. "Get back on track. Start going to class again, at the bare minimum. I guess it's too late for the summer classes now, but maybe take some extra courses in the fall."

"But…"

"Gabby, saying *but* to everything doesn't help. Mitchell, at the very least, needs time to cool off. If, sometime in the far future, you can make amends, great. But right now a heavy course load could be exactly what you need to distract yourself. You thrive on schoolwork, anyway. When does registration start?" I shouldn't have even thrown in the part about Mitchell, but this dog needed a bone.

"It already did. I didn't do it."

I get a lump in my gut because if registration already started, I'm sure she got shut out of most classes. We go on line to check. Some are open, but some of the ones she needs to graduate are already closed. "Okay, new plan. We go to the professors and beg. You've had spectacular grades up until this spring. You'll plead personal breakdown, ask for forgiveness, and beg to get in. And however many extra semesters it takes, it takes. It's better than living your life from your bedroom."

She pouts but doesn't argue.

We spend the next couple of days getting her into classes for September.

****

Gabby's improving a little every day, but the time's come when I have to figure out if I can extract myself from the situation. I've already taken five days off from work. But I'm afraid she's only doing well because I'm here. If I have to stay for her, I will.

I have to admit, being here has been a nice distraction for me, too. I haven't had to think about my lack of career opportunities, and I've forbidden myself to think about Griffin. It's taking everything I have to come up with good advice for my sister. I don't have time for thoughts about my own messed up love life, too.

But I do miss him. This is the longest I've gone without seeing him and before this week, we hadn't gone a day without speaking in I'm not sure how long. I wonder if he's upset that I left. Or if he's still so mad about me speaking to his father that he's glad to be rid of me.

On the bus ride here, I replayed every second of that dinner. And no matter how many times I go over it, I can't find a way I was to blame. Yes, I could have laughed a little less. And yes, I did find his father breathtaking. And yes, I could have minded my own business about his mother. But that doesn't mean I don't get what Griffin's been through. And it doesn't mean I'm no different from everyone else.

On the other hand, I know his father is his sore spot and he has a lifetime of reasons not to be able to control his actions around him. I should have said I didn't like him. Immediately, without pause.

Now that I'm considering an exit strategy, what's in store for me when I get back becomes all too real.

"Are you going to finish that?" Gabby asks, hoping to steal the bacon on my plate. I didn't even realize I'd stopped eating.

"No, have it." I'm glad she's got her appetite back.

"What should we do today?" she munches.

Yesterday, it was the mall. The day before, we went to the movies. Today, we need to talk.

"Gab?"

"Hmm?"

"Do you want me to stay?"

She stops mid-chew. Like it hadn't occurred to her I might have to go at some point. I'm not the only person who wants to block things out of my mind, I guess.

"You can't stay." She gulps down her mouthful. "You have a life in Manhattan." She says the words she thinks she should say.

"Not so much of a life. If you want me to stay, I'll stay." The house phone rings, but this is too important. Someone else can answer it.

"Do you want to stay?"

I pause before answering. "A part of me wants to stay. But that part is running away more than anything."

"What about your photography?"

"Whatever, it's just something to do. You're more important than anything else, Gabby. You're my sister and I'm here for you no matter what. If you need me here in Buffalo, then that's where I'm going to be."

She takes a minute to think.

"Frankie," my mother calls from the kitchen. "You have a phone call."

Chapter Twenty-Three

Griffin

When I went to Sam's Tavern the day after Frankie left and they told me she called in sick with no other explanation, I almost went ballistic. I hounded Sarah to go over every conversation they'd had about people Frankie knew in the city. I even called Taylor, thinking maybe she went back to Holly's House. But no one had heard from her.

Since Frankie usually works Wednesday nights, I returned to Sam's the next evening. She wasn't in again, but the manager did have new information. She'd called in asking for a few days off. Family emergency, he said. My heartbeat eased up for the first time in days.

Buffalo. Why hadn't I considered that? Within minutes, I had her cell in my possession and her home number, saved under Mom, committed to memory. Then I sat, anxious to call.

Sarah said don't. She told me to give her some time. I didn't think that was the right choice, but since I was aware not all of my actions have been rational when it comes to Frankie, I took Sarah's advice and tried to fill my days. I spent hours in the warehouse working on my pieces and hanging out with Antonio while he did his work. I met with my crazy client who likes to dress up her pets, figuring she could steal a few hours of my life. I had dinner with my friend Kaitlyn. I went to Sarah's apartment, but all I did there was listen for footsteps in the staircase that never came.

And then Taylor called requesting a sculpture for a new guest. I was eager for the work. It would occupy my hands and my head. It would give me some remission from myself.

Or so I thought.

I arrived at Holly's sooner than expected this morning, anxious to begin. I was getting myself set up in the sitting room when someone called my name. "Hi, Griffin."

I twisted in my chair toward the voice.

"Oh, hey, April. How are you?" I continued digging through my art bag for the pencil I was sure I'd brought with me.

And then it struck me.

I spun back around. April was talking to Taylor, with her profile to me. I bolted up from my chair and into the foyer. My bag fell off my lap and the supplies in it scattered everywhere.

"April?" I huffed. I braced myself.

She turned toward me in slow motion. My inspection started at her temples and probed downward. Nothing, nothing, nothing.

Then I reached her neck, just under her jaw. Red and purple marks, fingerprints no doubt. Definitely fresh.

I should have been compassionate. I should have welcomed her back. I should have asked if she needed anything.

But I didn't.

"How the hell did that happen?"

"Griffin," Taylor snapped.

"You went back?" I demanded, with disbelief.

April's face was guilty and apologetic, as if she was obligated to answer. "He begged me, Griffin. He promised he'd change. I felt like I had to try. We have a family."

"Yes, you have a family. You have a daughter! What about the moon?" I roared.

"Griffin!" Taylor seized my arm and hauled me into the sitting room, forcing the pocket door shut behind her. "What is the matter with you?" she fumed, with her teeth clenched and her voice low.

I was pacing, kicking at the supplies under my feet. "How could she go back to him? How could she do that?"

"That's not our business, Griffin. We are here to give support. Unconditional support. And we have to maintain professional boundaries, no matter what. You cannot do that ever again."

"Not our business? It's everybody's business."

"It's not. It's not my job, and it's not yours. It's her life. She alone can make those decisions."

"But she was out." I flung myself onto the couch, hunched over, and held my head. "She has a child," I sputtered. "What about her child?"

Taylor knew I wasn't just talking about April. She sat next to me and rubbed my back. She sighed with empathy. "I know it's hard. But this is reality. Sometimes they go back. We just have to be thankful that she's here again, asking for help. It's all we can do."

I lifted my head. "How do you stay so positive? How does this not eat you alive?"

She moved her hand to my shoulder. "Of course it does. Don't you think every time this happens I remember my mother in the same position? But I have to push forward. So I go to group when I'm down. Or I talk to my husband about it. I surround myself with people who remind me that there's good in this world, so I don't get suffocated by the bad and let it take over my life. You need to do the same, Griffin."

She was right. I'd waited long enough. I was calling Frankie. Screw her space. I needed to apologize. Immediately.

****

The phone rings three times before anyone picks up and with each ring my nerves are more scattered. Finally, someone answers and transfers me to Frankie.

"Hello?"

Her voice sends a wave of calm through me.

"Hey, you," I breathe. My voice is terse. My vocal cords feel strained, like strings on a guitar that are being pulled so tight they're going to snap.

"Griffin." I think she quivers, but it's hard to tell from just two syllables.

"Please don't hang up."

"I wasn't going to." I don't know why I thought she would. She's never behaved that way. I'm the one of the two of us who flies off the handle.

"I'm so sorry." I should have kept the speech I left on her voice mail. It was a lot more eloquent than whatever I'm going to say right now. But sorry felt like it had to come first, no matter what. "I should never have yelled at you like that. I know you were just being polite."

"Griffin. I'm kind of in the middle of something

important right now. I can't really talk."

She wasn't going to hang up, but she can't really talk either. That's not promising.

"Please, Frankie."

"I'm not blowing you off. I swear. I'm just having an important conversation with my sister, and it can't wait."

Gabby is probably the reason she had to go home. This could be legitimate. Still, I'm worried. "Can we talk when you come home?"

Heavy breath comes through the other end, but no words.

"You *are* coming home, right?"

She stutters. "Griffin, I-I'll call you back, okay?"

"Frankie…"

"Griffin, I've got to go. Please say goodbye so I know you don't think I'm hanging up on you."

"When will you call?" I'm afraid if I let her hang up all my connections with her will be lost.

"Soon. I promise."

"Okay. Goodbye, Frankie."

"I'll talk to you later, Griffin. Bye."

The line goes dead, which is how I feel.

I head back into Holly's House to accomplish what I intended this morning, before I got sidetracked. I had stepped out to make my call, but as I walk back inside, I try to maintain my focus and ignore the fact that April is back.

I spend the next couple of hours listening to a new woman. She doesn't want to talk about her present life. She discusses the one she left behind when she got married. She tells me how she misses it and would do anything to find her way back to the people she lost.

Even though I'm not supposed to get involved, I ask if she wants me to contact anyone for her. Taylor would probably be pissed if she heard me, but ever since I tackled that crazy husband, she's given me a little more leeway. I find that funny, since I'm the one who let him in.

The woman thanks me but declines. She's got to be the one to mend the fences, she says. I tell her I'm sure her family will welcome her with open arms. They'll just be happy she's back. I know if my mother lost touch with me because of my father, I'd take her back in a heartbeat, no questions asked. But she thinks it won't be so easy. Horrible words passed between her family and her husband, and she took her husband's side. Actions she regrets now.

Still, I can't imagine what could make me turn my back on my mother if she came to me, wanting back in my life after making a mistake. It would have to be something that destroyed me.

I want to do a sculpture for this woman, but what she wants more than anything, what seeps through her pores, is to be reunited with her past. That's what should be in her sculpture. But I don't want to sculpt that yet, because if it doesn't work out for her, the statue it will only bring sadness. I encourage her to contact them and assure her we'll pick up once again after she does. She likes the idea. It gives her the push she needs to call.

I'm glad.

It's the middle of the afternoon by the time I finish up at Holly's House. I've eaten nothing today and as I walk to the nearest bodega, my cell shakes in my pocket. Please, let it be Frankie.

When it is, I nearly stumble over the person in front of me. "Hi," I answer, too cheerfully.

"Hey. Sorry about before. It couldn't be helped."

"That's okay. I'm just glad you called back."

"Griffin, I would never not call you back."

"Frankie." The words rush out. "I have so much I need to talk to you about, but I can't do it over the phone. Are you coming back? If you're not, I need you to give me your address in Buffalo, so I can come there and explain it to you."

"I'll be back tomorrow."

The word tomorrow has never sounded so musical to my ears. She tells me which bus she'll be on and now all I have to do is find a way to kill the next twenty-four hours until she gets here.

****

I should give her time to get settled and unpack when she gets back to the city. It's a long ride and she'll need to unwind. Instead, I'm sitting in Sarah's living room, so I can check every few minutes to see if she's home. This woman has reduced me to things I never imagined I'd do.

Sarah keeps laughing at me, which I don't appreciate, but since it's her apartment I'm hijacking, I keep my nasty comments to a minimum.

"Who are you?" She's so sanctimonious I want to spit.

"I have no idea." I shake my head.

On my way down the staircase for the umpteenth time, keys jingle and my feet jump the last three steps in anticipation. I turn the corner and there she is, opening her door with her hip.

She's surprised to see me but covers it with a tired

smile. I follow her into the apartment, closing the door.

"I should have waited, I know. And if Sarah didn't live upstairs, I would have had to, so I'm completely taking advantage of the fact that you live near my friend."

"It's okay." She puts down her bags and collapses on the bed.

"How's Gabby?"

"Doing better. We can talk about her later. I need to say something to you."

"Let me go first. Please." Or else words might burst out of me of their own accord.

"No. Before you go, I have to tell you I am that person who does understand, Griffin. And just because I wasn't rude to your father doesn't mean I like him or think he's a good person or I'm not on your side. Because I am. Always."

I run both hands into her thick hair and kiss her lips, refusing to wait another second before I touch her.

"I know. And I'm so sorry, Frankie. I had no right to yell at you or blame you or anything. He just makes me so...so..." I kiss her again and she breathes in deeply. She must be able to smell me. I was in the warehouse all morning and even though I showered, somehow I can never get the smell off. She seems okay with it though, because she closes her eyes as she inhales, smiles, and sighs.

"Let's just forget it," she says and starts to pull my shirt over my head.

But I can't just forget it. I need to explain why I behaved the way I did before things go any further. And then, I'll have to let the chips fall where they may. "No, I've got to tell you what happened."

"Tell me after." She unzips my jeans.

I'm only a man and I'm only so strong. And I haven't slept with her in over a week. So I agree. But the entire time, I'm worried that once I tell her how I feel about my mother, this time will be our last.

****

"There are two parts to what I want to say. If you can still look at me after the first part, I think you'll like the second part."

"Okay," she smiles lazily, pulling the sheet up over her chest and giving me her undivided attention. "Shoot."

"It wasn't you I was mad at that night."

"That's what you were going to take a six-hour bus ride to tell me in person? I kind of knew that already, Griffin."

"No, I mean the whole thing with my father. That's not what initially had me on edge."

"I know you were nervous about me meeting your mother. You don't bring women home. I understand."

"Frankie, let me say this, okay?" I'm so thankful to be in her bed with her next to me, but if she keeps interrupting, I'll never get this out.

"Okay." She nods.

"Anyway, the whole week, I was nervous. Not about how it would go between my mother and you. About how things would go between my mother and me."

"What do you mean?" she asks, then clasps her hand over her mouth. "Sorry, go on."

I don't know how to say it any way other than just say it and then I'll judge her reaction.

"I hate her, Frankie." I pause to gauge her eyes, but

there's no expression in them yet. "I love her and I hate her and I pity her and I blame her all at the same time. I hate her for staying with him. I hate her for making me watch that all my life. I hate her for calling me when she needs help but defending him with her next breath. Even now, as a grown man, I still worry every time she calls.

"I'll always be there for her. I'll always see her as my responsibility. And as much as that might make you think I'm a good person, I resent her for it. Who would resent her? Hate her even? All I should feel for my mother is love and sadness about what she goes through. It eats away at me, yet I can't change how I feel. Who blames the victim? What kind of person does that make me?"

I assume she'll need time to process the fact that I'm not the selfless man she thought I was. She'll pause to compose herself, turning away to armor herself against being read. But her answer is immediate and sure and her eyes never leave mine. "It makes you human, Griffin. Human, which means..." She pauses and I think she's about to repeat the words she told me last time to make me feel better. But she shakes her head. Not at me. At her own thoughts, and she slaps her hand to her forehead. Then she talks out loud, I think to herself. "How did I not make the association sooner? It's so fitting."

"What is?'

"You have feet of clay, Griffin."

"I have what?"

"You've never heard the expression?"

I shake my head. I have no idea what she's talking about.

"It's an idiom. In one of my ancient studies classes, I learned this story from the Bible. There was a prophet who interpreted a dream the king of Babylon had. The king dreamt of a huge, powerful statue made mostly of gold and other strong metals, but it also had feet made of clay and iron. The feet were its unexpected, hidden weakness and the prophet said the dream meant the kingdom, though thought to be strong, was open to attack, which, ultimately it was. Now, when you discover someone you greatly admire or respect has a hidden character flaw, you say they have feet of clay. I guess it's meant as an insult, but I don't think of it that way, because everyone is flawed in some way.

"If that woman wasn't your mother and didn't make you watch what you did your whole life, you'd feel nothing but compassion for her, the way you do every single other woman you help. But you're not removed from the situation. You had to live it every day. It's personal for you, so you react personally to it. You need to allow yourself to be human and stop condemning yourself every time you realize you are."

I've carried this guilt around with me for so long that her words of understanding and validation free me in a way nothing else could.

"Feet of clay," I breathe. I pull her in close and nuzzle my face into her neck, finding another place where I'm at peace.

"What's number two?" she whispers into my ear.

"It's about why I've refused to sculpt you. And why I want to do it now."

This gets her attention and she bolts up. It's what she's been waiting for. I just don't know if I can explain it. She waits for me to start, lids batting nonstop.

"I've only ever been passionate about two things in my life, Frankie. Sculpting and you. When I sculpt, I release everything I have into my project. It's a catharsis for me. It's like my own method of purging. I don't hold anything in. When I'm with you, I lack some control but not to the point where it's been a problem. As it is, I act uncharacteristically and do things I normally wouldn't. If I combine the two…I don't know what will happen. I'm afraid I'll be too intense for you."

"There is no *too intense* for me, Griffin. I want everything you have. Can't you see that? I'm not some conservative person who puts her big toe in the water to test out how deep it is. Whatever's living inside of you is what I want. All of it. The good, the bad, and everything in between. As long as you're prepared to accept mine in return."

"Yours?" I laugh. "Yours can't compare to mine. But sure, bring it on."

"You don't know. I could have tons of crazy floating around in here. And you'll be stuck with it." She points to her head and sticks out her tongue as if she's insane.

I kiss her temple, chuckling. God, I love this woman.

Then she grows serious again. "What makes you want to do it now?"

"Because I know what it will mean, to each of us. For you, as long as I don't do it, there's an important part of me I won't share with you. And for me, as long as I can't do it, I'm still afraid to be totally in this. And I don't want to be afraid. I want more than anything to be able to give this to you."

"All right then, let's do it." She gives me an ear to ear, full-mouthed smile, letting me know even though she forgave me with just an apology, this gesture was worth making. "Should I wear something sexy?" she teases with a hand inching up my already-bare leg, creating the effect she was hoping for.

"Not if you want a sculpture," I say on a gulp as she finds her target. "But if you don't care"—I pick up the sheet and peek underneath, anxious to have what's about to be mine—"then wear exactly what you're wearing now."

****

Years ago, when I was tearing through women like days of the week, Mr. Rothman was concerned. He asked if I ever wanted to be in love. It was too risky, I told him. Casual dating had to be it for me.

He didn't like my answer at all. He said someday there would be a woman who forced me to question the doubts I had about myself. She'd make me want to believe I am the person he sees in me, instead of the person I thought I was destined to become. "When she comes along, son," he'd said, "grab her tight and don't let go."

As Frankie drifts off to sleep, I do exactly that. I wrap my arms around her stomach, and she backs up into me with a soft coo. And as I fall asleep, I conjure up all the strategies I can use to think of Frankie as a client when I sculpt her and not as the woman who makes me want to throw away any semblance of self-control I've got left.

Chapter Twenty-Four

Frankie

"I love you, too," I say before hanging up. When Gabby insisted I come back to the city and not hide in Buffalo, *I* insisted we speak every single day. That was my condition. Not text, not a quick check-in. An actual conversation. She may have started to get up and about when I was there, but she sees her life as being in a shambles right now and coming back from that takes time. Even if she brought this on herself, it's agonizing to watch someone you love suffer.

I think she tossed around the idea of asking me to stay. Having me there for support would be like a security blanket. But when my mother said Griffin was on the phone, I exploded with happiness. She must have picked up on it because as soon as I hung up she told me in no uncertain terms I was leaving. We went back and forth for a bit. I mean, whatever I feel for Griffin, no matter how deep, Gabby is my sister, and nothing would stop me from being there for her if she needed me.

Ultimately, I did want to come back. Not just because of Griffin, but because what my father said was right. I don't jump away from things; I jump toward them. Just because one guy was a prick, and maybe I'll meet some more, it doesn't mean I'll never amount to anything. I have to keep trying. Gabby knew this, and because she loves me as much as I love her, she made me return. I'm grateful for it.

It was obvious Griffin regretted his behavior from that night. His first two words held a tormented tone, and if I hadn't been at a pivotal point in my conversation with Gabby, I would have let him speak. By the time I called him back and heard how relieved he was that I was coming back to New York, any residual anger I'd had about that night was gone. I've never been one to hold grudges, anyway.

His offer to sculpt me was a much better apology than I'd expected or hoped for. It might be silly. It's just a sculpture. But I know how much it means to him, so to me, it's much more than a statue.

I'm rummaging through my closet as if this is our first date. It's ridiculous, because he's seen me in and out of everything I own, and it's not even like what I wear is going to be part of the sculpture. He concocts all that out of his head. But I want this to be perfect. I want to inspire him. Because in all the time I wanted him to do this, I had no idea how nervous it would make me. The sculptures he creates come from what he sees within his clients. And now, as I'm getting ready, I'm afraid he's not going to find anything interesting to create. What if he decides my beauty and intrigue are skin deep? I shake the thoughts from my head and shut my mouth so I'll stop talking to myself. I decided when I was in Buffalo that from now on, the only lectures I'll allow myself to speak aloud will be positive ones. Enough with the self-doubt.

I throw on a simple olive green tank top and cut off jean shorts. It's warm out, and the last thing I want to do is be a dripping mess while I'm trying to inspire him. When I get to the warehouse, I'm glad I chose this outfit. It's hot as hell, and there's no air conditioning.

I walk to the back and every step I take echoes in the space. I feel like I've never been here before, because now I'm coming as a client, not just his girl who wants to hang out.

"Hey." He approaches me, giving me a tentative kiss on the lips. He's jittery, as if he's the one who's going to be posing for hours. "Where do you want to be?"

"Wherever you think. You're the expert." I smile, trying not to show him how anxious I am. He thinks for a minute, then curls his fingers into mine and guides me to the couch. He places me sideways, on my hip and pushes my knees in a little so my legs are bent, resting in front of me. He hands me a throw pillow.

"Lay your head on this." He tucks one of my arms under the pillow. "Just be comfortable. Your position doesn't matter, but you seem a little jumpy, so I figured I'd get you situated. Put your other arm wherever it feels natural."

I lay it in front of me, though right now nothing feels natural. With the tip of his index finger, he slides the strap of my tank top off my shoulder along with the bra strap. He watches me lying there and swallows hard.

"I was going to tell you I did that so I could see the line of your neck better. But that's bull. I just wanted to do this." He leans down and sucks on the space where the strap was until my toes tingle. Then he backs off.

This session could be excruciating.

"Now I know why you get so much repeat

business," I tease, but he doesn't find it humorous.

"Frankie, I have never and would never touch a client."

"I know, Griffin, I was kidding. I know you're a professional."

"No." He shakes his head. "I don't care about that part of the joke. I just need you to know I don't do that. No matter who's in here with me, you'd never have to be concerned."

"I'm not."

I lie there for a while, but without my phone I have no concept of time. Griffin's got the Blues playing in the background, and as he works, his expression is more intense and focused than I've ever seen it, even when he's angry. His head is tilted down toward the table, and every time he scrutinizes me through his thick, black lashes without lifting his head, I feel as if my skin is transparent, revealing my every emotion.

He doesn't say a word as he sculpts, and I'm confused because I thought the whole idea was for me to divulge something about myself. "Don't you want me to tell you a story about my childhood or something?" I ask, after sitting in silence for what might have been half my life. I can't see what he's doing because he's got some supplies blocking my view. I don't know if their placement is strategic or it's just coincidence.

"You can talk if you want," he answers, distracted.

I start telling him a story about a game Gabby and I played when we were little, more for my benefit than Griffin's. When I make a joke at the end, I get no response. He's somewhere else, in that place he goes when he works. He didn't hear a word of my story.

After a while, his expression grows cloudy. His brows are drawn together in a frown and I have the urge to get up and kiss away those lines between them. His hands are frantic, shaking as he works. His chest is heaving and beads of sweat cover his forehead. He keeps swatting at them with the back of his hand, but they reappear in seconds. I don't know if they are from the heat or the tension. He wants me relaxed, but that's impossible when it seems as though he might ignite at any second. He's severe and smoky and incredibly sexy. I want to go to him, to make contact and give in to what's brewing across the table, but I stay put. I doubt he wants me going to him right now, interrupting his process. All I know is I've got a trail of sweat dripping down between my breasts as well, causing a wet spot on my tank top. I hope he doesn't notice it from where he's standing. I've tried to wipe it, discreetly, a couple of times, but there's only so much you can do when a person is watching you so hard you feel like they might maul you.

He said he doesn't touch his clients, and I trust him one hundred percent. Naïve or not, I believe Griffin would never do that to me. But the thought that all of his sessions are this intimate, with him reacting to his work and clients this way, brings me a small pang of jealousy. His next action, though, lets me know he doesn't.

Without warning, Griffin picks up the clay he was working with and flings it to the side. It lands on the ground with a thud. "Fuck, Frankie." He stalks over to me. In a split second, he swings one leg over me with his knee braced on the couch, while he stands on the other foot. He swipes his forehead again, trails his fingers down my own path of sweat running into my tank and swallows. He leans down, rushes his hands over my cheeks and clenches my hair. "I knew I wouldn't be able to keep it separate," he growls as his mouth claims mine.

The clay is all over his hands. I've come to love the smell more than anything in the world, but when it slides against my skin, smooth and hot from being worked in hands, it's a whole other level of sensual. My chest pounds with each desperate touch, and I'm thankful I waited for him to come to me.

We come up for air for a second.

"Shit, I'm sorry," he pants. "I'll go wash," he breathes into my mouth, but makes no attempt to lift his body from mine.

I must have clay all over my face and chest. The thought is exhilarating. He starts to release his grip on my hair.

"No, don't." I grab his wrists, wanting nothing more than to bathe in it. "I love it." I put his hands back in my hair and wrap my arms around him. He places one hand on my spine, turns me flat on my back and presses the full weight of his body down into mine.

And that's when a man I've never met before emerges.

From the first connection his mouth makes with my skin, Griffin is feverish. His eyes are as black as a panther's fur and his hands are everywhere, grasping at me, like he wants his flesh and bones to burrow beneath my skin and become a part of me. Every inch of him trembles. He can't take the time to lift my top and remove my bra, so he just yanks them both down over my arms to my waist while his mouth devours my breasts. I'm so surprised by this change in him, it takes me a second to catch up, but once I do, I match his frenzy, clawing so hard I must be leaving jagged marks on his skin. If I am, it's bringing him pleasure, because the guttural sounds coming from him are new to me and they alone are making me crazy to have him. His jeans make it only to his knees before I latch onto his hips and pull him into me, burying him. He takes a second to collect himself, before becoming completely unleashed.

If Griffin gave me his soul the first time we were together, he's giving me his demons now. With every clutch, every taste, every grind, he's emptying himself into me, transferring his darkness to me, purging himself. It's the most incredible thing I've ever experienced in my life.

Somehow, he manages to remove the rest of our clothes, and when we tumble to the rug, I don't even feel it. All I feel is him. Everywhere. He manipulates my body like it belongs to him, like my appendages are parts of his own body. He moves me in ways I didn't know possible, each one making me more delirious than the last. I've had plenty of experience before, but my body has never been possessed the way Griffin is owning me right now. Not even when I've been with *him*. When he unintentionally juts me forward and my head crashes hard into the leg of the couch, he freezes. He tightens everywhere but does not move.

"Frankie..." His voice is an agonizing whisper.

"Do. Not. Stop," I tell him, because if he's afraid of breaking me all of sudden, I'll die.

He muscles loosen beneath my hands, in relief.

We continue the delicious assaults on each other's bodies, neither of us willing to allow it to end. We've become insatiable and each time one of us finds a release, we hunger for another. A few times, I think my heart might give out, but somehow it manages to keep pumping.

Eventually, neither of us can find another ounce of strength. Griffin collapses on my back and even breathing with him on top of me takes more energy than I can muster. His breaths are as erratic as my own and it takes us a few minutes to be able to move.

When I turn over, he tries to brush the hair off my skin, but I'm covered in sweat, as is he, and it's stuck to me. He takes it between his fingers to pluck it off me instead.

"Frankie, I-I..." He looks remorseful and I'm shocked.

I try to erase his worry lines with my lips. "What's wrong?"

"Are you okay? Did I hurt you?"

"Hurt me?" I laugh. "Are you kidding? Were you here for the last two hours?"

His brows settle and the worry lines disappear. "I didn't want that. I had a feeling it would happen. I tried to figure out how not to let it, but I knew once I tried to sculpt you, I'd lose it."

"Griffin, why on earth would you not want that to happen? That was every woman's dream," I joke, but he doesn't find it funny.

He's afraid he was too rough.

I hold his face. "Everything you did, I wanted and I returned. And I loved."

"But we didn't even...I didn't take the time to..."

We didn't use a condom. Any of the times. I realized it about halfway through the first time, but I was too overwhelmed to want to stop. After that, what's done was done. I know it was stupid, especially after what my sister is going through right now. But in my heart, this is the man for me, for good, and if we're committed to each other we should be able to go without.

"I've been on the pill forever," I tell him, even though I know that's the least of what either of us should worry about.

"I'm clean, Frankie, I swear it."

"I believe you." I kiss him. "I am, too."

He pauses for a second to think and his expression transforms. "You mean, then, we don't have to use them?" He smiles like the devil himself, and his exposed dimples make him look entirely too naughty.

"I guess not any more." I grin back. We kiss, and if either of us had the energy, I bet we'd go again, but we don't.

Griffin studies my naked body.

"You haven't had enough?" I laugh.

"You're a mess. What are we going to do with you?" He smiles. But then something about his statement bothers him. He shakes his head. After a few deep inhales, he's okay. "What I meant was, I may have gotten you dirty."

The length of my body has smears of gray all over it. Remains of his touch. I might never shower again.

"I've never seen anything so beautiful." He's reflective as he streaks smudges of clay around me with a single fingertip. "If I could, this is exactly the way I would sculpt you. But that one would be just for me."

We don't get up from the floor. Our lips brush and our bodies stay tangled for quite a while. Griffin's pupils have gone back to the size of a regular person's. He traces his fingers from the base of my throat, straight down to my belly button over and over, deviating from their path to run over my breasts occasionally. He's airier than I've ever seen him and I've never felt more content or complete.

Or more grounded.

"I think we have a problem." He smiles after a long period of quiet, this time, with the dimples of an innocent child.

"What?" I kiss his cheek at the indentation.

"I'm never going to be able to sculpt you this way." His smile expands, exposing teeth. He skims his cheek over my breast, tickling it with his stubble and ending with a soft kiss. I giggle.

"Well." I play along. "I guess we'll just have to keep trying and see where it leads us."

****

For the next month or so, it leads us to roughly the same place again and again. I come to the warehouse under the pretense of Griffin trying to sculpt me. Antonio has a regular job, and Griffin is attuned to his schedule. We plan accordingly.

The duration of time between my arrival and when Griffin gives up trying to sculpt me has gotten progressively shorter as the weeks have gone on. He can't wait for me any more, and I'm glad because every second I spend on that couch without him touching me is torture.

The outfits I wear to the warehouse may have gotten shorter, as well.

Sometimes Griffin gives me his soul in the warehouse and sometimes he gives me his demons, but every time we're there, the sex is grittier than when we're at either of our places. Griffin understands I want to take all his darkness, but I think it's easier for him to share it with me around his clay.

Chapter Twenty-Five

Griffin

"This was a great idea, Griffin. We should do this more often."

My mother leans down and picks up one of the leaves that has already changed colors and spans the dull sidewalk like a mosaic. She twirls its stem between her fingers. I haven't seen her since our horrible dinner over a month ago. I had a meeting with a client that ran long today, so instead of heading to Brooklyn, I asked her to meet me in the city. She was enthusiastic about the idea, suggesting we walk through Central Park and have dinner around there. As much as I didn't feel like going all the way uptown, I knew it would make her happy, so of course I agreed.

We stroll and weave in and out of the other pedestrians, who are as unconcerned about reaching a destination as we are. My mother is lighthearted and I think getting together with her outside of that house is good for our relationship, because I'm calmer, too.

Or maybe it's just because I've been more tranquil lately.

Things changed for me the first time I tried to sculpt Frankie. I was trying. I was really trying to think of her as a stranger modeling for me and to get the work done. But seconds after she laid on that couch, I knew it was impossible. The angles of her body, her long legs, her lush hair falling over her shoulder, the way she was watching me work, the sweat glistening off her chest…all coupled with the way I had to think about the deepest parts of her to create something that represented her…in my workspace, my sanctuary, the place I let go of everything. It was too much. The second I left the safety of my sculpting table and made contact with her, it was all over.

I couldn't get enough of her. No matter how or where we touched each other, I couldn't get close enough, couldn't get deep enough. It was like I wanted to be inside of her, inside of her *being*. And I wanted her inside of mine.

Every inch of her was the perfect sculpture. Smooth and delicate, yet strong and sensual. Everything that I normally pour into my clay was seeping into her and she soaked it in, body and soul pleading for more. With every touch, I lost myself a little more, barely aware of anything except the way she was making me feel. Even when I cracked her head into the wood, it hardly registered. Just enough to hear her reassurance that she was okay.

Until afterwards. It registered then. All of it. How rough I was with her, again and again. How I smashed her head into the couch and kept going anyway. How I entered her bare. I don't know how I did that. I've never done that. Never even considered it. I know we're committed to each other and there's no one else, but how could I not check with her first? I'm not even sure how it happened. I was so overcome I didn't even think. I just needed more.

In the moments after, I feared she was going to

think I was scary or violent. But it's Frankie. I didn't need to worry.

The second she put my mind at rest was the second everything changed. I had let go. I released all of me to her, and nothing bad happened.

The world has been a little less gray since then.

"We should," I answer my mother. She smiles and her teeth twinkle. She is such a beautiful woman.

"When you were little we used to come up here all the time. Sometimes we'd go to the zoo and other times we'd just pick up hot dogs at the dirty water guy and bring you to the playground." She sits on a bench and crosses her legs, pulling her light sweater around her. She's in no hurry to move on. "Do you remember, Griffin?"

It's been a long time since I've allowed myself to reminisce, but on this cool, breezy evening, it doesn't sound so bad.

"The monkey bars?" I ask.

She smiles wide. "God, you loved those."

I did love them. I badgered my father to take me up all the time. "Come on! Please, Dad! It's fun."

My father griped a little, but I knew he would do it. He always did it.

"Fine, okay." He stood from the bench, rubbing my mother's knee. He tore off a piece of the big pretzel she was eating, popped it in his mouth and wiped his hand on his jeans. He walked to the monkey bars with me. I noticed some of the moms watching him and assumed, at the time, they were curious about what he was about to do.

He reached up and put a hand on each bar. Then he pulled himself up and over, so he was sitting on top. I stepped on the top rung of the ladder, and reached for the bars. As soon as I was hanging, my dad's large hands enveloped my wrists. With a quick tug, he pulled me up so I sat up there with him. The air smelled different. Fresher.

"How about we just do it this way instead this time, Griffin? It's safer," he said

"No way! I've been doing it the other way since I was four. If I could do it then, I can do it now that I'm six," I insisted.

"But you're getting too heavy, now."

"Pleeeaaseee," I whined.

"Okay." He sighed with a smile. He placed his palms on the top bars as he put his feet on the perpendicular ones. He checked himself for balance in a squatting position. "Okay, now you." He took both of my hands and held them steady while I came to my feet as well. He shook his head. "I can't believe I did this that first time. What was I thinking?" He laughed. It was a good laugh. All low and grumbly.

Carefully, he stood as we held hands. Again, he waited for balance. Then, he lifted me, one inch at a time, slowly, slowly, until I was sitting on his shoulders. He held my shins and I stuck my arms out to the sides to balance us the way he taught me.

"Check it out, Mom, we're as tall as the Empire State Building!" I yelled. I said the same thing every time.

She covered her eyes with both hands. "I can't look. Be careful!" She said the same thing every time, too.

The breeze blew my hair, and the sun shone on my cheeks, and I thought what a lucky kid I was to have him for a dad.

Huh. I'll be damned.

"Yeah, Mom, I did love them." I put my arm around her shoulders to fend off the chill, and she leans into me.

****

"Okay, I found something. But you can't go giving me false hope or anything," Frankie says as she enters my apartment.

"What did you find?"

She slaps a piece of paper on my coffee table. "It was stapled to a pole in Washington Square."

It's a flier about a farmer's market type of event in Stuyvesant Park. People will be selling food and clothing, and probably pictures.

"I was thinking maybe I could set up a table to show my photos. What do you think?"

As far as I know, Frankie hasn't taken a single picture since Scott Hannah crushed her confidence. Fucker.

"I think it would be a great idea."

"Do you think I can use the pictures I took with you-know-who or could I get in trouble?"

She doesn't use his name around me because she's afraid I'll fly off the handle. But I won't. I'm okay.

"I think screw him. They're your pictures. You took them. He never paid for them. Besides, let him try to come after you and explain why he didn't use them."

We check out the Stuyvesant Park event online and see if it's open to the public or if you have to register for space. I turn on my computer and as it boots up, I wrap my palm around the back of Frankie's neck and kiss her.

"What was that for?" she asks.

I shrug. "Because I haven't done it yet today."

She rests her head on my shoulder. The computer is ready. I type three letters before the search history comes up.

STU

Frankie gasps as she lifts her head off my shoulder, reading the words on the screen.

Studies about children who witness domestic violence.

"Griffin…" She doesn't say anything else and she doesn't need to. She's the only person who would have used this computer, other than me. I don't want her to see the pain she unintentionally caused me, so I stare at the screen.

She sniffles, and I know she must be crying, but I'm afraid if I see her tears, some might find their way into my eyes, and I will not have that.

"I wasn't…I just wanted to see. I was curious. It doesn't mean I think anything."

"What did you see?" My voice is low and identical to my father's, right before he explodes. But I'm not going to explode. You have to have something building inside of you to explode. And right now I'm a vast abyss.

"Nothing, really, it doesn't matter."

"No, Frankie, tell me what it said." Prove to me what I already know.

"Just the stuff you told me. Anger, drugs, depression, that kind of stuff."

I can't be mad at her. I'd been telling her who I am, and what blood runs through me, for months. How could I blame her for wanting to learn about it for herself? To know exactly what she was getting into? It's just that, lately, because of her, I've been forgetting. I've been feeling like a normal person who could have a normal relationship. And I've been *wanting* to forget. To convince myself I don't have to be the rule, I can be the exception. But here is a reminder of what I am, slapping me, and its source is the most painful part.

She grabs my face in her hands so I'm forced to look at her. Tears streak her cheeks. "I'm sorry. I shouldn't have done that. But it doesn't mean anything."

"You don't have to be sorry. You did nothing wrong."

"Okay, fine, but it still doesn't make me see you differently." She leans in to kiss me. I tap my lips to hers because I have no right to be mad, but there's a sadness in them she can sense. She pulls back.

"Griffin, I'm still here."

"When did you look it up?"

"The first night I met with Scott."

That was months ago. She read about what I could become months ago. And she's still here.

While the hurt remains, it shares space with a strange sense of security.

She's still here.

Chapter Twenty-Six

Frankie

How did I not delete the search history? I want to kill myself. I've never seen an expression like that on his face before. Like I took a knife and stabbed him in the back.

In a way, I suppose I did.

I mean, no, there's nothing wrong with me googling something. But why did I do it on *his* computer? Why didn't I wait until I got home and do it then? Idiot.

He's been doing so well, too. He's been happier, and I knew he'd be excited for me about the pictures in the park. He's been encouraging me to get back out and take some good autumn shots for a while now.

And then he had to go and see that.

The fact that I don't care about the articles has to mean something. It means he's worth sticking around for. It means I don't believe those articles describe him. It means I love him. I just hope he can see it.

But it's been over a week and though he says he's not mad and we've been together almost every day, there's been a small change in him. Some of the positivity he's carried around lately has disappeared, and he's been spending extra time alone in the warehouse. I've got to find a way to prove to him I don't give a damn what the research says, even if I was curious enough to learn about it.

Stuyvesant Park is much smaller than I expected. I find a tiny, unoccupied spot where I can stand some of my photos in a huge crate Griffin got from Jackson. I prop a couple around the crate. People throughout the park are selling all types of goods. One woman has a stand with a few cute wool sweaters, perfect for the coming winter. I might have to stop by later. Griffin offered to keep me company today, but I felt like he'd be babysitting. So I sit alone and wait, wondering if we're supposed to have licenses to do this. Maybe it's not legal. I don't really care.

People stroll by and smile at me from time to time. A couple even thumb through my crate and compliment my work. But no one buys anything.

My sister texts to see how sales are going. *Slow*, I tell her. I'll call her later so I can hear her voice, my way of judging how she's doing, but for now we text back and forth for a while to pass the time.

"Can you tell me about this one?"

A heavy, older man wearing a cap and scarf stands before me. He's pointing to my picture of the old hoop earring. As he leans in to see it, his foot hits anther photo and he trips a little, but he rights himself.

I put my phone aside and describe the shot. He nods, giving a *hmmm*, without opening his mouth.

"What are you charging?"

"Twenty-five?" I ask. Yes, ask. Griffin convinced me selling them for anything less than twenty-five dollars would be a bad idea, that people think they're getting what they pay for. But to even ask that much for my silly shot of an earring feels like a lot.

He laughs. "I assume that's a negotiable price?"

I nod.

"Well, I'll tell you what. I'm not going to buy one of your pieces, but I'll do something better for you."

Oh, here we go.

He picks up the picture I had blown up into an 11 x 14 print and studies it. "You've got some real potential here."

My brain groans. I've heard this before. Move along buddy, I consider saying. Instead, I wait to hear what bullshit line he's going to give me.

He puts down the print and inspects the rest of my work. "But your lighting is wrong."

Okay, I wasn't expecting that.

He refers back to the earring picture. He points out a better angle I should have taken the shot from—one that would have given the illusion of the refraction of light. He tells me which lens I should have used. I know nothing about these things.

"You've got good instincts..." He waits for my name.

"Frankie."

"You've got good instincts, Frankie. Your work is interesting. But you've got a lot to learn about technique." He reaches into his breast pocket and pulls out a card. He scribbles something on the back before handing it to me. According to his card, he's a director at a private photography school downtown. "You said you're charging $25. The classes cost more than $25 each, but if you give me this picture to use in class for critiquing, I'll give you the first class free."

I'm skeptical. "Why?"

"Because I'm always seeking new students, to

grow my business. I don't teach the classes, but I oversee the school. What better way to find new talent than searching local weekend street fairs?"

His reason sounds legitimate, but I don't want to get burned twice. Still, if I give him the picture and nothing comes of it, what have I lost?

"Okay," I agree.

"Great." He takes the picture in its plastic wrapper. "Beginner classes are every Tuesday and Thursday night at seven. Just call ahead and tell them you have a card giving you a free session. Then bring it with you and you can try out a complimentary class."

I don't like that he's calling me a beginner based on what he sees in my photos, but what did I expect? I've never been trained. I have to start somewhere. As soon as he walks away, I search his school on my phone to see if he's for real. Fool me once, shame on you. Fool me twice, I've got to be the biggest moron alive.

There's a picture of him on the website and a schedule of classes. And it says after about a dozen sessions, they help you make connections to get steady work. All in all, it sounds promising.

I don't make a dollar that day, but I think I might have stumbled into something more lucrative. Or, more accurately, it stumbled into me.

****

Griffin Googles him when I get to his apartment. Not just the school. The guy, himself. He's been a professional photographer for over twenty years in different parts of the country, has worked for some semi-influential people and even won an award for one of his shots. He took over managing the art school six years ago. Everything looks legit. The price per class is steep and Griffin offers to help out with it, but I won't have it. I'll ask for extra shifts at the tavern to make up the difference. I tingle a little at the thought of pursuing a career. It's the first time I can remember committing to something.

Aside from the man sitting next to me.

Griffin smiles as I blabber on about how beneficial this could be and how much I might learn. I've never been excited about the idea of learning something before. I think it's a very good sign.

"I'm proud of you, Frankie." He strokes my hair. I'll never take for granted the way he seems to ground himself by having physical contact with me.

"For what?" I ask. "I haven't done anything. I'm just going to take a class."

"For knowing what you want and going for it. For not letting a bad experience in your past dictate your future actions."

I'm not sure if he's referring to himself now or if this is all about me. But for the past week, I've been feeling like we took a step backwards in our relationship and it's bothering me. We need to move beyond this.

I lift the computer from his lap and place it on the table. I throw my leg over him and take the computer's place. I place my hands on his shoulders to get his full attention. As if he ever gives me anything less. "I have to tell you something."

He doesn't ask what. He just waits, always the patient soul.

I take a breath that I hope is filled with courage. "I'm in love with you, Griffin."

He opens his mouth. I'm not sure if he's going to

tell me he loves me, too, or say something else, but it doesn't matter. That's not why I'm telling him. I'm telling him because I want him to understand. I close his lips between my thumb and pointer.

"Don't say anything. Let me finish. I love you. I've told other people that before, but I was wrong. I didn't love them, because there's no comparison between how I felt then and what's going on inside me now. I don't care about any of that other stuff with your father. Not any more than you care about stupid stuff I've done. The fact that I hurt you is killing me. I didn't need a computer to tell me what I already know. You're everything I want in my life, and then some. Please don't let one little, ridiculous Google search hurt you and affect us. Being with you makes me happier than I ever thought I could be, and I wouldn't care if your father was Lucifer himself because I'm completely and totally in love with you."

He tries to open his mouth again, but I cover it with mine. "Shush," I mumble into his mouth before I peck his lips. Then I pull away. "I don't want you to say it back, if that's what you were about to do. When you say it to me, I don't want it to be an answer. I want it to come from somewhere deep inside you that absolutely must tell me."

We start kissing and his silent answer is palpable. Really, I've known it for a while even though he hasn't said it yet. He loves me, too.

Griffin lifts his hips to help me lower his jeans over them, but as I start to, his crotch vibrates.

"Excited?" I smirk.

He gives a single rough laugh at my terrible joke and shakes his head. He takes a jagged breath when I reach in his front pocket, but exhales when the only thing I grab is his cell phone, ringing in my hand.

"Do you want it?" I hold it up.

"Hell no," he grumbles, burying his face in my neck and hair. He snatches the phone from my hand, throws it on the couch next to us, and pulls my hips closer.

****

Coming down from being with Griffin always takes a while. A kiss is never just a kiss. Every touch penetrates below the surface, which makes it a lot harder to get up and go when it's over. Usually, we don't. We spend time woven together, long after we've both had our fill of each other. So when Griffin's phone goes off for the third time, it's very difficult to release him. I'm on his lap, chest to chest, with my arms wrapped around his neck as he palms the small of my back. My head is content in the crook of his neck.

"You should probably get it this time," I sigh, begrudging that irritating ringer. "It could be important."

"I guess." He sounds at least as unhappy about it as I am. I reach over and grab his phone without lifting my head as I pass it to him.

When he answers with venom in his voice, I think he's annoyed because our moment was interrupted.

Boy, am I wrong.

Chapter Twenty-Seven

Griffin

I'm pissed when my cell rings for the third time because I don't want anything pulling me out of my bubble with Frankie right now. She just told me she loves me and even though I already knew, something cracked inside me when she said it. Like I've been waiting all my life to hear those words from her lips and free me from myself.

I was going to say it back to her immediately, because God knows I do love her. But she wants me to say it of my own accord, not to repeat her words. It will mean more to her that way and I get it, since her words just meant everything to me.

There's only one person who would call me three times in the span of a half hour. And there's only one reason why. Which is what makes me so very mad when my phone sings the last time. It's got to be my mother, and she's got to be in trouble.

But when my father's number appears on the screen, my blood turns to fire.

"What do you want?" I snap.

"Griffin." There's panic in his voice. "It's your mother. You need to come to the hospital."

Frankie and I are dressed in an instant and though I really don't want her coming with me and witnessing firsthand the clusterfuck that is my life, I don't have time to fight with her about it. Besides, her presence keeps the red at bay, which I've got a feeling I'm going to need, so having her with me could be a good thing.

Unfortunately, I know my way around the hospital all too well and when I'm directed to my mother's room, it's clear that bringing Frankie along was a mistake. This visit won't be like the others. I won't be in the waiting room, finding out whether a bone is broken or just bruised. For one thing, my father is here. Scared and sheepish. And then there's the other difference. My mother is lying in a hospital bed.

Unconscious.

A nurse is checking her when we walk in. She tells me things I only half-hear. My mother fell. She's in a coma. Something about her vitals. All we can do is wait.

But I don't process most of it because my mother is in front of me, unconscious and my father, who obviously caused it, is standing here looking pale, sweaty, and guilty as sin.

The nurse leaves us and my father tries to explain himself. "Griffin, it's not what you think…"

"Shut the hell up!" I bark.

He's surprised at my outburst and seems to forget for a minute that he landed my mother in a coma.

"Watch how you speak to me," he spits back, with an anger I've heard too many times. Then he notices I'm not alone. "Frankie."

It's just one word that sets me off. Seven letters.

I'm about to scream at him not to talk to her, not to even look at her. But just the idea that my father is addressing Frankie after doing this to my mother sends my rage tearing through me at a force I've never felt before and my body moves of its own accord.

Taking one step in, my fist flies right into my father's cheekbone, sending him staggering into my mother. He places both palms on her motionless legs, tucked under the hospital blanket, to try to regain his balance. The fact that he's touching her enrages me more. I pull him off her by his collar. I completely forget where I am and what I'm here for as years of fury overtake reason. I hold fast to his shirt with one hand as I punch him with the other. Over and over. He doesn't try to hit me back. He just shields his face with his arm, as if he knows he deserves to have me beat the hell out of him and he accepts his fate.

The sight of his blood does nothing to calm me. In fact, if anything, now that I've got a taste for it, it makes me want to pound into him more. Somewhere in the back of my mind I hear Frankie calling my name, begging me to stop, but it doesn't register. I'm at my breaking point. There is no turning back for me.

Frankie calls for help and seconds later each of my arms is being restrained by a different man in scrubs.

There's commotion around me. Someone is asking my father if he's okay, which almost makes me break into hysterical, ironic laughter. Another voice is offering to call the police. My father declines, waving them off.

Everything around me is a blur. It's like when you're lying down at the beach, level with the sand and the ground is so hot the air just above it looks fuzzy. Except that's how the entire room is right now.

As my panting abates, everything comes into focus. My father's blood soaked face and shirt. The nurse reprimanding us. And Frankie, staring at me from the doorway.

Shaking.

Pale.

Terrified.

Of me.

It's written all over her face. I'm what I promised her I was all along. I'm an animal. I am my worst fear.

I am my father.

The nurse continues to scold us, but all I can process is Frankie. I know this will be my last moment with her. After what happened between us less than an hour ago, the thought of losing her makes me feel like I'm being sliced open and bleeding out on the floor. But she made me a promise.

If I ever frightened her, she'd walk away.

I want to say goodbye to her. I want to pull her into my chest and hold her until our muscles cannot withstand collapsing for another second. I want to kiss her until neither of us can breathe. Then and only then will I be ready to say goodbye.

But I can't do any of that. Because I see it in her eyes. They may be filled with fear, but they're also overflowing with love. And if I grab her, hold her, kiss her, she won't leave. She'll find an excuse to stay.

Just like my mother always does.

My next actions must ensure that Frankie keeps her promise, even though I know it will shatter me into so many pieces it will be impossible to put me back together.

She walks toward me. "Your hands." She reaches for the bloodied mess that I am. I pull away. I can't tell how much is my blood and how much is my father's, but I feel no remorse and it doesn't matter anyway. His blood, my blood. We are the same. We are one.

"I'm fine." My voice is harsh.

The nurse is shuffling the three of us out of my mother's room into a nearby waiting room.

"This cannot happen," she's saying at the same time Frankie is trying to take care of me. "You can't settle your problems here."

"We understand," my father says. "We're very sorry."

"As it is, only immediate family should be in here. Are you all immediate family?"

Here's my opportunity. I have to make her go.

"She's not." I point a thumb at Frankie but face the opposite direction. "She's just a girl I'm screwing."

Frankie lets out a sharp sound resembling a cry and I feel like I slashed her. I know I have to twist the blade, forcing her to leave me, alone, without the only person who ever made me feel everything I wanted to feel, but was terrified of at the same time. She was my one chance to prove I could be different. That I wasn't a statistic.

And now it's gone.

"Go home, Frankie. This is a family matter. You're not wanted here."

I once told her I never lie and because of that she should believe everything I say. Right now, I wish she could see through this. I wish she could see, even though I told her I never lie, what I'm saying right now couldn't be further from the truth. Because *she* is my family, not this man standing in front of me. And she's wanted here so much I think she's going to take my air with her when she leaves.

But for her sake, I have to be thankful she can't see through the lie.

As she turns and walks away from me without a goodbye or even a glance back, I lean into a nearby garbage can and hurl.

****

Sarah stays with me in the waiting room overnight. Even though she can't go in my mother's room, she holds my hand and sits with me in silence. Neither of us mentions Frankie, but she knows what happened. Frankie's the one who told her I was here.

My father and I take turns sitting by my mother's side. I'm having to fight back thoughts of killing the man each time he walks in there, the doting husband. But Sarah rubs my back when she sees my tension rising, reminding me if I fight with him again, they'll throw me out and then I won't have any access to my mother.

I can't stomach the sight of her, lying there. I'm filled with a heavy, burdensome sadness, which is rivaled by anger that she allowed it to come to this. I feel like I should be leaning over her, sobbing, but I'm too empty inside, even with all of the emotions, to shed a tear. Or maybe I'm too scared that if I cry, it will mean I'm losing her and that's not something I'm willing to accept. When it comes down to it, I have no idea what I'm feeling. I'm just a jumbled mess, wishing I could be anywhere but here, and anyone but me.

At some point, my father mumbles something about getting some rest. He leaves, telling me he'll be back in the morning. As if I give a shit if he ever returns. Sarah falls asleep, her body warped into the position of the chair in the visitor's lounge. The nurses let us stay, ignoring the fact that visiting hours are long over. I'm grateful because I have nowhere to go, anyway.

Sarah wakes after a few hours of uncomfortable sleep. She rubs her eyes and gets her bearings. It's very early and the sun hasn't finishing rising yet.

"Maybe you should go home. I'm sure they'll call if there's any news."

But what am I going home to? All I'll do there is obsess over losing one, maybe both, of these women I love.

"I'm okay here, Sarah, but you go. Get some sleep. I'll be fine."

She shakes her head. "I'm not leaving you, Griffin." She takes my hand again and rests her head on me. We stay like that for most of the day.

In the evening, Sarah and the nurse on call convince me to go home, take a shower, and get some rest. They'll call me the second there's any change, the nurse assures me. Reluctantly, I agree. I'm not doing anyone any good here, and if I have to look at my father—who made his reappearance this morning—for one more second, I might get banned from the hospital, anyway.

"Do you want to come over?" Sarah asks on our way out.

But I can't go there. Unless Frankie moves, I'll never be able to go there again. I shake my head.

Sarah understands. "How about I come to your place?"

I give her a weak smile. "I'll be all right, Sarah, but thanks. Go home and take a shower. You reek of hospital." I try to say it with humor, but I miss my mark.

"You sure?"

"Yeah, I am. I need some time alone. But thanks."

She kisses me on the cheek to say goodbye and tells me she'll come by and check on me in the morning. I promise I'll call her first if I hear anything.

****

Every inch of my apartment is flooded with Frankie, places I held her, conversations we had. If I had one wish, it would be to go back twenty-four hours, not answer my phone and run somewhere far away. Before I could ever find out about my mother and before Frankie could get a glimpse of the side I've been trying to deny. I can't believe I had to let her go. In my mind, I knew it would come to this from the very start. I knew what my destiny was and that you can't hide from the inevitable. But deep within my chest, in the chambers of my heart, I pleaded that I was wrong. That I could outrun the demons passed down to me that threatened my happiness.

Ultimately, my pleas went unanswered.

My thoughts flip-flop between sickness at turning Frankie away and angst about my mother, more helpless in that hospital bed than I've ever seen her. I'd almost rather think about losing Frankie because the realization that my mother might not come out of this and I might lose her this way rips me into a thousand shreds. Every time she's been hurt, it's torn at me a little more, one string at a time. But this will very possibly leave me in tatters. And without Frankie, there's no chance of being woven back together.

The apartment is too small and the walls too tight, so I go down to the warehouse, hoping to find some air to breathe. But even the warehouse is filled with shadows of Frankie, and I'm pissed at myself for allowing her to infiltrate my asylum.

Antonio is working behind his divider. He has no idea what's going on with me. He rattles on about things that seem important at the moment but are insignificant in the long run. I welcome the distraction, even though I know as soon as he stops talking, I'll be right back where I started.

He asks how things are going with Frankie. When I give a simple, evasive shrug because I don't have the strength to admit she's gone, he changes the subject. After a while, he wraps up for the night and heads out, leaving me alone with thoughts I'd give anything to erase.

I force myself to sculpt, which is simultaneously bringing relief and pain, until my hands are numb and I can't see straight. I curl up on the couch and pull the blanket I brought here weeks ago over my legs. My body gives in to an exhausted, much needed sleep.

But my subconscious brings me no reprieve. I dream of my mother playing a game with me. I almost lose, but am victorious at the last second.

"Great game, Griffin." My mother's frame floats just above me.

"Thanks." I'm modest, but inside I love that the board is all mine. "Wasn't looking good for me a second ago."

"Kind of like life," my mother responds. "Everything can change in a blink. You never know how things will go from one minute to the next. There is just one thing that's consistent and won't ever change."

The one thing I find predictable is my need to watch my father's moods.

"What's that?" I ask.

She nudges my shoulder with her hand. "That I'll always love you, silly. Even when you're grown and married with kids and you don't have time to come take care of your old, pathetic mother, I'll still love you every minute of every day."

****

I wake to the soft tapping of rubber soles on the floor of the warehouse. At first, I think it's my mother walking, because I'm still foggy with dream. I shake my head to clear it and remember, with a sunken stomach, where my mother lies.

Then I realize Sarah said she'd come in the morning. She must have gone upstairs and found I wasn't there. I remain still with my eyes closed. Knowing Sarah, she'll just sit by me and not interrupt my sleep, or my thoughts. She's good at being quiet when everything inside me is too loud.

The figure stands over me, though, waiting for me to show any signs of being awake, and I know it can't be Sarah. When I open my eyes, I doubt whether I've even woken up.

Chapter Twenty-Eight

Frankie

I'm tentative as I make my way into the warehouse, but my feet still make a soft patter on the concrete. I've got a feeling I'm going to get one shot at this. One shot to convince him.

I have to do it right.

He's asleep, more peaceful than I thought he'd be, considering what's going on in his life right now. I take a minute to watch him sleep, knowing as soon as he wakes, the calm will disappear.

He's plastered with disbelief when he sees me standing in front of him. I don't understand that. Did he really think I'd just walk away because of what he said? Did he think, after all these months, I wouldn't be able to tell he was lying to protect me?

Joy radiates from him as he becomes more alert, but he tries to hide it with a coldness he thinks should be there. For my own good.

It's too late, though. I already feel it.

"What are you doing here?" he asks as he sits up.

"I wanted to see how your mom's doing. Actually, how you're doing."

He takes our blanket off and throws it to the side. "I'm fine, Frankie." He crosses his arms over his chest, shielding himself from me.

"You're not fine," I correct. "And I know what you're doing, so just stop."

"If you know what I'm doing, then you also know why I'm doing it. I told you this all along, Frankie. This is who I am. Who I'm destined to be. You witnessed it yourself. So go away. Do what you promised." He turns away from me on the couch.

I shake my head. "You're not destined to be anything, Griffin. You're wrong. Look. I want you to see what I brought." I walk to his sculpting table and inch a piece sitting in the middle of it to the side. I lay down a stack of papers. "Here. You want to see what I was doing on your computer? You want to talk statistics? Come see."

My words catch his attention. He joins me by the table. Our arms brush, and I'm happy to have him this close to me again. It's been a little over a day since we parted, but knowing I couldn't be there for him when he needed me, until I took care of this, made it feel much longer. At least he had Sarah by his side.

I spread my papers over his worktable and read from them. "A child who witnesses domestic violence is at least twice as likely to commit violent acts against a partner as an adult...they exhibit increased risk taking...witnessing domestic violence is the strongest predictor of juvenile delinquency...they experience higher than usual levels of frustration...harbor anger toward the mother for triggering or tolerating the abuse...strongest risk factor of transmitting violent behavior to the next generation..."

"I know all this, Frankie. It's what I kept telling you. Why are you showing me what I already know?" He pushes the papers away with the back of his hand.

He's hurt that I'm rubbing this in his face, like I'm doing it to be cruel. But he's got to let me get to the next part.

"Right. Now show me where it says it's a certainty you'll become abusive."

He releases an aggravated sigh. "Oh, come on. You know it's not going to say that."

"Of course it's not," I answer, hoping to prove my point. "Because these are just possible outcomes, Griffin, not pre-destined futures." I pull a second set of papers from my bag. "Now look at these."

I've printed off one success story after another of famous people who came from abusive households, but have gone on to do wonderful, charitable things. He skims each story. He frowns, but I think it's a frown of hope, if there is such a thing, and not sadness.

"If you want to believe one side, you've got to at least acknowledge the other," I tell him.

He gets to the last one and sets it on top of the rest, in a mess all over the table now. I wait in silence, not wanting to interrupt his thoughts. Finally, he turns his attention to me. "But these aren't my stories, Frankie."

Now I smile. "No. But these are." I pluck my final stack of papers out of the bag.

"What are they?" He takes the pile.

"These, Griffin, are your stories. These are the stories of the things you've done, told by the people you've done them for."

He's flushed with confusion. "What do you mean?"

My throat tightens before the words are even out of my mouth. "The other night, when you sent me home, I called Taylor. I told her you needed a boost and asked her to share a story or two about how you've helped the women there. She did me one better. She contacted some of the women you sculpted or got furniture and whatever else for, and asked them to share thoughts about you. She didn't tell them why, just that she was doing something for you. She thought they'd each give a couple of words she could remember and pass on to me, but their responses were so extensive she had to write them down. She spent the last day compiling their stories. I offered to help, but she wouldn't let me talk to them, for confidentiality reasons."

I pause to catch my breath while he marvels at the lengthy pages in his hands. He reads them over, one at a time, placing each page behind the others as he finishes. He's engrossed, and my heart pounds against my ribcage, because I know what he's reading. I've memorized almost every word. Paragraph after paragraph discussing how Griffin gave these women hope. How he helped them to remember they were beautiful. How he affirmed that they had value, that they deserved better, that an alternate future was possible. How the furniture and children's toys made starting over much less daunting. They went on and on about things Griffin may never have thought about, and certainly would never take credit for.

The woman whose husband Griffin fought at Holly's wrote a passage thanking him, crediting him with saving her life. Griffin shakes his head, like he thinks she's exaggerating, but it doesn't matter. It's the way she feels. When he comes to the last entry, he pauses. It's written by a woman whose sculpture Griffin hasn't done yet. She says he encouraged her to reunite with her family, which she might not have been brave enough to do if it hadn't been for him. But she did and her family embraced her. She says she's awaiting the day she sees Griffin again because now she's got her story for him.

He places this sheet behind the others and stares at the stack, his hands shaking. He clutches them in his palms and they crinkle a little under the pressure.

I lay my hands over his to help steady them.

"I don't know what to say," he eventually whispers. His adam's apple bobs as he tries to swallow his shock.

"This is who you are, Griffin," I point out. "You are not him. Would your father dedicate his life to giving these women tiny pieces of themselves? You know he wouldn't. This is you. In black and white. Every word on these pages is who you are, who you will always be."

He rests his forehead against mine, slumping his shoulders. He's drained. His voice is smaller than I've ever heard it when he utters his next words. "But you saw what I'm capable of doing."

"Yes, I did." I pull my head from his. I take his jaw in both hands. "I saw a man capable of killing to protect the women he loves." I'm sure the fact that I counted myself in the *women* he loves isn't missed by him, but his expression of pure grief makes it impossible for me to say anything less.

"You were afraid of me." He might fall apart as he says this.

"No." I shake my head. "For someone capable of seeing clear into my soul, how could you so badly misinterpret what I was feeling?" I pause for effect. "I wasn't, not for one split second, afraid *of* you. I was afraid *for* you. I was afraid you were going to injure him, or kill him or something and you'd get arrested. Or worse, you'd have to live with that guilt."

The change throughout this body tells me he believes me. He pulls me into a tight hug and buries his head in my neck. His body trembles and his breaths against my neck are clipped, but no tears fall from his eyes as we move to sit down on the couch. We hold each other for as long as it takes Griffin to digest that he is really the person everyone described on those pages.

****

"So, the women I love, huh?"

We've spent most of the day on this couch, doing nothing but holding each other and talking. Griffin checks his phone every so often to make sure he hasn't missed a call from the hospital, but other than that, his hands haven't left me.

I freeze at his words. "What?" I ask, in a lame attempt to stall for time.

"You said I was capable of killing to protect the women I love. Women. Plural." He waits for me to answer his non-question with a smirk. He wants me to acknowledge the fact that I proclaimed he loves me. I assumed it.

I could backpedal and claim I didn't mean it, but we're too far beyond that for me to try it, and there's no point anyway. I know he loves me, even if I didn't intend to announce it to him. I will not withdraw it. I just shrug and give an embarrassed grin.

Griffin chuckles and pulls my head to his for a kiss. "You couldn't have been more right. I do love you, Frankie. So very much. Even though I didn't want to. At all."

"Nice!" I swat his shoulder. "Real nice."

He laughs. "You know what I mean. I know you wanted me to tell you when it wasn't an answer to you saying it. When I felt like I had to say it. I've needed to tell you for so long, but I was afraid when I said it, things would change for us." He sits on his knees to face me. "But I'm not going to let it. I'm going to..." He points toward the stories about him. "I'm going to keep being this person, okay?"

I smile. "You don't need to convince me, Griffin. I know who you are. But I was wrong about something."

"About what?"

"I was wrong when I said you had feet of clay. Well, kind of wrong, anyway. Griffin, you've taken what makes you flawed and turned it into something invaluable to other people. You may not realize what an accomplishment that is, but obviously everyone else does. When I said you had feet of clay, I should have stressed to you it was feat with an *a*, because what you're doing with your life is definitely a feat. F.E.*A*.T."

He gives me his warmest, widest smile, but doesn't answer me, of course. "Speaking of clay," he says, standing from the couch and walking over to his table. He reaches over the mess of papers and picks up the statue I'd moved aside.

It's a statute of a woman sitting on her knees, looking through the lens of a camera. Long wavy hair falls all around her face and the camera, making her expression unreadable. In front of her is a tiny flower just beginning to bud. Behind her is a man, crouching against her. His open palms lie on her hips and his forehead rests against her back. You can't make out his face either but I don't have to be a detective to figure out this one. My statue, our statue, is magnificent. I approach the table and run my hand down the statue Griffin's spine. The clay is damp, so, this time, I wrench my hand back, not wanting to alter it in any way.

"I tried to get it right, again and again. But it just didn't work with you by yourself. I couldn't see it without me in it. I'm sorry."

"Why would you be sorry?"

"Because it's supposed to be entirely about you."

"This is entirely about me. This is perfect."

He shakes his head. "Not perfect."

I examine it more closely to find what he's talking about. And then they appear. Tiny imperfections. A crack in the clay. A line going the wrong way on a fold of skin. Griffin's disjointed signature on the pedestal. Nothing that takes away from the overall effect of the piece. Nothing anyone would notice unless they were searching for mistakes. Which I am.

Griffin's work is ordinarily impeccable, so maybe he was too upset to focus. Or maybe the imperfections are the result of rushing it. I'm a little disappointed mine is the one to have them, but still, he did it and that's what I wanted. "It's still exquisite."

"They're meant to be there, Frankie."

I should have figured that. Griffin doesn't do anything haphazard. Just like when he told me the placement of his tattoos wasn't random. Everything's got a reason. But what is it?

And then I know.

"They're flawed."

He nods. "They have to be. Because that's normal,

right? It's okay?" he asks. His low voice is breaking, begging me to say yes, to tell him that even though he's flawed, he's all right. More than all right. He's amazing.

I place my hands on his cheeks, over his thin stubble and his infrequently revealed dimples, and rub them with my thumbs.

"Yes, Griffin. They're beautifully, normally flawed. But even with all of those flaws, they'll never shatter, you know. Because what's holding them together is strong and resilient. And forever."

Chapter Twenty-Nine

Griffin

Eighty-three hours after my mother was admitted to the hospital, I receive a call letting me know she's awake. A comforting, cool breeze passes through me. Frankie's been by my side every second for support, but now she waits in the visitor's lounge while I talk to my mother.

I walk into her room. She's alert and the IV has been removed from her hand, but her skin is grainy and her eyes are glassy. The bandage wrapped around her head makes her look frail. I'm flooded with relief that she's conscious, but trepidation and anger nip at the heels of my relief because now that I see she's okay, I know exactly what I have to say.

I kiss her on the cheek when I reach the side of her bed and she grabs my hand.

"I love you," I say.

She lets a tear fall and puts my hand to her cheek.

"But I have to tell you something. This is the last time I'm coming to this hospital for you."

My declaration takes her by surprise.

"Griffin." She tries to speak, but her voice is hoarse as she tries to sit up. She must be in a lot of pain, because she releases my hand and clutches her head as she lays back against her pillow. My heart aches for her, but it's battling resentment. I don't think there will ever come a time when my love and hatred for my mother will not be at odds with each other. The thought disturbs me.

"Shhh." I help her get comfortable. "Don't speak. It'll just hurt you." I pause to collect my courage. "I've done this too many times, Mom. I've watched you let yourself be hurt over and over and you refuse to do anything about it. Whatever your reasons, I can't be here to pick up the pieces of you anymore. I don't have it in me. If you want to let him kill you a little more each time, then there's nothing I can do about it. But I won't help you. I won't bring you to the hospital and I won't sit in the waiting room to see if you're okay. Because this"—I gesture up and down her battered body—"isn't just killing you. It's killing me, too. I love you, Mom, more than I can ever say. I love you so much I have to walk away before it destroys me."

But as I leave her room and hear my mother choke out my name once more, I'm confident of two things. One, my mother will go back to my father as soon as she leaves the hospital. And two, no matter how strong and determined my words were, no matter how much I want them to be true, the next time I get a call saying she's in the emergency room, I'll be right by her side.

****

When I was a child, my mother once asked me not to cry over her. My crying made her feel worse, and she knew I only wanted to make her feel better. She taught me that the way to make her feel better was to bring her some ice wrapped in a towel, so the cold didn't sting her skin.

I haven't cried over my mother since that day.

Crying didn't help her to heal, so I found other ways to deal with what was going on inside of me, for better or worse. But when I leave her hospital room, I only make it about a dozen steps, past the next room and the nurses' station, before I need the wall for support. I lean back against the wall and slide to the floor, wrapping my arms around my knees. I lay my head in them and shed the tears I've denied myself for almost two decades.

Chapter Thirty

Frankie

Damn, the wind is whipping right now. I pull my hat lower on my head. I'm learning that winters in the city are a little different from those in Buffalo. For one thing, in Buffalo, we don't have these huge slush piles on every street corner after the snow starts to melt. They seem shallow but are actually bottomless. I found out about them the hard way, once I was calf deep in wet muck without boots on. A mistake I'll never make again.

I pull off my glove to answer Gabby's text, before cramming it back on. Though I'm used to cold weather, most of my winter stuff is still in Buffalo. I'm going to pick up all of it when Griffin and I go home next week and Griffin meets my parents. The introduction is well past due.

"Hey, you," he growls from behind, which he follows with a warm kiss on the back of my neck. Somehow, it doesn't feel so cold out anymore.

"Hey, you." I turn and smile.

"How was class?"

"It was great. We learned about tilt-shift today."

Griffin's face is blank, which means he has no idea what I'm talking about, naturally, because until today I didn't either. But he listens steadily, as always, as I explain it while we walk.

These classes have been more beneficial than I ever thought they'd be. I get a little embarrassed that I assumed I knew what I was doing before. But as my father says, you don't know what you don't know until you know it. I never even knew what *that* meant until now.

My instructor has given me great tips each class and has seen a lot of improvement in my work, as have I. He says after a few more sessions, it'll be time to start exploring job opportunities, which has me psyched out of my mind.

"So where are we going?" I ask as we turn a corner.

"She picked the place." He leads me down into the subway. "Somewhere new," he smiles.

It's not Monday and we're not going to Brooklyn, but we are meeting Griffin's mother for a late dinner.

Monday dinners are a thing of the past. It's one of the compromises Griffin and his mother have made over the last couple of months.

Griffin was broken when he left the hospital the day his mother woke up. He knew he wouldn't cut her off, and, of course, he didn't really want to. He just needed some of the immense hurting to subside. So, with my encouragement, they discussed ways Griffin thought it would be easier to have her in his life. Getting rid of dinners where he was sitting in a house, surrounded by bad memories, hoping his father wouldn't come home, was the first one. Instead, she meets us in the city every once in a while. Though things between them are still very rocky, the dinners are a lot less stressful for him. They choose new places each time, creating better memories. It certainly doesn't fix his mother's situation. But at least Griffin can have some positive thoughts of her, even if they're accompanied by constant worry.

I also encouraged something else, even though I knew it was risky after the last time I brought it up. I told Griffin we should do some research about why women remain in these dangerous situations. Griffin was concerned with learning the statistics about himself. Maybe it was time to hear about the other side.

At first, he was mad at me for suggesting it, assuming I was validating her choices. But we worked through it as I showed him that wasn't my intention. I just wanted to find a way for him to have a more positive relationship with his mother. Together, we learned there are a multitude of reasons women stay in these relationships. Reasons neither of us had imagined. He may never know the true reasons his mother chooses to stay, and I'm certain he'll never accept it. But I think hearing the perspectives of women in similar situations helps him to realize the decision may not be as simple as he thinks. He still struggles with his conflicted feelings about her. But he tells me it's easier to deal with because he's got me by his side, helping him, guiding him.

And that's exactly where I intend to remain.

"I hope it's good. I'm starving." I stick my phone in my purse.

"How's Gabby?" He assumes she's the person I was texting. She usually is.

"She sounds okay. She had a date this weekend."

"First one?" he asks, brows raised.

"Yeah. Since Mitchell. She met the guy in class."

She said the date was kind of boring, but I'm glad she's getting back out there, even if this isn't the guy for her. It's a step in the right direction.

We exit the train station and approach the Italian restaurant, steps away. Griffin squeezes my hand tight for reassurance, as he does whenever we see his mother. It amazes me every time he uses me for support, because even though I'm starting to figure things out and find my ground, I still see myself as a girl who is innately flighty. But I'm coming to understand that's not how Griffin sees me at all. We may each have our own cracks and imperfections, but together we find our stability. Together we mold into something better.

Together, we are shatterproof.

Epilogue

Griffin

I skim my hand over the plaque at Holly's House and take in an exaggerated breath of air. I haven't been here in a while and it feels good to be back, doing something important. Taylor gives me her usual, welcoming hello and motions for me to wait in the sitting room. I make myself comfortable, listening to the soft music and inhaling cinnamon.

I don't know how many stories I've heard within these walls or how many more I'll hear. I do know that, no matter how many times I'm here, no two experiences will ever be the same, no one choice will be better or worse than another and every single woman I meet with will possess an inner beauty that I'll do my best to expose.

It doesn't get any easier, hearing about their lives. But each time one of Holly's guests starts down a new road, the sky around me becomes a little brighter. And when the darkness rolls back in, I've got Frankie, my moon, to light my path.

Years ago, after finishing my first sculpture here at Holly's, Mr. Rothman asked how it went. I smiled as I recalled my time with Vera. "When she saw the statue," I told him, "her whole face lit up. It was like she was happy inside for the first time in a while, and it was because she saw a promise in the clay. I know it sounds stupid. It's just a statue."

Mr. Rothman tilted his head. "There's nothing stupid about it, Griffin. You gave her a vision of what she was, what she could be again. For someone hoping to start over, a vision is everything."

I just shrugged.

"One day, Griffin," he said, "one day you'll understand what you're doing and how much it means to people. I don't know if it'll be tomorrow or somewhere far in the future. But I hope, when you understand it, you allow yourself to accept it. Because maybe then you'll realize the man you truly are. Not the man you're afraid of being, but the one who lives and breathes inside of you. Because that man, son, is someone I greatly admire."

I cleared my throat to push down the emotions rising at his words. I didn't think I'd earned them yet, but hoped that maybe I could beat the odds. Maybe someday in the future, I'd be like him. Maybe one day, I'd be worthy of his admiration.

I'll always wish places like this didn't need to exist, but as long as they do, I'll be here. To help in my small way, to show our futures are not predetermined, to unearth dreams long forgotten. And in doing so, I'll keep reminding myself exactly who I've been, all along.

A word about the author...

K. K. Weil grew up in Queens but eventually moved to Manhattan, the inspiration for many of her stories. Weil, who attended the University of Albany as an undergrad and NYU as a graduate student, is a former teacher. Although she still loves New York City, Weil now lives near the beach in New Jersey, where she is at work on her next novel.